T0147146

The West Side Kids in
The Space Aliens Are Coming
The Space Aliens Are Coming

Sixth Book of The Series

David Dorris and Michael Boblit

authorHOUSE®

AuthorHouse™
1663 Liberty Drive
Bloomington, IN 47403
www.authorhouse.com
Phone: 833-262-8899

Published by AuthorHouse 10/04/2022

ISBN: 978-1-6655-7183-8 (sc)
ISBN: 978-1-6655-7184-5 (hc)
ISBN: 978-1-6655-7182-1 (e)

Library of Congress Control Number: 2022917896

Print information available on the last page.

APPRECIATIVE NOTES FROM DAVID DORRIS AND MICHAEL BOBLIT

The content of this book came from ideas and research of episodes about the phenomena of extraterrestrial beings and UFOs. It took about 11 months to accomplish the publication of the book. In these months, many people were involved. David and I would like to thank these people. If we missed anyone, it was not intended.

We would like to thank our wives, Sally Dorris and Carol Boblit. Both have shown great patience and understanding of our focus in the book, working long hours to get this book completed and published.

We would like to thank Christopher Murphy for using his pictures and store front as one of the settings in the book. Burlington By The Book; 301 Jefferson; Burlington, Iowa 52601. (319)753-9981.

We would like to thank Benjamin Hendricks for allowing us to use his picture for the character of Scooter.

We would like to thank Officer Dustin Edkin of the East Moline Police Department for using his name in a couple of chapters.

We would like to thank our book reviewers for taking the time to read the book, writing the review and giving us permission to place them in the book. These people are Diane Conners, Jim Boblit, Robin Rollins, Tina Gibbs and Robert Whitney.

We would also like to thank Norah Bell, our young artist, for creating the book cover and supplying us with illustrations to place in the book.

We would like to thank people crucial to this book project: Raven Tan as our Check-In- Coordinator, the Publishing Service Associates, and the rest of the AuthorHouse team.

CONTENTS

Chapter One

THE RETURN OF THE LOTTERY TICKET INCIDENT

The story continues from the book, "The West Side Kids in A Pocket Full of Wishes."

"Wait! Don't go yet!" insisted Kelly. "Isn't that both Chris and Michael in the store? Hannibal, I want you to come in the store to talk to my brothers about our one million tax free deal. I want them to know you gave me the fifty million dollar winning lottery ticket when you didn't have to and about the evil people chasing us to Burlington."

"Come on girls, let's go into the store so I can feel that I finished my job," instructed Hannibal.

"Hey brothers, I brought some company," beamed Kelly. "Hannibal is alright because he brought Betty and me here with the winning lottery ticket."

Hannibal, I want you to meet my brothers. This is Christopher Seven Murphy and this is one of my other brothers, Michael Eight Murphy.

"It's nice to meet you Chris," acknowledged Hannibal. I already know your brother, Michael who goes by the name, Dr. Zodiac."

"It seems like everybody has a nickname but me," reckoned Chris. I'm told that everybody at your detective agency has a nickname, but not me. Why not me? Just what are the names of your men at your agency?"

"Well, I started out the nickname as Hannibal that my dad gave me," beamed Hannibal. "Scooter was given his nickname by his parents. Then, when we formed a baseball team in second grade and all the kids on the team wanted nicknames, they heard ours. Let's see. There is I'm Not Sure, Because, Who, What, I Don't Know, Smiley, You Don't Say and Whatever."

"Well, I want a nickname, like them," insisted Chris. "But what do you think it should be?"

"That's a good nickname," laughed Hannibal.

"What's a good nickname?" asked a confused Chris.

"What you just said," chuckled Hannibal. "What Do You Think?"

"What do I think? Just what are you talking about?" challenged Chris.

"Your nickname," declared Hannibal.

"I think that's a good nickname," laughed Kelly.

"What nickname? That's what I'm trying to find out," reckoned Chris. "What should my nickname be?"

"Older brother, read my lips," jested Michael. "Hannibal says your nickname should be, What Do You Think?"

"Oh, now I get it," replied Chris as he kept hitting his head with his right hand.

"You did it Kelly. Isn't this a wonderful day? You made this the happiest day of my life," praised Michael. "You know how long I waited for this? I didn't expect you back until tomorrow."

"It sounds like you were having your usual good times. Michael and I thought you were crazy to go to Davenport. If you can understand this, when you told me that you were going to go to Davenport to get the lottery ticket, it just made me ill," growled Chris. "When you have a problem, you confront it. You knew what you had to do and you did it. In the case of the winning lottery ticket, you and Betty did everything the best. Michael and I did everything the worst."

"I know we have a relationship that we don't tell each other what to do," reassured Kelly.

"Is that what you're telling us?" asked Michael. "Chris and myself

2

thought that you should give up before you left for Davenport. There is one thing about progress. You never can tell what is going to happen."

"I thought you were right, but I had an idea and decided to go with it anyway. Because you failed, you didn't have to blame me. You're only a failure if you believe it. You have to believe in yourself. It was just mind over matter. I had a fight of my own to go to and I had to fight back," admitted Kelly. "There is one thing about doing nothing. You can never tell when anything is going to happen."

"Kelly, you can't take all of the credit, reasoned Betty. Hannibal and Scooter are both alright. If it wasn't for Hannibal and Scooter, you wouldn't have the winning lottery ticket in your hands to give to your brothers. You were totally helpless. I think you need to thank these guys for helping you. Hannibal and Scooter had the can-do, never-giving-up, won't-stop-for nothing attitude. It was the most amazing job they did. What they did was a master stroke."

"Hannibal, it's nice to have you here. I don't know how to show you my appreciation for helping Kelly. Is there no end to your thoughtfulness? Would a handshake be good enough?" offered Michael.

"Oh, it was nothing," smiled Hannibal.

"I'll never forget you for this," added Betty. "I'm sorry I can't be with you. Will I ever see you again? It would be lovely if I could know you better. I can't resist your fatal charms. Before you leave will you take me in your arms and hold me, thrill me and kiss me?"

"OK, Betty. Close your eyes. Pucker up your lips," requested Hannibal. "Ho ho. Ha ha. He he. Good bye."

After Hannibal left the store, Betty stammered, "Strange things are happening. Hannibal doesn't seem to like me or dislike me. I think he just gets nervous around me. It just doesn't seem fair. "

"Betty, take it easy, Hannibal will come through," encouraged Kelly. "Look, Hannibal is coming back in the store."

"Kelly, you better tell your brothers everything, because we may be having more trouble coming our way," cried Betty.

"What other problems could there be? We have the winning lottery ticket and now we're all going to be rich," stated Michael.

I'll tell you in one short sentence," answered Hannibal. "Jerry Dickerson, his mob, Dr. Fine and Charlie, The Chill."

"Oh, them," replied Michael. "What is this all about? How did they find out about the winning lottery ticket?"

"I'll tell you what Betty and I went through, so you can say aha, aha," teased Kelly. "First Dr. Fine and Charlie, The Chill tried to kidnap me when I tried to run out the back door of the West Side Kids' Detective Agency. After we walked past the garage, there stood Jerry Dickerson. He took me from Dr. Fine and Charlie, The Chill. Jerry blindfolded me and took me to his apartment. His girlfriend Delores went through my purse and found the winning lottery ticket."

"Her name is Dixie, not Delores," corrected Hannibal.

"OK. Dixie went through my purse," Kelly continued to say as Tim walked into the store. "After Jerry realized the ticket was a winner, he started to question me about some sort of silly lamp with a magic genie. He wanted me to go back to the West Side Kids' Detective Agency to find the lamp and bring it to him. He said that if I did, he would trade my ticket for the lamp. If I didn't do as he asked, he would tear up the winning lottery ticket.

Then strange things were happening. It was amazing that I didn't see anything. I didn't hear anything and I didn't know anything, because for some odd reason, next I was standing in front of Scooter and this guy by the name of Pockets in the kitchen of the West Side Kids' Detective Agency and I don't know how I got there. Then I began to believe that Jerry Dickerson was right about a lamp with a magic genie."

"Jerry Dickerson really did a job on Kelly. He was playing a game with Kelly to make her think that there are lamps with real magic genies," added Hannibal. "When I talked to Kelly about lamps with magic genies, Kelly insisted that I had one. Jerry Dickerson is driving me nuts about these lamps with magic genies. There is a lot of speculation in Jerry's mind that I have a lamp with a magic genie. I don't like this Jerry Dickerson. He's a dirty rat. Now, you I like.

I think Jerry was just trying to find a reason to keep the winning lottery ticket. That is why Jerry tried to follow us back to Burlington. I had Scooter lead Jerry on a wild goose chase in our SUV. I bought the Ford Taurus in Blue Grass and brought the girls safely back to Burlington. I was really proud of Scooter taking Jerry on a wild goose chase. He is my friend. Nobody can have one better.

Since I don't have a lamp with a magic genie, I have a new deal with Kelly. For one million dollars tax free, my share of the winning lottery ticket, I gave the ticket to Kelly. I was suppose to bring the girls back to Burlington safely for one million dollars. What are you going to do now that you have the ticket? When are you going to cash it in?"

"I know one thing I am going to buy with my share of the winnings," bragged Kelly.

"I am going to buy some nice golden earrings. Chris bought me some golden earrings and he should be embarrassed, because strange things began to happen and when I wore those golden earrings Chris gave me, my ears turned green."

"Kelly, your ears didn't turn green," boomed Chris.

"Did to," insisted Kelly.

Chris then began to open up his mouth and hollered like this "Those golden earrings were very expensive and they did not not turn your ears green!"

"Chris, you are absolutely right. Those earrings didn't turn my ears green except when I wore them."

"Boy, oh boy, oh boy. Here we go again. Hannibal, if you wait right here, I will call the lottery officials right now," assured Michael as he picked up the phone of the book store. "I don't want to take any chances of losing it to Jerry Dickerson or Dr. Fine."

"Michael, how many times have I told you not to use the store's phone," laughed Chris.

"What phone do you want me to use?" asked Michael.

"You can use any phone you want. Just don't use the store phone," jested Chris.

"What phone can I use?" insisted Michael.

"It doesn't make any difference to me. Any phone you want. Just don't use the store phone," scolded Chris.

"Fine. Just fine. If you don't make up your mind, you're going to drive me nuts," screamed Michael.

"OK. Anyway you want it. Here, let me give you a quarter. Go outside that door and you can use the phone in the phone booth," instructed Chris.

"Chris, you are always a comedian. You know that phone isn't hooked up," insisted Michael. "How would you like me to disconnect you from the lottery ticket winnings?"

"Hannibal, They're at it again! yelled Kelly. "They just never stop."

"I didn't know that," admitted Hannibal.

"I knew that," reassured Kelly.

"I understand that," acknowledged Hannibal. "Scooter and myself are always doing the same thing. Don't pay any attention to them. That's what friends and brothers do."

"Well, I don't understands why Chris and Michael don't get along. I want my brothers to be more like you." insisted Kelly.

"You do? I mean you do?" asked Hannibal.

"What's the matter Chris? Don't you ever relax? Leave Michael alone. He's mentally disturbed," reasoned Kelly.

"What's disturbing him?" asked Chris.

"You are," declared Kelly. "Stop that. You're making him nervous."

"Well, he's making me nervous," boomed Chris.

"Chris, you never change," chuckled Kelly.

"I would never treat my brothers and sister like that," added Tim.

"Don't believe a word Tim says," laughed Kelly. He's the worst of my three brothers."

"Am not," replied Tim.

"Am so," insisted Kelly.

"Stop it Kelly and Tim," demanded Chris. "There are customers coming into the store."

"Chris, can you get any books about lamps with magic genies? Well, can you?" asked Hannibal.

"Take it easy. You don't have to explain or prove anything to me. I understand," reassured Chris. "There is something I like about you and I am going to trust you."

"I think Jerry resents me. In fact he hates me and` he gives me the creeps," insisted Hannibal.

"That's a very interesting story. The only advice I can give you is to never go hunting with Jerry," laughed Chris.

"I just talked to the lottery officials," boasted Michael.

"How did it go?" asked Kelly.

"Ho ho. He he. Ha ha. Our ticket is a winner," boomed Michael. "This is the happiest day of my life. I'm going to Des Moines tomorrow by bus to cash in the winning lottery ticket."

"Hannibal, I have a splendid idea. Can we hire you for one more job?" begged Kelly."This is ridiculous because Michael has lost his memory of a day of the week. Would you accompany Michael to Des Moines to cash in the ticket? I want you to look after him. If you do, I think we can give you another one million, tax free."

"This is my lucky day. It sounds like a good idea to me, because right now, I am so poor that I can't pay attention, so I'll do it," yelled an excited Hannibal. "Right now, I think I'm going to stay at the casino hotel here in Burlington to celebrate. My problem is that I'm broke from buying that Ford Taurus. Some people have a high regard for my signature. I wish the bank did.

A couple of months ago, I asked the bank to loan me $10,000.00.

I volunteered to give them my note for the $10,000.00 and said I would pay them back in three months. I told them if I didn't pay them back in three months, they could keep my note. Is there anyway I could get an advance payment as to what you owe me? Say $500.00."

"Let me see what I have in the register," answered Chris. "This winning lottery ticket is getting expensive. It sounds like you're a man that is about to come into money, because you must be expecting money. It looks like I have $500.00 to give you. Thanks again."

"Thank you sir," beamed Hannibal. "I think I'm going to stop at a drive through and get me some tacos."

"Why don't you order ahead," suggested Chris.

"No, I would rather have some tacos," teased Hannibal. "Michael, I will be picking you up tomorrow in front of the store at eight o'clock. I will be leaving now. See you later, What Do You Think.

Chapter Two
THE HIGH HOPES INCIDENT

After Hannibal left the store, Kelly said to Tim, "What's eating you?"

"I was thinking what you said about Hannibal having a lamp with a magic genie," exclaimed Tim. "From what you told us, I think Hannibal has convinced you that there is no such thing as a lamp with a magic genie. He was trying to depict that he didn't have a lamp with a magic genie. That was far from the truth. I think his story is phony. We'll soon find out."

"Come to think of it, I think you are on to something, Tim," reasoned Michael. "There is just something wrong with his story that Kelly told us. You don't go from one place to another in a couple of seconds without realizing what happened to you. It was like a whirlwind visit. I sure would like to know how it happened. I know. It happened to Chris and myself."

"The West Side Kids have to have a lamp with a magic genie," insisted Chris. "Michael, that can be the only explanation as to how we came back to Burlington and not knowing how it happened. It also explains losing our memory and losing Tuesday.

It was really a weird circumstance that we appeared out of nowhere. That was the most notable cause of absolute terror. There is so much about the experience as we can imagine, it that makes you feel alone. That is no way to live."

"Tim and I are here to support you and Michael, because you are not alone in this," insisted Kelly.

"It happened that way, because the West Side Kids have a genie. They are ordinary people doing extraordinary things with a lamp and a magic genie. It was pretty smart of them, wasn't it? Now that I remember that, I know that I am right," reasoned Chris."

"On top of that, I know this Jerry Dickerson and Dr. Fine, " assessed Michael. "They wouldn't be after the lamp with the magic genie if it weren't true."

"I see. I think I've got the answer," reckoned Chris. "When I went to Davenport to get the winning lottery ticket, I found a pot. No, it was a lamp and I threw it in the waste basket.

Scooter would know if it was a lamp when he saw it. I'm sure he didn't know there was a genie in the lamp anymore than I did. He pulled the lamp out of the waste basket and I sold it to him for $5.00. Neither Scooter and myself knew he was getting a bargain."

"I bought the lamp at a yard sale. I always had it in the back of my mind that there could be a genie in the lamp," exclaimed Michael. "Let me say one word. If you're not interested, I'll never mention it again. The word is lamp."

"No, Michael, you might as well forget about the lamp. I'm not interested. OK?" insisted Chris.

"Maybe I need to say more words. The West Side Kids have my lamp with a magic genie and I want it back," demanded Michael.

"No, I strongly advise you to forget the lamp with the magic genie," reasoned Chris. "Besides our winning lottery ticket, it's just as good as having a genie."

"Ouch! What do you mean that having a winning lottery ticket is as good as having a genie? What in the world are you talking about? What did you say? Let's have it," challenged Michael. "I just don't know what you are talking about. Why do you keep saying no every time I want to do something? I think you are being mean and insensitive. Now, I am going to open up my mouth and holler like Hannibal. I don't like you, you dirty rat."

"It's time we had a heart to heart talk, because there is something else I want to explain to you. If I explained it once about you forgetting the lamp and the magic genie, I've explained it to you a thousand times," recalled Chris.

"Then does that mean, if you explained it to me a thousand times to forget the lamp with the magic genie, you've only explained it once?" reasoned Michael. "I want to go to Davenport to get my redemption by bringing back the lamp with the magic genie."

"I guess you're not going to understand this. I'm not sure of anything, because I don't know how to make you understand," scolded Chris. "Can a leopard change his spots? Would a leopard change his spot? Can a leopard change a five for two tens? Who let that leopard in here anyway?"

"What? Here we go again. I don't believe it," smiled Michael.

"I don't believe you don't believe it," admitted Chris. "You shouldn't be the one to complain. We are all going to be an overnight success since you bought the winning lottery ticket. We are all going to start having an intense and meaningful, good life, because now we will be living the life of Riley.

In addition to a complicated life, there will be impossible conditions. Nobody is going to try and take our winnings away from us except maybe our family, friends and greedy people who have the love and obsession for the fortunes we have. Then, we might run into some people that might be off the beaten path."

"So what about it. They can't do this to me. I want the gravy, instead they can have the beans. When the time comes, if these people try to take advantage of me, then it will be time to put the gloves on, because I mean business," insisted Tim."It might even be a little fun."

"Tim, you should know that money can't buy life. Where do you want your body sent? If they ever chase you, the first thing you better do is surrender. This is no pool hall. It's a store where I sell books," laughed Chris. "Some people say that when you are rich, you get used to it."

"How long does it take to get used to it?" asked Tim.

"Well, I'll tell you a few things. That's the problem of the rich. There is nothing we can do about it and it can't be helped, even if we had a pocket full of wishes. I'm beginning to think we're better off not having a winning lottery ticket or wishing we had a magic genie."

"You're telling me that I don't have a chance to go to Davenport because you're banning me to go to Davenport and not giving me a choice?" begged Tim. "Why are you so reluctant to help me?"

"This is not a good time. If you have any social engagements in Davenport, I think you better have your secretary cancel them," proposed Chris. "I think you should have to wait awhile."

"When is a good time?" growled Tim. "This is really a very important thing for me to do."

"Tim, that's the only thing you care about. You have a strange attraction to the genie and you're going to do everything in your power to get the lamp with the magic genie. You're looking for more trouble than you can handle. You're beginning to sound like you're becoming a mental case and I don't know if I can talk to you anymore about this because you have a stiff brain," reasoned Chris. "Someday, you're going to have a tragic ending by blowing your brains out."

"If you ask me, I think he has already done it," laughed Kelly.

"Kelly happened to luck out to bring back the winning lottery ticket. With Michael and I, it was another story," Chris continued to say. "There are no words to describe the severity and evilness of Michael's deeds. Michael believed in the supernatural and it turned on him and me."

"I think my skills to get the lamp and genie are uncomparable skills to yours and Michael's," boasted Tim.

"I still think you better leave well enough alone," scolded Chris.

"Is there a way out?" growled Tim.

"I have no idea," declared Chris. "Don't you think you should give this a little more time? What do you expect?"

"So what's with you? Anyhow. That is no consolation what you are telling me. Why are you so mad at me?" bellowed Tim. "I find it hard to believe that you won't help me. You never give me a hand when I need it. What's the matter with you? Don't you ever stop being angry at everything? You are very rude. I don't think you want to help me because you're just as madcap as ever."

"I have to be honest, because it will turn out exactly the way I know it will," reckoned Chris. "You are a little pushy and also very arrogant. What I'm trying to say is, you live by the sword. You die by the sword."

"Well, nonsense. Well, what are we waiting for? Haven't we uncovered enough evidence about the lamp with the magic genie? I want the lamp with the magic genie. What are we going to do about it?" boomed Tim. "I must get them back and I'm going to Davenport to get them both. If I handle it right, there is a good chance I can bring back the lamp with the genie.

Kelly, since you were at the West Side Kids' Detective Agency, would you draw me a diagram of the house so it would give me an idea where to look for the lamp?"

"You seem to think that you can pickle your nose. You can pickle a friend. But don't pickle your friend's nose or something like that. I think your brain is yea thick," insisted Chris. "I don't like this new idea. When you come up with an idea, why do you always dump it on me?"

"Because you're my brother and my best friend," smiled Tim.

"I don't want to be your best friend," answered Chris.

"You talk about my idea of being my best friend as if it was a dirty word," reasoned Tim. "Am I asking for so much? I have time on my hands, so I'll be your best friend because you can't make friends to save your life. Don't you like my idea?"

"I'm certainly glad you appreciate me and I don't like it at all," scolded Chris. "We were friends before. Now, you're my responsibility."

"What did I do now to make you say that?" asked Tim.

"That's just not necessary for you to go to Davenport, because a few things have gone wrong when Michael and I went to Davenport. If you try to get the lamp and the genie, you're going to make this your life's work. You'll live, you will definitely live without the lamp and the genie," reasoned Chris.

"If that's all that's bothering you, I will take care of it myself," promised Tim. "If I get the lamp and the magic genie, the possibilities are endless. Not only can we have what we want, look what we can do for Burlington. OK. You are right. Like it or not, this was my idea and I have responsibilities. The only thing left for me to do, is what I have to do."

"I agree with Tim," proclaimed Kelly. "It's really not a bad thought. Come on Tim, you can do it. I have a hunch that you can find the lamp with the magic genie and bring it back. I know the house and I know how Hannibal and Scooter thinks."

"I guess if you feel that strongly about it, you can try it," offered Chris. "What do you intend to do about this matter?"

"Well, how do you like that? See, it's not so hard to give," beamed Tim. "That's all I need to know. It's weird to be left off the hook and to be put in 2nd place and have you be sympathetic toward me at the same time."

"OK, Tim. Come on. Let's go. What are you waiting for?" asked Chris.

"I know the house even better," boomed Michael. "I think if Tim wants to go to Davenport to get the lamp and the magic genie, I will accompany my brother to Davenport."

"What did you say, Michael?" growled Chris.

"I said that if Tim wants to go to Davenport to get the lamp with the magic genie, I will go with him."

"Oh, that's dumb. Michael, haven't you forgotten something?" asked Chris. "You're getting a little too careless with your thinking. Absolutely not. No, you certainly can't go to Davenport with Tim, because you're going to Des Moines with Hannibal tomorrow."

"I get you. You're way ahead of me. You're right. It is dumb. I just wasn't thinking," answered Michael. "Tim, before you go, can you wait for me to come back from Des Moines? I wish you would wait until I can go with you.

Now that I think about it, Tim won't need me to go to Davenport with him, because Hannibal will be with me. He just doesn't want to run into Hannibal. All Tim has to do is deal with Scooter. Well, I admit it. I like the idea."

"Then, it's settled. I heard enough to make my decision. I'm handling things myself. I am going to pack my clothes and leave for Davenport right away while I have a better chance to get the lamp with the magic genie. The sooner, the better," declared Tim. "I think you have heard everything I have to say."

"I think I've heard enough," laughed Chris. "Words are for fools who haven't said enough. Before you make a decision about going to Davenport, you should post this on Facebook to see how many likes you get."

"I don't need the likes on Facebook," answered Tim. Everything has already been said."

"Then you better have a plan, a good plan," insisted Michael. "You've got to be crazy to do this. Remember, you're going to have to compete with Jerry Dickerson and Dr. Fine to get the lamp with the magic genie because they are twisted human beings. What are you going to do now?"

"I would rather go skiing and let them eat their cake," replied Tim.

"Oh wow. Oh wow. I've never known you to ski," said a surprised Michael.

"I never have. But I would rather ski than to go to Davenport. None of these people in Davenport knows who I am. That will be in my favor," smiled Tim.

"Just watch yourself and don't be too overconfident, because when we went to Davenport strange things began to happen," noted Chris. "We don't want you to return to Burlington like my little brother, Michael and I did with the loss of your memory. You're taking a big risk."

"Don't put the blame on me. I'm used to long odds and I'm willing to take that chance, because I think I can pull it off," boasted Tim. "I just want all of you to know that anything Kelly can do, I can do better. Maybe you want me to do things different than you did?"

"It doesn't make any difference to me what you do," replied Chris.

"I know you want me to do something different. Just what do you want me to do that's different?" asked Tim.

"It doesn't make any difference to me what you do," repeated Chris. "Do anything you want to do."

"Tell me what you want me to do that's different," insisted Tim.

"Nothing. If you don't make up your mind, you're going to drive me nuts. What are you going to do about it?" boomed Chris. "Must you wear those glasses?"

"Only when I want to see, " explained Tim. "I can't see without them."

"I see. Tim, You are so full of it," replied Kelly. "Then you better wear those glasses, because you don't realize it, but you have a big job ahead of you. A big, big job."

"Kelly, from what all of us has talked about, I think it's going to give me a chance to do the big, big job," assured Tim.

"OK, go for it. I know you can get the job done because you are a Murphy," exclaimed Chris. "There is something we didn't talk about and that is the rest of the West Side Kids you will be dealing with. Remember, there are eight of them to deal with."

"I didn't know that," insisted Tim.

"I knew that," reasoned Michael.

"I knew that," added Kelly.

"I never thought about that," reckoned Tim. "I guess I'll have to deal with them one way or another when I get there. One thing is for sure, I know about them, but they don't know about me. I've got work to do. They are in for a big surprise and I think they will leave me alone. Because of that, I won't have any trouble getting the lamp with the magic genie.

There is nothing like being prepared. I'll be there when they least expect it. The strange act of providence will protect my secret. If I act fast enough, they won't have time to stop me. They will be surprised alright.

Tomorrow, I'm going to their detective agency to get the lamp. I don't have time to explain. I better get ready to go and now I have to run to get the lamp with the magic genie."

"You can take off, wise guy. Good-bye kid. Hurry back," requested Chris.

"Here we go again," boomed Michael. "Tim, I hope everything turns out that you hope that it will be."

"How do you like that? Now, what's Tim up to?" asked Kelly.

"Search me. It's sure not clear to me," answered Michael. "It sounds like trouble. If there is trouble, Tim is going to be right in the middle of it. That's all I know."

After Tim went out the door, Kelly began to yell, "Tim, come back Tim! Come back!

As Tim started to drive away, Kelly ran out the door and continued to yell, "Tim, come back! Come back Tim! Come back!

Burlington By The Book, front view

Chapter Three

THE INCIDENT OF THE GREAT ESCAPE

The next day, Tim pulled up to the property of the West Side Kids' Detective Agency. Tim decided to sit in his car to see if anybody was in the house. After sitting in his car for a half hour, Tim climbed out of his car and walked over to the house. He then began to look through the windows and started humming, "A hunting I will go. A hunting I will go. Hi ho the dairy-o, a hunting I will go."

Then he said to himself, "Where is that wabbit I'm looking for? I hope to find the wabbit, I mean lamp today. So far, I don't see it. It's got to be someplace in the house. It's probably in the kitchen. How do you like that? There it is. Na, it can't be. By golly, it is the lamp. The lamp I have come for, is sitting on the kitchen table.

There is nobody in the kitchen. Now it is time to sneak in the kitchen to get my lamp. This is going to be easier than I thought."

Tim then walked through the back door and approached the kitchen table. As he picked up the lamp, he said to himself as Pockets walked into the kitchen, "What's up Doc? You're a sight for sore eyes."

"Hey, put that lamp down!" yelled Pockets. "That's my lamp."

"Not anymore," insisted Tim. "Now the lamp is mine. Now, I'm taking the lamp with me and getting away with murder."

Tim then began to walk out the back door with the lamp as a puff of smoke filled the lamp.

Hearing Pockets yell, Scooter ran to the kitchen just in time to watch Tim leave with the lamp. A race began as Tim raced to his car with the lamp, with Scooter following.

Sitting in his car down the street, Jerry Dickerson and his gang watch as Tim with the lamp climbs into his car and then drives away. Jerry Dickerson then begins to follow Tim.

Scooter climbs into his car and follows Jerry Dickerson and Tim.

Parked down the other side of the street is Dr. Fine and Charlie, The Chill. After they watch what happens, they follow Tim, Jerry and Scooter. And the race is on to Burlington.

Tim calls Chris at his book store and tells Chris about the lamp and Jerry Dickerson following him.

Scooter calls Hannibal, who is with Michael Murphy in Des Moines and tells him about Tim taking the lamp and Jerry Dickerson following him.

"I don't know who that was that took the lamp," said an excited Scooter to Hannibal. "It looks like he's leading us to Burlington. How soon can you get to Burlington?"

"Michael and myself are an hour and a half away," explained Hannibal. I will step on it and try and get there sooner. I don't know how I'm going to go faster with all the traffic on the road. In the meantime, call the West Side Kids and have them follow you. We may all end up in Burlington."

"I know who has the lamp," insisted Michael. "It was my brother Tim, who went to Davenport to get the lamp from you and Scooter. None of us ever figured that Jerry Dickerson and his mob would be following Tim back to Burlington."

"I never figured you or your brother Tim would even believe we had a lamp and then come to Davenport to get our lamp," replied an angry Hannibal. "Scooter bought the lamp from you. Your brother Tim had no right to take the lamp from our house. I could have kept your $50,000,000.00 winning lottery ticket, but I gave it to Kelly to give to you. One thing I know is, cheating won't get you far in life. So it just seemed fair and I thought it was the right thing to do.

Boy, oh boy, oh boy. This must be the most unluckiest day of my life. When we find Tim, I want you to help me get the lamp back. The genie in the lamp, Pockets, is a member of the West Side Kids' Detective Agency. I don't care if he is a magic genie. Pockets is my friend and I want him back. His friendship is worth more than his magic could ever be."

"I'm sorry my brother took your lamp," apologized Michael. "Tim and me thought you was holding out on us. Chris tried to discourage Tim and me about taking your lamp. He told us that just because we think we're going to have a good life and we're going to be rich, that being rich or having a lamp could cause us many problems. That is no way to live. Money can't buy life. We wouldn't listen to Chris about this and didn't understand what he was trying to tell us.

Now I will help you get the lamp back. Before I can do that, we have to deal with Jerry Dickerson. I better call Tim and warn him that he is being followed by Jerry Dickerson. Then, I better call my brother Chris and tell him to make Tim give you back your lamp."

As Scooter is talking to Hannibal. Jerry sees Dr. Fine in his rear view mirror and calls him.

"Dr. Fine, This is Jerry Dickerson. I don't know who this Mug is in front of us that has the lamp. I know you want the lamp as much as we do," exclaimed Jerry. "We are both having trouble grabbing the lamp from Scooter."

"Well, well. That's a surprise; you calling me," insisted Dr. Fine. "What's happening to you? I thought you hated me."

"I'm particular who I put in with. Let's make a deal and go on this as partners, instead of fighting over who gets the lamp," suggested Jerry. "Instead of being more complicated, I think it would be a little more effective and faster if we work together. We would be working for the same end at that. What do you say?"

"That is a good idea if we work together. I'm willing to help anyway I can. Why are you telling me all of this?" asked Dr. Fine.

"That all depends on you. The game is not over yet," answered Jerry.

"What makes you think so?" asked Dr. Fine.

"All I want is a chance to work together," offered Jerry.

"I'm for it," reassured Dr. Fine. "If we can get the lamp, the genie should grant all the wishes we want. How do you propose we get the lamp? You had your chance to get the lamp before? What stopped you?"

"A few things have gone wrong and I have no idea," replied Jerry. "All I know is that, since this Mug doesn't know who we are, that may be our chance to get the lamp. That Mug has to see us pretty soon. Just stay a safe distance behind us, so you won't be spotted. It's not going to be a picnic.

Now remember, if anything happens and we fail to get the lamp, because this Mug turns the genie on us, it will be up to you to grab the lamp from this Mug. The West Side Kids made a pack of fools out of all of us by using the genie. They used the genie and got us all messed up by having our heads shaved and losing our memories."

"He can't turn the genie on us," reasoned Ace. "Remember, only Scooter and Hannibal, together, has control of the genie. That is something we shouldn't overlook."

"Oh sure. Now I get it and now I'll find out for myself," reassured Jerry. "Scooter is following me and Hannibal is no where to be seen. That Mug in front of us has to stop pretty soon. I don't think we will have any trouble with Scooter.

Now, it looks like this Mug is going to Burlington. I just wonder if he knows Michael and Chris Murphy."

"It's possible," answered Dr. Fine. "We will just have to see where he leads us. How far do you think Burlington is from here?"

"I just saw a sign that says thirty-nine miles to Burlington," replied Jerry. "If he goes to Burlington By The Book in Burlington, that will be our opportunity to grab the lamp. If that's the case, me and my boys will try to park our car in front of the store and go in first to try and grab the lamp."

"Are Charlie and myself going after this Mug into the bookstore with you?" asked Dr. Fine.

"We need to be prepared to what we can and must do. Whatever goes on in the store, my men will take care of it," explained Jerry. "After we go in, the most effective way to support us is to wait in your car a few minutes to see what happens next. If we get the lamp, then you and Charlie, The Chill grab Scooter when he gets out of his car.

After that we will all go to Davenport as fast as we can and go to my apartment. Then we need to get Hannibal to come to my apartment so that Scooter and Hannibal together will turn the lamp and the genie over to us."

"Whatever you say. Charlie and I are prepared to help you. In a nutshell, aren't we running a high risk? What if Hannibal and Scooter turns the genie against us?" asked Dr. Fine.

"They won't, because when we get back to Davenport, we will kidnap one of the gang members and not tell Scooter and Hannibal what we did with him," replied Jerry. "Those boys care very much about each other. I don't think we will have any more trouble with them. Hannibal and Scooter will sacrifice the lamp for the safety of one of the members of the gang."

"I like your plan. It looks like we are finally going to get the lamp," declared Dr. Fine. "What if this Mug goes someplace different than the bookstore?"

"We'll deal with it, if that happens," answered Jerry. "I really think this Mug is going to the book store. In case you get lost, do you have the address to Burlington By The Book?"

"No, I never have been there before," replied Dr. Fine.

"The address is 301 Jefferson in downtown Burlington," answered Jerry.

"OK, I'll see you when and if we get to the book store," replied Dr. Fine.

Thirty minutes later, Hannibal and Michael pulled in front of Burlington By The Book and went into the store.

"Hi, Chris," greeted Michael. "What's the word? Did Tim tell you he had the lamp? He did a great job. I didn't think he would make it here with the lamp."

"Yes, he did and he should be here in a couple of minutes. I would sure like to know when he is going to show up," replied Chris.

"What's your hurry?" asked Michael.

"I just can't stand this waiting, waiting, waiting," answered Chris. "I hope no customers come in the store after he gets here."

"Jerry and his gang is right behind Tim. He is looking for the lamp. I think I'll have some fun and let him find it," exclaimed Michael. "Chris, is that baseball bat still in the store room?"

"It's somewhere in that room," assumed Chris.

"Then I have a plan. This is going to be mighty tough for Jerry and his pirates. Jerry is a tin horn crook and he is really asking for it," insisted Michael.

"This, I have to see," boomed Chris.

"OK. Let's get ready for them. I'm going to wait in the store room at the end of the store with that baseball bat," explained Michael. "Hannibal, there is a hallway at the end of the store that leads to the art center and bathrooms. You wait there. Chris, when Tim comes, send him our way with the lamp. Jerry and his gang will follow Tim and when they do, I will hit each one of them on the head with the bat. When they reach the hall, Hannibal, sock them a good one. Chris, after they walk past you, call the police. Hannibal, there's Tim. Let's go.

As Michael and Hannibal ran to the end of the store, in walks Tim and Scooter.

"Tim, run out to the hallway in the back of the store! Hurry!" yelled Chris.

"Hey mister, you've got my lamp and want it back," screamed Scooter, as he followed Tim to the back of the store.

Next, Jerry, Ace, Lefty, Danny, Shorty and Mugs came rushing through the front door of the store as Dr. Fine and Charlie, The Chill watched from their car.

"There he goes with the lamp! Look at him run! yelled Jerry. "Get that lamp!"

As Jerry walked past the supply room, Michael hit him in the head with the bat and Jerry staggered out in the hall as Scooter raised his arms and yelled, "Get him Hannibal"

Hannibal then socked Jerry, knocking him down.

As Ace, Lefty, Danny, Shorty and Mugs passed the supply room, Michael hit each one in the head with the bat as Scooter repeated, "Get him Hannibal! Get him!"

Each one then walked blindly in the hallway, where Hannibal socked each of them in the jaw where they all fell down on each other.

The Blue Jinn s then appeared in the hallway and grabbed the lamp out of Tim's hands. He then rubbed the lamp and a puff of smoke came out of the lamp.

"I don't know who you are," said Scooter to the Blue Jinn s. That's my friend Pockets and that's my lamp. Give it back to me," ordered Scooter.

"Who is this stupid, crazy human being ordering me around like that?" asked the Blue Jinn s.

"That's my friend Scooter. Don't do anything to him," begged Pockets. "He has been very kind to me. That is Hannibal standing behind me. They have both been very good to me."

"You and your lamp are coming with me," proclaimed the Blue Jinn s.

"Before you take me away, can I grant Scooter and Hannibal one wish?" asked Pockets.

"Just one quick wish and we're leaving," replied the Blue Jinn s.

"Because I always wanted a lamp of my own, with a magic genie, I wish Hannibal to be put in a lamp and replace you as my genie," wished Scooter.

In a flash, a second lamp appeared with Hannibal inside it.

"Let me out of here! Let me out of here," screamed Hannibal.

"Hannibal, you wanted a lamp and now you have one," laughed Scooter.

"Rub the lamp and let me out!" yelled Hannibal.

"Hannibal, I will rub the lamp if you want to come out of that broken down tea pot and that you promise me that you will follow my rules. One of my rules is not to do anything stupid," insisted Scooter. "You have to grant me all my wishes and quit calling me stupid. Now, I finally have a pocket full of wishes of my own."

Chapter Four

The Incident of Hannibal, The Genie

Scooter is standing in the hallway of Burlington By The Book store. He has Hannibal now in a teapot replacing Pockets, the genie. Pockets, the Blue jinn s and the lamp vanished in a puff of smoke.

Kelly screams, "What a sight at the end of the hallway."

All of Jerry's gang, Ace, Lefty, Danny, Mugs, Shorty and Jerry, himself are moaning in pain.

"It serves them right to rush into my brother's book store and to try to steal the lamp with the magic genie. Are you alright Michael?" asked Kelly.

"I'm doing fine," assured Michael, alias Zodiac. "I'm checking my bat for any dents. Chris says the police should be coming any minute now. We should make sure Jerry and his gang don't wake up and try to escape."

Tim not believing what he had seen questions, "Who was that blue character that took the other stranger and disappeared with the lamp? I see no trace of them being here and Hannibal is missing too."

Scooter laughs, "Ho ho. Ha ha. He he." and says, "Strange things have happened. I have a pocket full of wishes and I know where Hannibal is."

Chris interrupts Scooter and alerts the family, "I hear the sirens of the Burlington Police cars coming."

Scooter then moves out of sight around the corner of the hallway and rubs "the teapot" to have Hannibal appear.

Standing in front of Scooter, Hannibal whined, "I am the slave of the broken down teapot, I mean lamp, and I will grant you your wishes. What would you wish for, gold, silver, dancing girls, to be put in a teapot of your own? I better not let you wish to be put in a teapot of your own, because if the Blue Jinn s finds out, he will never let you out of the teapot."

"I know you have to say those things. What are you trying to do? Do you think that's funny offering me to be in a teapot of my own?," asked Scooter.

"I know you know I have to say those things. Now, since you had me put in the lamp, I'm not upset with you. I just wanna kill ya.

Now, I'm a genie, I have to say all of that. I just added that you could wish for your own teapot for laughs," declared Hannibal. "Keep me out of the lamp, please. I will follow all of your rules and grant you, your wishes. I am sorry Pockets had to leave suddenly with the Blue Jinn s. I will miss him, because you did another stupid thing and wished for me to be a genie to replace Pockets."

"Right now, I need your presence," begged Scooter. "How are your fists?"

"My fists are a little uncomfortable, but I am fine." reassured Hannibal.

The Burlington Police arrived at the book store in three squad cars. After being startled by the sirens, people from other businesses, in downtown Burlington, stood around the silenced police cars to watch the exciting action. Three Burlington Police Officers entered the bookstore with their tasers in hand. They identified themselves and explained why they were there.

Meanwhile, Dr. Fine and Charlie, The Chill are in their car, parked along the other side of the street. Due to the chaotic event developing at the bookstore, they decide to leave the scene and go back to Davenport.

Scooter whispers to Hannibal, "Hannibal, my best buddy, I could just scream. That's a fine mess I got myself into. Why does everything always happen to me?"

"You could just scream?" moaned Hannibal. "Everything has happened to me. First you wished me into this lamp and now I'm the genie of this broken down teapot. Next you're calling me your best buddy. Right now as your best buddy, Mr. Master, I'm going to help you get out of this fine mess that you got yourself into. Now, I have work to do and I believe I must start with this wish, if you agree with this."

"Don't tell me. I'll agree to anything you want to do. You don't even have to go back into the lamp anymore. Just hurry up and make the wish before I get into bigger trouble," demanded Scooter. "What about it?"

"Nothing about it, my master. Here it goes. I hope it works because I haven't done this before," reckoned Hannibal. "I wish to have Ace, Lefty, Danny, Mugs, Shorty, Dr. Fine, Charlie, The Chill, Chris, Michael, Tim and Kelly, wiped out of their memory of the lamps and the genies and Pockets and the Blue Jinn s appearance. I want Jerry Dickerson to remember, so he will be a crazy person for believing in genies."

Hannibal murmurs, "As your best buddy, Mr. Master, I just completed the wish that I hope that will get you out of trouble, master of my lamp. Now, if it worked, only you, the West Side Kids and Jerry will only know of genies and their abilities."

While Hannibal and Scooter are still out of sight, one police officer asks, "What's going on here? Everyone stay where you are with your hands up."

The other two officers walked to the back of the store and saw bodies laying on the hallway floor.

Officer Bill Conner bellowed, "Why are these people moaning on the floor?"

Tim bursts out, "They rushed into the bookstore to steal my brother's winning lottery money. We thought they were going to get aggressive, so Michael and Hannibal protected us and our property. They gently batted and punched them onto the floor."

Officer Conner replied, "I see. When they wake up, we will arrest them. Next, we will need statements from all of you. Who is the owner of Burlington By The Book?"

"I am," replied Chris.

"Do you confirm with all that has been said and witnessed here so far?" asked Officer Conner.

"Yes indeed," insisted Chris. "We were protecting my brother's winnings and ourselves."

"Excuse me, sir," replied Officer Conner. "I need to tell Officer Johnson to hold back the crowd assembling here at the front door.

Officer Johnson, tell these people to disperse and go about their business shopping in downtown Burlington."

"I'm right on it," promised Officer Johnson.

Officer Conner then calls for several ambulances to take the injured Jerry Dickerson and his gang to the local emergency room for evaluation. When the injured woke up, Officer Conner read them their rights and told them why they were being arrested.

Officer Conner then instructed the third Police Officer to meet Jerry Dickerson and his gang at the ER and to call for backup. Officer Conner thought he needed more help watching over the numerous gang members with the head injuries.

Officer Conner next told the Murphy family, Hannibal and Scooter that they may be questioned at the hearing of those being arrested tonight.

Officer Conner then said, "I will need your names, addresses and phone numbers. After you give them to me, you can leave. The Burlington Police Department will contact you, if needed."

Chapter Five

The Incident At The Goldfish Palace Casino

Without telling anybody, Scooter and Hannibal decided to go to the Goldfish Palace Casino in Burlington. Hannibal and Scooter, with the lamp, then left the bookstore and went to the Goldfish Palace Hotel, where they checked in for the night. Although, they didn't bring any extra clothes with them, they went up to their room.

After they went into their room and sat on the bed each one had picked out, Hannibal asked Scooter, "Are you ready to go gamble and make money our way?"

"You bet your lamp, I'm ready," answered Scooter. "Now that you're a genie, we will never have to be the nice guy, because we can do things our way."

"What do you mean?" asked Hannibal. It always pays to be a nice guy and there will always be people we can help as detectives, like we helped Betty and Kelly."

"I know what I said, but I didn't mean how I said it," replied Scooter. "What I meant is that since you're a genie, we can just have fun with it, by pranking people. Yet, we should always use your powers to help powerless people that are in trouble."

"Scooter, I always knows you have a heart of gold. That's the smartest thing I ever heard you tell me. OK boy. Let the games begin.

Let's get it done," insisted Hannibal. "Since we don't have much cash on us to gamble with, we have to go to the ATM."

After getting the money that both of them needed to gamble with, Hannibal recommended to Scooter that they should go separate ways in the casino. Hannibal's thinking was that they could try to win on more slot machines if they do it that way. Perhaps, they would have a better chance in hitting the jackpot on one of these machines.

"Gambling isn't part of my life," explained Hannibal. "Scooter, you are due for better chances to win since you lost our deposit money and you felt like making it up, by selling your car. Even though you are an easy going and light heart-ed man, I don't want you to feel a range of negative emotions. Before you drop that first quarter in a slot machine, you need to just stay calm and boost up your confidence. Then you need to pump yourself up and prepare yourself to win some money.

When you went to sell your car to Friendly Freddy, he tried to take advantage of you because he could see you were a very happy-go-lucky type of a man and very stupid and an idiot."

Scooter was then baffled by the whole fiasco of what Hannibal said. Being absolutely appalled and displeased, Scooter commanded Hannibal to quit calling him stupid and an idiot. Scooter then demanded that Hannibal apologize or he was going to put Hannibal back in the lamp.

"First you was gushing over me about being a happy-go-lucky type of man and then you call me stupid," boomed Scooter. "I don't understand you. What do you do that for? This is an outrage. I was waiting for something like that to happen.

I'm going to punish you severely. You're going to sing a different tune when I put you back in the lamp. You won't get out of that lamp. Not for a long time. That is my final decision. P-H-Y-N-U-L decision."

"Hannibal then began to think deeper and began to apologize as his anxiety heightened to a whole new level by saying, "I guess I do have egg on my face. I must be slipping in my old age. To make things perfectly clear, I still have the habit of calling you stupid. That's not the kind of cooperation I meant to have and I'm sorry. I was determined to help you solve your problem with Friendly Freddy and decided to start with the direct approach."

"It's OK. Just relax. I'm not going to put you back in the lamp since you apologized," smiled Scooter. "I'm glad you came to my rescue and straightened out Friendly Freddy, because everything got flipped upside down.

Friendly Freddy was unreasonable with me and absolutely terrifying. I was nervous and anxious about this interaction with Friendly Freddy. He was intimidating me on a one-on-one encounter. The most frustrating part of the situation seemed to be more and more stressful to deal with Friendly Freddy.

"If Friendly Freddy was my friend on Facebook, I would have definitely unfriended Friendly Freddy" as both of them began laughing. "I still need a new car, but I'm not going to buy it from Friendly Freddy.

This is a beautiful, colorful and noisy casino," Scooter continued to say as his heart began to race and as he began to think which slot machine could be a winner. "Everyone looks like they are having fun."

"I agree," replied Hannibal. "Now let's see if we can be happy. I think we should pursue around the casino. We better be careful and handle this operation with great care. You go to the left of the casino, while I go to the right. If that doesn't work, I think we should kick for the extra point."

"What are you, a wise guy or a truck driver?" laughed Scooter.

"No, I'm your best buddy, friends to the end Mr. Master of the lamp," chuckled Hannibal. "Now, go do what I told you before I wish you in the lamp. Well, what's it going to be?"

"To be or not to be is the question. Alright, alright, Don't rush me, I'm going," cried Scooter.

After slowly maneuvering around the Goldfish Palace Casino, they saw slot machines and game boards. People were smoking in areas designated for smoking. Being the detectives they are, they also noticed strategically, located cameras around the casino. After scouting the casino, Hannibal and Scooter met halfway on the floor.

Scooter then tried to find Hannibal through all the smoke and yelled, "Hannibal, where are you? I can't find you anywhere in all this smoke."

"Ditto," replied Hannibal.

"How did you find me?" asked Scooter.

"You was feeling down in the dumps, so I checked all of the dumps," answered Hannibal.

"We need to move away from all of this smoke. It's so hard to breath in here," exclaimed Scooter. "Get me a pail of water, so we can put out the fire."

Hearing what Scooter said, a man playing a slot machine behind Scooter, got up out of his chair and got on his knees behind Scooter. He stuck a match and attached it behind Scooter's shoe and lit it.

"Ouch, ouch," yelled Scooter as he jumped up and down trying to put the fire out as the man laughed.

Seeing what the man did to Scooter, Hannibal said to the man, "Don't touch my friend. You have to go through me first. When it comes right down to it, I should get first crack at him.

There is one man too many in this casino and I think it's you. I don't know who you are, but you have a surprise coming. Now just go home," and immediately Hannibal wished the man to turn into a twelve year old boy. "I don't think we're going to have any trouble with you anymore. It's better to burn out than to fade away," laughed Hannibal.

A security guard then approached the twelve year old boy and asked him how he got into the casino. Being confused as to what just happened to him, the twelve year old boy showed the security guard his identification.

Looking at the identification, the security guard, said to the boy, "That won't wash. That's not you. You have to leave the casino immediately."

After the security guard and the boy left, Hannibal asked Scooter, "Are you alright? We have to be very careful what we do, because we can't stay out of the range of the cameras and the security guards."

Scooter then whispered to Hannibal, "I wish to win a bundle of money playing the slot machines today."

"What?" asked Hannibal. "Speak up boy. With all that noise in here, I can't hear you. You need to quit whispering or I'm going to have to learn to read lips."

"I said I wish to win a lot of money playing the machines," boomed Scooter. "Is that loud enough for you my best buddy?"

"Scooter, keep it down. Do you want everyone to hear you?" laughed Hannibal. "Most of the people who gamble don't walk out of the casinos with a lot of money. You sound like a man that is just about ready to come into money. I can help you with that. Your wish is my command you, you jerk, I mean best buddy, Mr. Master, of the lamp. Now that I'm a genie, we can pull all the pranks we want. How much money do you have to start with?"

"Just a minute and let me count it," answered Scooter. "I have two twenty's and a ten."

"That should be enough to start with to win from these slot machines," insisted Hannibal. "What slot machine are you going to start with?"

"I like the Double Triple Diamond slot machine in front of me. I know I can win big on this one," answered Scooter. "The best man always wins."

"Oh you're crazy. Nobody ever wins," reasoned Hannibal. "Come on. You can do it. I am prepared to do what I can and must do this for both of us to win on these slot machines. Remember what I told you. I couldn't be in a better position. I'm going to be positioned close enough to the slot machine where you are playing at."

"Do you think it will work?' bragged Scooter.

"Just do what I tell you and play three quarters at a time and I will line up The Double and Triple Diamonds for the win. Now, let's concentrate. It's free for the taking. After we win on this machine, we have to be careful and move along to another machine of your choice, so we are not noticed by the security guards."

After playing three different machines and winning $1,200, Hannibal says to Scooter, "That's my boy. Now let's moves to the Pyramids in Egypt slot machine."

After putting three quarters in the machine, The Queen of Egypt appeared on Scooter's lap. Scooter puts his arm around The Queen of Egypt and hits the button on the machine. The machine begins to spin and Scooter screams, "Come on-Beetle-Bomb!"as it stops, an excited Scooter screams again as his heart began pounding and he yells, "Oh Boy, Oh Boy! Is this exciting news! The Jackpot! It seems to be one surprise after another. I won again! You're a sight for sore eyes. Come to Papa! I've got plans for you!" Looking at Hannibal with evil in his eyes, Scooter roared, "It's mine. All mine."

Answering Scooter, Hannibal replied, "Don't give me that look. I invented it. You have to give me the money, or else."

"Or else what?" asked Scooter.

"Or else, make it my day. I always wanted to say that. How would you like me to punch you in the nose? Then, that can be all yours."

"I'm not interested in giving you the money, you noodle head," cried Scooter.

"That word just jumped out of the gutter and into your mouth," declared Hannibal.

"I'll put you back in the lamp and that will teach you to hit me," threatened Scooter.

"Why bother? You don't have to teach me. I already know how to hit you," clarified Hannibal. "You agreed to everything, before we started to gamble."

"I'm sorry Chief. OK, I'll do it. You take the money. You can have all of it, you, you dirty rat. I'm better off without it. After one day of gambling, I have already been stabbed in the back.

Besides, I have something better sitting on my lap. She is a cute, adorable, grabbing attention, Queen of Egypt. Now this, I like," hollered Scooter. "Can I have some more money to play some more machines?"

A lot of noise is heard throughout the casino and people begin to gather around Scooter and Hannibal, including several security guards, who came unannounced as the slot machine was ringing up credits over a $1,000.

One huge, muscular, security guard standing at 6' 4" interrupted the increasing number of people in the crowd, by demanding them to clear the area around the Pyramids of Egypt slot machine and go about their business. Then the security guard saw the Queen of Egypt sitting on Scooter's lap and said to himself, "That's strange.

Impossible. Na, it can't be.". Then he began to rub his eyes in disbelief. When he was finished rubbing his eyes, the Queen of Egypt was gone.

Joe then said to Hannibal, "Did you see what I saw?"

Hannibal looking at the security guard's name tag, which read Joe and then Hannibal asked, "What did you see?"

"There was a girl dressed in an Egyptian costume sitting on this guy's lap and now she's gone, "insisted Joe.

"What girl? What are you talking about?" answered Hannibal. "What have you been drinking? There was no girl sitting on Scooter's lap. How long have you been working here today? Your eyes are playing tricks on you. You sound like a mental case and strange things are happening. I think you're nuts and need to cheer up and be happy and give me a smile. Be happy and that will make your life worthwhile. It's hard to be sad when you're laughing. Then I think you need to go home and rest."

"Maybe you're right," answered Joe. "But for now, I came to assist you with your winnings."

Hannibal then began to explain to Joe by saying, "I am with my master, I mean with my best buddy, who is my best friend in all my life and to the end. You're just the man we're looking for. We want to know how to cash in the credits."

"Oh, you do, do you?" replied Joe. "You need to go to the finance office to cash in your credits and to fill out the paperwork for tax purposes. Bring the cash vouchers with you and I will personally take you there, so that you don't get lost."

As Joe leads Hannibal and Scooter down the hallway to the finance office, Joe then begins to ask Hannibal and Scooter who they are and how long they will be visiting the casino and the city of Burlington.

Hannibal then began to explain to Joe, "Scooter and yours truly are from Davenport where we own a private detection agency."

Interrupting Hannibal, Scooter corrected Hannibal by saying, "We own a private detective agency, which is spelled d-t-e-c-t-e-d-i-v-e agency. Not d-t-e-c-s-h-o-n agency. Hannibal doesn't speak English none so good. Hannibal and myself really enjoy coming to Burlington to gamble. We intend to come to Burlington to gamble and visit Burlington By The Book. This time, we had a race to get to Burlington By The Book. I came from Davenport, while Hannibal came from Des Moines. I followed Tim from Davenport and."

"And I beat you there," Hannibal continued to say.

"When you arrived at Burlington By The Book, you beat a lot of people. Now, I bet you wished this never happened," laughed Scooter.

"So you are detectives,?" asked Joe.

"That's what the sign says on our office door," laughed Hannibal. "Every time Scooter and myself came to gamble before, we lost a lot of money. This time we were lucky and won our money back.

Last time we came, we played a slot machine called Lucky and had high hopes on winning. We thought the machine would come through and instead we lost all of our money, because everything got flipped upside down.

Before that when we came, we played on a machine called The Space Aliens. After we lost all of our money on that machine, a sign would say, "There goes another spaceship". We thought the machine was out of this world and it took our money with it.

Then we had a bad meal at your restaurant here and did our impression of old faithful."

"Here we are," said Joe as he opens up the door labeled The Goldfish Palace Casino Accounting Office. "If I can be of further service to you, let me know. Have a great time with the accountant."

Chapter Six

The Incident of Losing A Winning Credit Voucher

The accountant introduced herself as Jane Dixon. Jane had dark short hair to her shoulders, tan skin, a smaller person than Joe, not skinny or overweight and was wearing a blue dress.

Jane invited Scooter and Hannibal into her office by saying, "This is an opportunity to meet fine people like you. Come on in gentlemen. As I see your faces of hope and integrity, you must be here to cash in your credit vouchers?"

"You better believe it, Pilgrim," laughed Scooter. "What's on your mind, Babe?"

"Don't call me Babe," screamed Jane. "I'll have you know that I was married and I stayed with my husband to the end. He was an unforgettable lug. I married him for his looks, but I loved him for what was left over. I was going to say something even though he was seeing another woman."

"Whoa! Torn between two mammals. No wonder he passed away," laughed Scooter. "I think the parade of life has passed you by."

"I have a big responsibility. Before I can pay you anything, I have to determine if your winnings were fair and there was no cheating involved. None what so ever. It's my job to look at the camera footage where you, Scooter, was sitting at the different slot machines. Isn't that you?"

"What is this that you are looking at," asked Scooter.

"Spy stuff," answered Jane. "I spend a lot of time thinking of the hereafter. When I check the camera footage, it will tell me what you're here after. It will expose you to any antics you tried to pull off."

As Jane begins to look at the footage, a few minutes of zoom viewing where Scooter was playing several slot machines, she sees that the machines were moving to the maximum winning positions before Scooter even touched the play button or pulled the lever.

"And where were you, ah Hannibal is it?" asked Jane.

"Who, me? You talking to me?" asked Hannibal.

"Yes, Hannibal, why certainly I'm talking to you," insisted Jane. "Are there any other Hannibals in this room?"

"OK. I admit it was me, you was talking to," answered Hannibal. "I was playing some other slot machine, two rows over."

Jane then looked at Hannibal and Scooter and began to wonder how this could have happened.

Scooter then declared, "I must have used the hand away from the view of the camera angle to push the play button."

"Even if you did, the camera would have caught your movement," explained Mrs. Dixon.

"I didn't know that," answered Scooter.

"I knew that," answered Jane. "And I can see that you didn't move the opposite hand either when the machine was a second away from winning. Somehow, I think you cheated the machine. Hannibal, what do you have to say about this?"

Answering Mrs. Dixon, Hannibal smiled and said, "Those cameras can really tamper with your mind. I don't know what you are talking about and I can not say how it happened and that's the truth. Come on. Come on. It was just a mistake. Maybe you should ask the slot machines. Maybe I'm a magic genie and wished for the machines to win."

"This is ridiculous. That's cute, very cute and pathetic. You are either crazy or a liar and I don't want any part of you. One thing for sure, I know somehow you and Scooter cheated," challenged Mrs. Dixon. "If you want to cheat, cheat fair. One thing I hate is a crook.

That was sort of an accident that I caught you. That is a little unusual. It's not easy to prove, so I can't prove it. I'm more and more sure of it. It's just a matter of time before I wear you down. There is something strange about this. I don't know how you did it, but you know how it happened.

I've heard about enough. There is no such thing as magic genies and it is highly unrealistic. If there were, you certainly don't look like one. I have to call them as I see them. For now, my decision is that the casino will not accept your credit voucher. Both of you must leave the Goldfish Palace Casino immediately.

Hearing this, Scooter blurted out, "Can't I come to your buffet anymore and make a pig out of myself by eating all the fish I want? You're discouraging me to bits."

"No, you certainly can not," vowed Mrs. Dixon. "You're missing the point. You know I can't do that. What makes you think you are so special? There is nothing worse than a sore winner and more like a pirate or bandit. You sound like a couple of crazy nut buckets, because you made a mistake and thought you were men coming into money.

There is something strange about both of you. You both have shifty eyes and I just can't trust you. That's how it looks to me and I'm just not taking any chances. I'm not walking on eggs with you. As of now both of you are banned from the Goldfish Palace Casino and you can take your appetite somewhere else."

"Hey, what's the idea? It's not my idea. You're going to blame me and I get drunk on rye bread. It was his idea," boomed Scooter.

"That's the worst thing that can happen," exclaimed Hannibal.

"That's wall to wall sense. Now I get it," reasoned Scooter."Who are you going to believe, him or me? So count me out."

"I know it was my idea. I get that. Those are my sentiments exactly," insisted Hannibal. "One of these days Mrs. Dixon, you're goina to blow the whistle and your teeth are going to fall out."

"You convinced me that you're the perpetrator of all this," acknowledged Mrs. Dixon.

"I want a second opinion and speak to your boss about me being an alleged perpetrator," insisted Hannibal.

If you want a second opinion, I think you're ugly too. You have an ugly face and that's why you never got married. My boss isn't competing with me on my decisions," answered Mrs. Dixon. "He goes along with my decisions and leaves them up to me."

"Hannibal, I was afraid of that. Everything has taken a drastic turn," growled Scooter. "This reminds me about what happened to my cousin, who lives in Alaska. He was put in jail for striking gold."

"Why would they put your cousin in jail for striking gold?" asked Hannibal.

"Because the gold he struck was Sheriff Gold," answered Scooter. "Now, I think we over did it. We should have had better shoulda planning."

"What is this shoulder planning you're talking about," asked Mrs. Dixon.

"Shoulda planning is about, should I have better shoulda planning on hitting the play button or should I had better shoulda planning on pulling the lever," beamed Scooter. "Because of our shoulda planning, we've been caught by the standing guards.

Mrs. Dixon, are you saying we can't succeed at this? I was thinking of seeking your help and would like to ask you for your support, even though I can stand up for myself."

"Oh, poo. What on earth are you talking about? What kind of guards did you call them?" asked Mrs. Dixon.

"Standing Guards," replied Scooter.

"Why should we have standing guards?" asked Mrs. Dixon.

"Because the guards would have to stand up if you didn't have any chairs. You would sure save money, a lot of money on chairs," laughed Scooter. "Hannibal, this is another fine mess you got us into. This is the last in a long series of screw ups and the last straw. How could we let this get by us? We need to be level headed and mature about this, so I'm not going to tell you I told you so."

"Scooter, you're too nice. Now stop it. I think your name should be Slash. What we did was daring, exciting and now it's avoidable. I'll see what I can do to fix that for you," explained Hannibal. "Mrs.

Dixon, Thanks, but no thanks. This is the last time we're going to take money from you."

"I know," replied Mrs. Dixon.

"I'm a doorman and I thought with winning all of this money, I could have a better life," explained Hannibal.

"You mean to tell me that you're a doorman," replied Mrs. Dixon. "Well in that case, there's the door, man."

"Scooter, don't you fret. Now I'm going to remedy the mess we're in. Mrs. Dixon has a surprise coming," smiled Hannibal. "OK, Mrs. Dixon, that's enough. Since this is a casino without pity, there is no need to wish you a nice day. There is no point of us hanging around here anymore. I have one wish for you and Scooter will definitely agree with me."

In a flash of time, Jane Dixon was wearing a torn dress, with messed up hair and her make up was melting. Jane's memory of the footage on the camera disappeared along with her memory of Hannibal and Scooter being in her office. Jane's name tag and all of her identification had her name changed from Jane Dixon to Jane Doe.

Feeling her face with wet make up, Jane thought there was something different. She took out her compact and looked in the mirror of the compact and screamed. The reflection in the mirror was an old, ugly woman.

"Who wuz that woman," laughed Scooter.

With a smile on his face, Hannibal then said to Scooter, "I love it when a plan comes together. Why didn't you think of that, useless? I don't think we will have any more trouble with Mrs. Jane Dixon."

Then Hannibal and Scooter did an about face and ran out of the office, down the hallway onto the casino floor, through the entry gate and into the hotel lobby to check out. The security guards' shirts and pants disappeared. While standing their in the underwear, they waved good-bye as Hannibal and Scooter raced past them to the Goldfish Palace Casino lobby.

Chapter Seven

The Incident of Checking Out With Brenda

Standing there at the counter, Hannibal and Scooter present themselves for checkout. The lady sitting at the front desk has long blonde hair, brown eyes, tan skin and was wearing a combination yellow and white sleeveless dress. Her name tag said Brenda.

Looking up from her computer, Brenda smiled and asked, "How may I help you gentlemen?"

"I don't know about Scooter being a gentleman, but we need to check out fast," bellowed Hannibal.

"What room were you in?" asked Brenda.

"The room number was 286," answered Scooter.

"Well OK. It says here in the computer that with taxes you owe $137.25.

"I have an uncle that lives in Texas," insisted Scooter.

"No, I mean money, dollars," replied Brenda.

"That's where my uncle lives, Dallas, Texas," laughed Scooter.

"OK, Hannibal, I paid for the ice cream cones yesterday and now I have a cash flow problem. Could you make me liquid again and pay for the rooms?"

"Oh, wow. What a nice guy you are. Why don't you go into the casino kitchen and jump into the blender. You bought two cones and ate both of them, yesterday," jested Hannibal.

"We have to do something to pay for this room. That was a swell dump we stayed in," insisted Scooter. "Let me see that bill. Quiet, I can't hear myself read. I can't see. I can't see. I'm blind! I'm blind!"

"What's the matter with your eyes? Is there something wrong with your eyes?" gasped Hannibal.

"Let me look in the mirror at my eyes," insisted Scooter.

Brenda then handed Scooter a mirror.

"Now, I see what's wrong. I just have my eyes shut, but my head is cut off." said Scooter as he began to panic. "It couldn't be! It Couldn't be!"

"This just can't be. Cut it out and hold the mirror up closer to your face, dummy," instructed Hannibal.

"That was lucky. Now, I can see the bill and I got my head back," said a relieved Scooter. "What should we do? I know, you pay for the dump we stayed in."

"Scooter, give me that bill! Let go of it!" demanded Hannibal. "Scooter, do you like to play games?"

"I love to play games," answered Scooter.

"Then open up your eyes and give me that bill or I'm going to annihilate you," boomed Hannibal.

Taking a deck of cards out of his pocket, Scooter separates the cards and says to Brenda,"Here, pick a card."

Brenda picked a card out of the deck and looked at it.

"You can keep it. I have fifty one left," laughed Scooter.

"Scooter, you're a card, yourself. You're just full of jokes and you kill me," laughed Brenda.

"I guess I will have to use my credit card to pay for the room." insisted Hannibal.

"That will just be fine," said Brenda.

After processing Hannibal's credit card, Brenda got up from her chair and walked to the printer, to make the hard copy receipt of the transaction to give to Hannibal. As Brenda was walking to the printer, Hannibal and Scooter saw that she was wearing a mini-skirt.

Scooter blurted out, "Nice legs you have, Brenda. I would follow you anywhere. The one thing I like about you. You are so down to earth. I can't resist your fatal charms and I welcome you with open arms."

"How long are you going to be open?" laughed Hannibal.

"I don't know. What time is it now?" asked Scooter. "Brenda, I'm going to do you a big favor and ask you to marry me and after we're married I can see you bending over the stove. Only you can't see the stove."

"I don't know if I can resist you. You are kind of cute at that," answered Brenda.

"I have to get married fast," proposed Scooter. "I have a lot of numbers of other girls I've called, but haven't had any luck. My rich uncle told me that if I could get married in a week, he would give me $5,000,000.00.

"You talked me into it," insisted Brenda.

"Well, say something else to Brenda," instructed Hannibal.

"Help! Help!" yelled Scooter. "I'm sorry Brenda. I'm afraid I can't do this. I don't need the money that bad."

"This is great stuff. You two are so funny," laughed Brenda. "You two know each other so well that it's scary and it helps you make a terrific comedy team. You sound like Abbott and Costello."

"We fool around like that all of the time," laughed Scooter. "Oh, oh. Hannibal, we've got company and have to get gone, fast. I can see the security guards coming this way in their underwear. Can I say one thing? Help! I wish I was dead. I think I'll get my wish. The rats are back and I don't want to be the cheese. I think we better beat it.

Good-bye Brenda. We've got to leave. That warehouse fire isn't going to last forever. We want to go see it and wouldn't miss it for the world.

I'll be back to marry you another day after you buy that stove. Until then, take care of those legs and see if you can find a good deal on a new stove. What am I saying?"

"Now get going, kid," demanded Hannibal. "I don't know how it looks outside, but we have to run."

"I'm with you Hannibal," exclaimed Scooter. "I've got travelin' muscles. Just watch our dust."

Hannibal and Scooter then ran out of the lobby and went into the parking lot.

As they entered the parking lot, Scooter bumped into a drunk.

"Why don't you watch where I'm going?" asked the drunk.

"I'm sorry," replied Scooter.

"Somebody bumped into me yesterday carrying a grandfather clock and I asked him why he didn't wear a wristwatch like everybody else," said the drunk.

Holding up his bottle of wine to Scooter, the drunk said "Here, have a drink. Everyone is always a few drinks behind and I'm buying. Drinks are on me. I like to put molasses in my wine. That sweetens it up. Here's to wine, the rose colored glasses of life."

"I'm sorry, sir. We are just on our way to a fire," confided Scooter to the drunk. "We have to find our car in a hurry."

The parking lot of the Goldfish Palace Casino was full of vehicles. The waves of cars were constantly changing and it was difficult to see where Hannibal's $500 Taurus and Scooter's Dodge SUV were parked. The sun was positioned towards the west main entrance of the casino parking lot where Hannibal and Scooter were standing after being chased out of the hotel. Both Hannibal and Scooter raised their open hands to their forehead to shade the sun.

"OK. Where is the car?" gasped Scooter.

"Let's walk straight ahead and hunt from here," instructed Hannibal.

"Do we have a license to hunt?" asked Scooter.

"We don't need one. What we really need is a baseball cap and sunglasses," answered Hannibal.

"That's one thing I know for sure," answered Scooter. "I think it will be easier to use the panic button on the key fab to find my Dodge."

"I don't have a panic button or a key fab," admitted Hannibal.

"That's because you have a cheap $500 Taurus," acknowledged Scooter. "That's why we need to find my Dodge first and then we can drive around the parking lot to look for your cheap Taurus."

"That sounds like a great plan. Do you want to hear my slogan? I wrote it myself,," proposed Hannibal. "My motto is, I like it when a plan comes together. I'm beginning to think you are a real master of the lamp."

Oh, you are just saying that, so I won't put you back in the lamp," insisted Scooter. "I don't know why we have to go through all of this just to find our cars, since you are a genie and all. Besides, there are two cars to drive back to Davenport and two of us."

Hannibal and Scooter then began to run around the parking lot, hoping to hear the panic noise from the Dodge SUV before they ran out of steam. Finally, Scooter locates the sound of a car in distress near the outer limits of the parking lot.

"There is my Dodge SUV, Hannibal. I found it," yelled Scooter. "Let's get in my Dodge and go hunt for the Ford Taurus."

"I believe I parked my car by the light post," insisted Hannibal.

Yah, there are so many light posts in this parking lot, that it is like a forest of many trees," exclaimed Scooter.

After a few minutes of driving around the parking lot, Hannibal smiled and shouted, "There's my car, parked between a red Ford Escape and a dark green Honda Civic! Look at that back tire! It's flatter than my head!"

"OK, I'll drop you off by your car and help you change your tire. By the way, do you have change for a tire?" jested Scooter. "After we change the tire, we can leave for Davenport," instructed Scooter. "Luckily our drive is mainly north so we won't be depending on sunglasses, which we forgot to bring with us."

OK, Scooter. I'll meet you at The West Side Kids' Detective Agency in about an hour and a half," replied Hannibal.

Chris Murphy in store reading a book

Chapter Eight

THE INCIDENT OF DREAMING TOGETHER

It is now 7:30 a.m. and Scooter wakes up from a dream. His upper body springs up and he shakes off the drowsiness and then wipes his eyes. He gently moves out of the bed and wonders where he is. Then he remembers that he spent the night in the casino hotel.

Scooter then stands up and tiptoes past the next bed where Hannibal is sleeping and walks into the bathroom. Since he didn't bring another set of clothes with him, he begins to wash his face and under his arms. Next, he combs his hair and his mustache. While he is doing this, he begins to think that he could be anybody he wants to be.

Scooter then walks out of the bathroom and past the bed where Hannibal is sleeping. He begins to get dressed and puts on his blue jeans, the same dark socks, his brown shoes and a striped yellow and brown collared shirt.

Now that he is ready for the day, he wakes up Hannibal and says, "Hey Hannibal. It's time to get up. The day is half over. Are you going to sleep all day? Were you dreaming that you were at a sawmill? You was breathing heavy and hard and sure was sawing logs this morning."

"I was?" asked Hannibal. "Did I wake you up?"

"No, I've been up since the crack of noon," answered Scooter. "Of course you didn't wake me. I woke up on my own. I wouldn't stay in bed any longer, unless you can make money in bed."

"Now I remember. I woke up in the middle of the night, because I couldn't sleep," reckoned Hannibal. "I think that Mexican food we ate for supper kept me awake and I stayed up for a while. What was you doing in the dark room?"

"Reading," answered Scooter.

"How could you read in the dark?" proposed Hannibal.

"I went to night school," exclaimed Scooter. "I was going to ask you if you had something I could put over my ears since you snore."

"I know I don't snore, because I stayed awake one night to see if I did and I didn't snore all night.

Then I went back to bed and began to dream, because I had a hard days night and began sleeping like a log. What my dream was about will explain the heavy breathing. It was one of the wildest times of my life. First, I began dreaming that I lived in a yellow submarine. Next, I was dreaming that I was Chuck Norris learning about CPR and I brought the dummy to life. Then my dream changed about being a genie. This is something Michael Eight Murphy, alias Dr. Zodiac would like to know.

The Blue Jinn s explained to me in my dream that he was a genie that is known as a Jinn s, who are supernatural beings. Jinn s don't have a lamp they live in. They are not wish-granting benevolent servants. They are taken very seriously and are real tangible beings.

Scooter, get this. These Jinn s can change their shape, fly through the air and make themselves invisible."

"You mean like superman?" asked Scooter.

"Scooter, just let me finished," demanded Hannibal. "These Jinn s can appear humanoid or even human and they possess great powers. If that's the case, we better make sure the Blue Jinn s never gets mad at us."

"I had a horrible dream last night about us gambling and we deserved what the woman in the casino office was going to do to us," explained Scooter.

I'm afraid to ask. How did it go?" asked Hannibal.

"We won a lot of money on three different slot machines. I can't say it was a pleasure to be in her office, because it wasn't. The woman in the casino's office would not pay us any of the money on our credit vouchers. She sure was a tough old lady and she banned us from coming back to the casino. When we arrived at the casino's office, we was the good and after we was caught cheating we was the bad.

Before we left the casino's office, you wished that her dress was torn, her hair and make up messed up and she lost her memory of us being there and she became an ugly old woman.

We had all that money in the palms of our hands until we were caught cheating on the slot machines we played on."

"Oh yeah," answered Hannibal.

"After that, we went to the casino hotel to check out," Scooter continued to say. "Then there was this beautiful girl, named Brenda, who helped us check out. I told her she had nice legs and wanted to marry her, because Uncle Columbo told me that if I got married in a week, he would give me $5,000,000.00."

"Oh yeah," beamed Hannibal.

"Brenda accepted and then the security guards started to walk our way," declared Scooter. "I told Brenda that we had a warehouse fire we wanted to see and ran out into the parking lot. Wasn't it a wonderful dream? I'm glad that was just a dream. I'm more interested in Kelly."

"It was just another one of your stupid dreams," proclaimed Hannibal.

"What did you say that for," boomed Scooter.

"For waking up. On the plus side, since there was no cause and effect, it never happened. That sounds worth a bad dream," reassured Hannibal. "Now let's do something that is wild and exciting. Even though I'm still tired, let's not let a minute go by without something crazy happening and go down to the casino and gamble the way we planned."

"Before we do that, we need to call Chris Seven Murphy, known as What Do You Think, at his book store, Burlington By The Book, to arrange for a time to meet with him and his family, before we go back to Davenport," suggested Scooter.

"I sure hope Betty will be there. It would be a good for a start of my day," smiled Hannibal. "Today can be a beginning of our wildest days even though there is an element of risk. Let's go down to the restaurant to get some breakfast. Boy, good ole hotcakes. I sure do love them. That's what I'm going to get, but first we need to get some money from the ATM machine.

Now that I'm a genie, we don't have to strive for quality. We can shoot for the moon. We have achieved what any American would dream of. Since we have arrived, we can coast. Now that you have a handle on it, I've decided to let you decide what machines we're going to play on with your wishes.

Before we do that, I have decided to discontinue the anything you want wishes that Pockets offered you, such as dancing girls, gold, silver. I'm going to give you some choices. You can have the bare essential package, where you can have just three wishes. You can include your three wishes with two undecided wishes or you can have the gold package where you can only wish for gold."

"Wait a minute. Hannibal, don't play with me," commanded Scooter. "If you do any of those things, you have gone too far. There are a hundred ways you can humiliate me and I don't want the roof to fall on a lot of good memories. Don't be low and insensitive. You can call me stupid. You can call me a quitter.

I may allow you to take back the low and insensitive, but not the stupid. Just remember. When we get to the bookstore, I don't want you to say anything stupid. I want you to be on your best behavior. Well?"

"Well? What if I do say something stupid? Are you going to put me back in the lamp?" asked Hannibal.

"No, I'm going to pat you on the back, because I'm lonely and ask you to dance," growled Scooter. Of course I will put you back into the lamp.

Remember, I can do that whenever I wish or whatever I wish. You will have to grant me those wishes even though we are still best friends."

"I didn't know that," insisted Hannibal.

"I knew that," answered Scooter.

Chapter Nine

The Mystery At Round Lake Park Incident

While Hannibal and Scooter were having fun at the Goldfish Palace Casino, Dr. Fine and Charlie, The Chill were at the Round Lake Park, west of Davenport. Their car was found at the park and they were missing.

That morning, the park manager was informed by several campers about the strange incident of the parked car. The park manager then went to investigate the car and found nobody inside. He then wrote down the license plate, make and model of the car and went back to check the guest list of people who own cars, trucks and campers. Not finding the car or the people who owned it, he then went back to the car and placed a yellow flag on it.

Seeing the park manager, camper Harry Morgan said, to his wife, "This picture I took last night, give it to me. Don't look at me like that. I have to show the park manager and quick."

Harry then walked over to the park manager and said, "Strange things were happening last night. I thought it would be important to show you this picture I took last night. I think I saw my life flash before my eyes. I never saw so many stars. Then I thought the roof fell in when I saw a flying saucer and took this picture."

After looking at the picture, the park manager then began to ask the campers more questions about the car and became suspicious of foul play. Not knowing what else to do, he called the Scott County Sheriff's Department. Hence, the scene of the Scott County Sheriff's investigation began at the park.

Deputy Sheriff Juan Gomez answered the call and drove to the campground in a new black and white Ford Explorer. As the deputy pulled up to the park manager's office, the park manager, Howie Brosky came out of his office to meet with the deputy.

"I'm Howie Brosky, the park manager. Thanks for coming in such a short time."

"I'm Deputy Gomez," smiled the deputy. "Tell me about this empty car that you called about."

"Several campers came to my office to tell me about a parked car with nobody in it. They heard a car pull up late last night, beside a wooden area. Nobody has seen the occupants in the car or get out of the car," answered Howie. "They told me that during the late night, the campers closest to the woods heard humming sounds. One camper saw a light that illuminated inside a camping trailer, where campers were sleeping. Since it was so late at night, that camper thought it was security patrolling the park grounds calling for a fire bell of the night. I wasn't sure to make of it, so I called you."

"You're not the first one to call. We have received several calls needing our immediate attention about concerns of missing people," replied Deputy Gomez.

"Let's take a look at the empty car."

The deputy and the park manager then went to the car parked by the woods.

Pulling up to the car, the deputy and the park manager got out of the deputy's Ford Explorer and looked through the windows of the car.

"Yep, it's empty," assessed the deputy. "The keys are still in the car. Let's check the trunk. Nobody here. Where are they? I will have an investigative research team out here to talk to any eye witnesses, search the campgrounds and the woods. Do you know of anyone who has heard or seen anything suspicious?"

"Come to think of it, there is a couple in lot 17 who showed me a picture that he took last night, of what he claims to be a flying saucer," replied Howie, the park manager. "They say they heard a humming sound and saw a bright light in their camper."

"Now we're getting somewhere," boomed Deputy Gomez. "We have found cases like this that there were very little evidence of what happened to missing people. I better talk to these people and make a report. I need to get a tow truck to pick up this car and take it to the station."

Walking over to lot 17, the deputy saw the couple sitting outside of their camper.

"I'm Deputy Gomez. I understand that you experienced some strange, weird, happenings and I hope with your explanation, I will find the answers."

"I already have the answers for you," said an exited Harry Morgan. "I have proof that flying saucers really do exist and I took a picture of one last night."

Looking at the picture, Deputy Gomez exclaimed, "That's not a flying saucer. That's a paper plate. It does jump out at you and the evidence speaks for itself. You can still see a little potato salad and beans left on the plate. It must have flown through the air by the wind. We're talking about mysterious things that happened last night, not flying saucers."

A disappointing Harry replied, "Oh, golly gee. I thought it was a real flying saucer and I had something important to show you."

After interviewing other campers, who describe what they heard and saw to the deputy, Deputy Gomez then reported his findings to the newspaper reporters who were at the scene.

After Deputy Gomez left the campgrounds, Howie thought about the local rumors of missing people.

The next day, Howie found out that the investigating team located two cell phones under the front seats of the car that was towed into the police station.

One cell phone indicated that Dr. Fine had a missed call from Jerry Dickerson. The other cell phone indicated the owner, Charlie, The Chill.

Howie Brosky and the Scott County Sheriff's Department now know the names of the missing people who owned the car.

But, where are they? No wallets of the missing people were found.

The Davenport Quest reporter placed the story in the newspaper, along with the pictures of Dr. Fine and Charlie, The Chill, told of the event that has been happening at the Round Lake Park with the names of the missing people. The public was requested to report any information they had to the Scott County Sheriff's Office.

Before this happened, a chapter was written about Jerry Dickerson and his gang with their experience with the Burlington and Davenport Police Departments. Jerry describes Dr. Fine's car to the Burlington Police.

After the Round Lake Park and casino-hotel experience, Hannibal and Scooter went to Burlington By The Book to meet with Chris Murphy and his family.

Tim, Kelly and Chris Murphy in the Burlington By The Book

Chapter Ten

THE INCIDENT OF MEETING WITH THE MURPHYS

Three hours later, Hannibal and Scooter arrived at Burlington By The Book. As they went through the front door, there were Chris, Michael, alias Dr. Zodiac, Scooter's girlfriend, Kelly, Hannibal's girlfriend, Betty and Tim. Tim and Betty were cleaning up the mess that Jerry Dickerson and his crew made from the day before.

While Tim and Betty were putting the books back on the shelves, as Scooter and Hannibal entered the store, Hannibal greeted everybody and said, "Hi all. What's up? How is everyone doing today?"

"I'm doing just fine," answered Chris.

"I'm doing OK. I'm just tired," added Kelly.

"Have you come to help us?" asked Betty. "If you have, your timing is right because we're just about through cleaning everything up."

"After the police came, I never seen that many people in the store for a long time and where we ended up with a mess," insisted Chris.

"What happened?" asked Hannibal.

"I thought it was a crazy idea," explained Chris. "The whole town came to our store just to see how many people would fit in our store at one time. After they left, we had a big mess to clean up."

"One thing is for sure. The town can never leave town," laughed

Scooter. "What happened to Jerry Dickerson and his gang after we left?"

"They were taken by the police to the ER at a Burlington Hospital for treatment," explained Michael. "They were diagnosed of having bruises on their heads with concussions. Before they could be released to the authorities, they had to stay in the hospital 24 hours for observation."

"My twin brother, Michael and Hannibal will have to answer for their violence and damages to Jerry Dickerson and his gang. I don't understand it. Why you two would want to stick your neck out, is beyond me," added Chris. "Jerry Dickerson and his crew were released from the hospital today, with prescriptions for their very painful headaches. The doctor said that she would have arrangements for follow-up evaluations with a doctor in Davenport. Both Michael and Hannibal will have to pay for Jerry and his gang's medical bills.

But I do have great news that will knock your socks off. Hannibal and my brother will not be arrested for assault, because they were protecting our property and defending themselves.

The Burlington Police called the Davenport Police about their crimes in Burlington and what they were told about their crimes in Davenport. It was agreed that Jerry and his boys would have to answer to their crimes in both Davenport and Burlington. Since these men live in Davenport, they will be transferred to the Scott County Jail until a court date is scheduled.

Hannibal, you, Michael, Scooter, Tim and Kelly are to be in court to testify to the events of the crimes."

"Hey Chris. Is that a tie you are wearing or a napkin you forgot to take off?" laughed Scooter. "Would Michael and Hannibal be charged with assault if they had used pepper spray on them?"

"Very funny, Scooter," laughed Hannibal. "And you told me not to say anything stupid, before we got to this store."

"Jerry is quite a character, himself, isn't he? He doesn't care how he looks. He lets his drinking do the talking for him. I don't think he tries to be a character, because he is one," insisted Michael.

"Since we have all that money from the winning lottery ticket, I think Hannibal will agree with me that it was worth giving Jerry and his rats a whipping. I could see the fear in their eyes when I started to hit them with the bat. They thought they were intrepid, but I didn't think they were very smart. They are pushy jerks, who are obnoxious balls of slime.

I sure would have like to have some salt that I could have sprinkled in their wounds. But sigh, our next choice was to accuse them of kidnapping, trespassing and stealing."

"I know. I know just how you feel," admitted Hannibal.

"I was told that Lt. Columbo has come to Burlington and will be in charge of taking these clowns to Davenport, today," added Chris.

"Speaking of Davenport, I think it's time for me and my best buddy, what's his name, to be heading into the sun and going home," reckoned Hannibal as he approached Betty. "Betty, when Kelly comes down to testify at the Jerry Dickerson trial, would you be coming with her? I would sure like for you to get a closer look at our detection agency and then show you around Davenport. I would surely like to show you all the streets, alleys and sidewalks. You can stay at our detection agency as long as it takes to do that."

"Hannibal, it's time to leave for Davenport. Let's git going," laughed Scooter. "Why don't you write her a nice long letter when we get back to Davenport? After she gets it, she can read it for herself."

Scooter, followed by Hannibal, then went out the front door and stood in front of their cars.

"Love, love, love," laughed Scooter. "I don't know how you're going to get along with the traffic on the roads if you think of your true love, Betty, on the way home. Take your lamp with you and pay attention to the traffic and I will meet you in Davenport in about an hour and a half."

Chapter Eleven
Back To Davenport We Go Incident

The north drive home was a tiring struggle for Hannibal. Hannibal arrived back home, before Scooter. After Hannibal pulled up to his home at the West Side Kids' Detective Agency, he sat in his car reminiscing the day's strange happenings and he waited for Scooter to come home. At the same time that Hannibal pulled up to his home, Jerry, Lefty, Ace, Shorty, Danny and Mugs arrived in Davenport with Capt. Columbo.

After Jerry and his gang were taken into the police station, Capt. Columbo explained their rights to them again and told them they can remain silent if they wished. If they need lawyers, they will be assigned to them.

"Jerry, I'm sure that since you was a Davenport Police Detective once, and all of you know this since you have been in jail before, you know the procedure in processing and incarcerating," assured Capt. Columbo. "There are a lot of crooks with guns around this town and so few brains."

"I guess we're going to be looking pretty in our orange jumpsuits again," declared Jerry. "One thing is for sure, I don't want to be locked up in the same cell as Shorty. His behavior can be unbecoming a human."

"Since you are the leader of this gang, you get one phone call," explained Capt. Columbo.

"Somebody intelligent has to lead these people," insisted Jerry. "They would be lost without me. They can't plan anything or even organize a party by themselves."

"You couldn't plan a party without your girlfriend, Dixie. You told me that you gave up drinking once and that it was the worst afternoon of your life," insisted Ace. "If you're such a great leader, why are we all in jail?"

"I think we need to just be silent and quit fighting among ourselves," demanded Lefty. "I'm the only cause I'm interested in."

"I don't want to hear anymore fussing, ladies," laughed Capt. Columbo. "Jerry, since you are allowed to make one phone call, use that phone on the wall."

Jerry then walked over to the phone on the wall and dialed Dr. Fine's number. The phone rang and rang, but Dr. Fine did not answer the phone.

After waiting fifteen minutes for Scooter to arrive, Hannibal decided to take his lamp with him and go into the West Side Kids' Detective Agency's front door into the living room where the West Side Kids were hanging out.

Once inside, Hannibal greeted everyone by saying, "Hello gang. Boy, it's good to be home. What's been happening since I have been gone.?"

"Hey, look who's here," replied What, as each one of the gang walked up to Hannibal and patted him on the back and told him that his experience was well done.

"Scooter and myself did manage to get the job done, we set out to do," beamed Hannibal."I had a good day today. All of you do know that we are all 2,000,000.00 dollars richer. Jerry Dickerson and his skunks are all no good crooks and are going to be put into jail.

Do you know what's at the end of 2,000,000.00? Zero, zero, zero... and nothing; a circle with a hole in it. The only point in having this much money is that you can tell some big shot where to go.

Did Scooter get back yet? Has anybody seen Scooter? His SUV is not parked in the back lot."

"No, he hasn't returned yet," answered You Don't Say. "He has called to tell us that we need a team conference in the main living room. How did you luck out gambling yesterday?"

"Scooter and myself almost won a lot of money at the Goldfish Palace Casino," answered Hannibal. "Because of the security cameras, we had to give it all up. Then this old lady instructed Scooter and myself to exit the premises and never come back."

"That's very unfair," replied Who. "Just who does she think she is?"

"I know that," replied Hannibal. "I will tell you later how it all happened. Unfortunately, we won't see Pockets again."

"That's so sad," reasoned I'm Not Sure. "I can say for all of us that we liked Pockets. We felt he was part of the team. A very valuable part of the team!"

"I just heard a car pulling up to the back door," interjected Whatever. "I bet its Scooter."

"I know that," added I Don't Know.

After turning the engine off, Scooter climbed out of his SUV and walked to the back door. He opened up the outside door to the kitchen and saw no one in the kitchen, cooking. As he came through the door, he looked up to see if anybody was on a ladder, painting, to prevent an accident.

A pail of water was setting on top of the door and turned over, with water and the pail landing on Scooter. Soak en wet, Scooter went into the living room, where everyone was gathered.

"What took you so long? Was you out for a swim?" laughed Hannibal. "You look like mother nature spit on you."

"I was waiting for my chance to get Scooter back for taking the ladder from me while I was painting in the kitchen," laughed Because, as he walked up to Scooter and patted him on the back and said, "It was just a curse that was going to happen to you. It looks like I got you. Bullseye!"

"Why you. What was you trying to do, break my neck? I'll murder you for this, Because," insisted Scooter.

"Why are you getting so sore?" replied Because.

"I was only kidding, Because," insisted Scooter.

"Break it up you two! Scooter, where have you been?" asked Hannibal.

"I stopped to talk to some buffalo," answered Scooter, as everybody began to laugh.

"What?" exclaimed What. "What did you do, get lost Buffalo Bill and was asking for directions as to how to get home?"

"Very funny, What. What do you know about buffaloes, anyway?" asked Scooter, as he was standing there soak en wet. "It so happened that the buffalo told me what they found out about and was giving me a hint of some unusual things going on in this area."

"Where would you see buffalo in this area?" asked Smiley.

"There is a ranch just east of Blue Grass on highway 61, where they raise buffalo for meat," answered Scooter.

"What was you doing down on highway 61? How could a buffalo talk to you, Buffalo Bill?" asked Smiley.

"I'll tell you how they do it, Chief Rain In The Face," argued Scooter. "They stomp their hooves into the ground, which told me something is wrong on Earth. Then the buffalo, all in unison, lowered their heads and snorted profusely. This meant that I needed to investigate what they was telling me and soon. It was sad to see what they had to tell me, but I thanked them anyway."

"What's a buffalo got that I haven't got?" asked Smiley.

"A long tail," laughed Scooter.

"I didn't know that," insisted What.

"I knew that," jested Smiley. "The other day, the chickens were making the same motions. They had a meeting with the black sheep and the sheep said bah, bah, bah. It must be what Scooter was told by the buffaloes."

"Wow!" yelled Because. "That's heavy. It sounds like all the animals on Old McDonald's farm."

"Now that we know something is wrong, we need a plan," declared Scooter.

"Yah, that's right," insisted Hannibal.

"I want to hear what happened at Burlington By The Book," questioned I'm Not Sure.

Answering I'm Not Sure, Scooter began to tell the story about how they stopped Jerry Dickerson and his gang from getting the lamp with Pockets, the magic genie.

"You can relax. Hannibal and me was never under arrest by the Burlington Police Department. The Blue Jinn s came out of nowhere and demanded that Pockets go back into his lamp. Before Pockets went back into his lamp, he asked the Blue Jinn s if he could grant me one last wish and the Blue Jinn s and Pockets disappeared."

"Well, hold on one second. What did you wish for?" asked What, as he became curious.

That's when the huge bombshell was dropped.

"The wish that Pockets granted me was for Hannibal to replace Pockets as a genie and to be put into a broken down teapot of his own," explained Scooter with a heartbreaking confession. "This isn't the only thing to consider here. I didn't think that Hannibal was going to be a real genie until after Hannibal was put into the teapot, I mean lamp.

I couldn't get that through my head until he yelled for me to rub the lamp to let him out. Before I did that, I had to frantically examine to figure out what happened and face the truth.

I want to make it clear that at first I was happy with the arrangement as it was. I thought now we can do things together and get into all the mischief we want. I didn't know if that was going to last and that is when I gave Hannibal the rules to get out of the lamp. I told him that he needed to promise me that he would not do anything stupid and to quit calling me stupid. He was to grant me all the wishes I wanted. That is the way it has to be or I would put him back into the lamp.

I know this sounds dreadful and makes it very tough for listening. There is no other way to look at it. I can understand your reaction and if it was me, I would be devastated."

"Why all the long faces? You plan on attendin' a funeral," declare Hannibal.

The gang then began looking at Hannibal and began to realize, he is now a genie as they responded to the insane news. For a minute, you could sense the resentment after the truth was finally revealed. Once they had time to get their head around the news, then they connected with each other. The devastating departure of Pockets didn't spell the end of the unbelievable tale. After losing Pockets to the Blue Jinn s finally grasping the impossible choice. A gut wrenching admission came forward. The West Side Kids are all now happy to have a genie of their own.

"What is there to eat? I'm really hungry," asked Scooter.

"The refrigerator is loaded with TV dinners," replied Who.

"Why would I eat a TV dinner? We don't have a TV," reasoned Scooter.

"Now, have you been promoted as the leader of the West Side Kids' Detective Agency and Hannibal's master?" cheered Whatever.

"No, I'm going to spend my money on a buffalo ranch and raise buffaloes," replied Scooter. "I have already thought of that. Of course I'm going to be the leader. Now that Hannibal is a genie, I'm taking over. I am the new leader. Follow me and I'll lead the way.

My first order of business is that you are not to tell your family, your friends or any people of authority what I told you about what the buffalo told me. Now we are more than a detective agency. We are secret agents and we have to be tough."

"You mean like James Bond?" asked I Don't Know. "Do we all get numbers as secret agents?"

"No, we're more like Scooter Hickenbottom's secret agents," answered Scooter. "And if I give you numbers, I'm not going to tell you because that will be a secret. Like I started to say, what I told you is not to leave this room.

The next order of business is about the tax free, two million dollars that Hannibal and I made by taking Kelly and Betty safely to Burlington. It will be my job to get the money from Michael, alias Dr. Zodiac Murphy. I will personally see that the money is transferred into the West Side Kids' Detective Agency account."

"You don't say. Two million dollars. That dough is for us. We can sure use some of that. At last, we can start living like gentlemen," smiled I Don't Know. "Are you going to really have it put into the agencies account, instead of gambling it away?"

"Don't worry. I'll manage. I may be stupid, but not that stupid!" insisted an angry Scooter. "My plan is that we all put our heads together and think about what the detective agency needs. Let's get busy here. Now everybody shut up and start talking."

"Gee whiz, Scooter, It looks like Hannibal is out of a job. Now you are the new leader of the West Side Kids' Detective Agency. What does Hannibal have to say about this?" asked Who.

"Are we going to need money for us to be secret agents?" asked Because.

"What's the matter with you guys?" asked Scooter. "What do you think, you need a glass slipper instead of a bone head?

Don't answer questions, before I can think of asking them. One question at a time and don't be answering any questions. My ears are giving me heart burns. I don't want you to be mixing me up with all of those questions and answers. The more I know, the less I understand."

"Knock it off. you eight balls. There is a lot of questions to be answered. What it takes to answer these questions, Scooter doesn't have, so I'm going to help our new leader out by answering these questions," exclaimed Hannibal while he was thinking, "We can't have a weaker mind running this agency. If some of his stupid ideas are good, I'll go along with it. If I don't, instead of getting his permission, I will do things my way. It's easier to apologize afterwards and wish his way out of any mess he gets us into.

You're wasting your time asking Scooter all these questions, because he doesn't have any brains. Brains, brains. My head is crawlin' with em! I'll answer your question, Who, and everybody else who needs to shine a light on the jaw dropping truth and I'll explain so even you can understand it. I'll tell you what I have to say about Scooter. I have a new home now inside a lamp, thanks to Scooter. To say it was a massive dilemma is an understatement. It was like somebody electrocuted me with rage and utter devastation.

Now, I want to reflect on my relationship with Scooter. Scooter was unafraid that mistakes were made as he assessed the breakdown of friendship. Scooter is going to demand a lot out of me and I have to live up to his standards. It's not easy and I wouldn't wish this on my worst enemy. My tongue is tied and my jaws are stuck, I can't talk back to him anymore, so Scooter doesn't put me back into the lamp and I have to beg him to let me out.

I want all the right things for the right reasons and for it all to fit into place. I will work 100% with my master, who is now our new leader. Since Scooter has taken over my position as leader of the pack, everyone should respect him, like me. I will grant him all the wishes that he wants. Well, that's that."

Chapter Twelve

The Incident of Kelly Testifying In Court

It is now a month later and court is in session.

"Order in the court," bellowed the clerk.

Before the judge came out to sit on his bench, Scooter blurted out, "I had a friend who lived in a court, Lincoln Court. He always had order in the court."

Hearing what Scooter said as he came to sit on his bench, the judge asked,"Who said that? I don't want any more outbursts or you will be in contempt of court and fined. I'm ready to hear the case.

Jerry Dickerson, you are charged with three counts of kidnapping and lying to the court about a genie being in a lamp. Are you responsible for this? How do you plead?"

"Not guilty, your honor," replied Jerry.

"Ace, Lefty, Danny and Mugs, you are charged as conspirators of criminal acts. Are you responsible for this? How do you plead?" asked the judge.

"Not guilty," replied all four of the gang.

"I was waiting for a witness that just flew back from a ravioli convention and then said, "Boyaredees arms tired" declared the prosecutor. "He is known as Father Delay. Since he has not arrived here at this trial, I will have to start with another witness, without father delay. If it pleases the court, I would like to introduce one of my four other main witnesses."

Kelly Murphy, would you step forward and take the stand?" asked the judge.

The clerk then walked up to Kelly and held a bible in front of her.

"Raise your right hand and put your left hand on the bible," asked the clerk. "Kelly Murphy, do you swear to tell the truth, the whole truth and nothing but the truth?"

"I do," answered Kelly.

Jerry's lawyer was then asked by the judge to come to the stand, to question Kelly.

"Wait a minute Kelly Murphy. It was all a mistake that you accused my very nice clients of kidnapping you, by taking you against your will from the West Side Kids' Detective Agency's kitchen to his apartment," insisted Jerry's lawyer. "Aren't you exaggerating a little bit. I'm not asking you to make Jerry the goat. Let's understand each other. In fact, Jerry, who is very friendly just invited you to come to his apartment to have lunch with his girlfriend, Dixie Doneright. Shouldn't kindness, decency and skill be rewarded?"

"NO, no, that's all wrong. Are you nuts? That is stupid. This friendly Jerry, as you call him, and his men did indeed kidnap me," answered Kelly.

"Who else would do something, so insensitive, so stupid, so low like that? Isn't it true that it was Dr. Fine and Charlie, The Chill who were the ones that took you from the West Side Kids' Detective Agency's kitchen against your will," quizzed Jerry's Lawyer. "All you should be thinking about is what the good things Jerry did for you. It was Jerry and his boys that rescued you from Dr. Fine and Charlie, The Chill and then invited you to have lunch with Dixie Doneright? What you are saying about Jerry would crush him."

"NO. No. It was Jerry and his men that caught Dr. Fine and Charlie, The Chill taking me past the garage of the West Side Kids' property," answered Kelly, as she began to cry.

"Kelly, weep all you want if it makes you feel better. No more questions," replied Jerry's lawyer.

"Mr. Prosecutor, your witness," said the judge.

"Kelly Murphy, as you told this court of law about how your kidnapping took place, would you continue to tell how Jerry and his men found you and took you from Dr. Fine and Charlie, The Chill?" asked the prosecutor.

"Well, it was like this," answered Kelly. "After Dr. Fine and Charlie, The Chill took me around the garage, to the street, Jerry and his gang just happened to be standing there with guns, I was then taken to Jerry's apartment, where Dixie Doneright was. Instead of having lunch with Dixie, she took my purse and dumped the contents on the table. Then she found the winning lottery ticket. I didn't tell them it was a winner.

There is something peculiar about Jerry. He did make a good guess that it was a winning lottery ticket and told me he would destroy it. When I asked for it back, he made a deal with me. He told me that if I would go back to the detective agency and find a lamp and bring it back to him, he would trade me the ticket for the lamp.

Next thing I knew, I was standing back in the kitchen of the West Side Kids' Detective Agency in front of this Pockets and Scooter and I don't know how I got there. Sometimes when you go away and come back, things aren't as they used to be."

"This lamp that you talk about, do you really think there is a genie that comes out of it?" asked the prosecutor.

"That's silly. There is no such thing as genies," answered Kelly "Those friends of his must have poisoned his mind, because a genie can't be coming out of a lamp, unless you have been having too much to drink or crazy, like Jerry and his friends."

"Have you pressed charges against Dr. Fine and Charlie, The Chill?" asked the prosecutor.

"No, I haven't," answered Kelly. "No harm. No foul."

"That's all the questions I have for Kelly," exclaimed the prosecutor. "Judge, may I have my next witness, Scooter Hickenbottom, to take the stand?"

Chapter Thirteen

The Incident of Scooter Testifying

"Scooter Hickenbottom, would you step forward and take the stand?" asked the judge.

"OK, I will", answered Scooter, as he walked up to the chair by the judge and picked it up. "Where do you want me to put it?"

"NO! no!" boomed the judge. "Put that chair down! You have to be sworn in by the clerk first and then you have to sit in the chair."

"Judge y boy, what comes after 75?" asked Scooter.

"76" answered the judge.

"That's the spirit," laughed Scooter.

"What do you mean, that's the spirit?" asked the judge.

"Everybody knows that judge y boy. The spirit of 1776. The Revolutionary War," explained Scooter.

Hannibal, then got up out of his chair and walked up to Scooter and demanded to Scooter that he was to quit clowning around.

"Scooter, this is a court room and not a circus. Now pay attention to what the judge is telling you to do. I think you need to project a strong prospective attitude. A cheery smile can do a lot to stimulate the jury. Do you read me?" demanded Hannibal. "Sorry judge. My name is Hannibal Columbo and I have tried to learn Scooter everything I can about being polite to others. You can believe what Scooter tells you, because he doesn't have a dishonest bone in his head."

"Who is this man? What is he doing here?" demanded the judge. "Don't you realize that you are in a court of law. Go sit down before I fine you for contempt of court."

"The clerk then walked up to Scooter to swear him in. Holding out a bible in front of Scooter, the clerk said to Scooter, "Remove your hat."

Scooter then took his hat off with his right hand.

"Raise your right hand," instructed the clerk.

Scooter then put his hat back on and raised his right hand, accidentally hitting the clerk with the baseball bat.

"I'll sue you for this. Will you put down that bat? Give me that baseball bat," demanded the clerk.

"Oh, superstitious, huh?" replied Scooter.

"Remove your hat," instructed the judge.

Scooter then took his hat off again with his right hand.

"Raise your right hand," demanded the clerk.

Scooter then put his hat back on and raised his right hand.

"Will you get rid of that hat?" ordered the judge.

Scooter then took off his hat and threw it to Hannibal, where the hat landed ten feet from Scooter on the floor.

"Will you go pick up your hat?" ordered the judge.

Scooter then got up from his chair to go pick up his hat.

"Take the stand," ordered the clerk.

Scooter then walked over to the chair and started to pick it up.

"Don't think of picking up that chair," ordered the clerk. "Turn around and put your hand on the bible."

"I told you to get rid of that hat," ordered the judge.

"Will you make up your mind?" asked Scooter. Scooter then took off his hat and threw it to Hannibal again where it landed on the floor next to him.

"Now we can begin," insisted the clerk. "Do you swear?"

"No," replied Scooter. "But I know all of the words. Nobody swears at me, because I have a picture of my mother in my pocket."

"Don't play with me! Let's start again!" demanded the clerk.

"Scooter Hickenbottom, do you swear to tell the truth, the whole truth, and nothing but the truth?" asked the clerk.

"If I say I do, does that mean we're married?" asked Scooter. "I don't even know you."

"Just say I do and quit the nonsense," ordered the judge.

"Sure, what have I got to lose," answered Scooter. "Jerry Dickerson and his boys are like the mosquito who went to the dentist to improve his bite and are dirty rats. You and judge y boy, I like.

"You don't call the judge, judge y boy. You show him the respect in a court of law and call him, Your Honor," instructed the clerk. "Don't be giving me the double talk. This has gone far enough. You're making a monkey out of this courtroom. Kindly speak louder and speak the vernacular."

"Is that so? You mean like in the Boy Scout Creed, On My Honor?" and then pointing to the baseball bat, Scooter boomed, "That's not a vernacular. That's a baseball bat."

"I object. Judge, can we have what this, this gentleman has just said stricken from the record?" asked Jerry's lawyer. "It is merely to influence this broad minded, intelligent jury as to what has been said so they can all come to an unbiased opinion that my clients are innocent of all the charges."

"Sustained," replied the judge. "Mr. prosecutor, your witness."

Walking up to Scooter, the prosecutor said, "Well, so far, so good. What is your name?"

"Scooter Hickenbottom," answered Scooter.

"Have you ever been indicted?" asked the prosecutor.

"Not since I was a baby," proclaimed Scooter.

"What are you doing here?" asked the prosecutor.

"Talking to you. What are you doing here?" asked Scooter.

"You don't ask the questions. You just answer the questions," instructed the judge. "Mr. Prosecutor, proceed with the testimony."

"What is your occupation?" asked the prosecutor.

"I work with Hannibal Columbo, at the West Side Kids' Detective Agency in Davenport," replied Scooter. "Hannibal always calls it a detection agency, but it's a detective agency. Hannibal no talk English very good. His days of good grammar went."

"I object!" yelled Jerry's lawyer.

"Says who? What are you always butting in for?" asked Scooter. "Get back into your hole, you ground hog. While you have been talking, my brains have been spinin'. Who died and made you a detective? I believe I have the floor. If you are through, I would like to pass on a little choice information to ya. You did your talking and now it's my turn. If you think that is too much trouble, stay out of it. If your smart, I'll never talk to you again.

You can't hold me here as an accomplishment to the crime, because I never accomplished anything in my life. I got no talent. I just loaf. It can't be for fragrancy, because I ain't fragrant. I'll take this case to the Extreme Court."

"Just answer the questions and tell the truth," boomed the judge.

"What were you doing in the bookstore, known as Burlington By The Book on the day that Jerry and his gang busted into the store?" asked the prosecutor.

"I object! Tell Mr. Scooter to skirt the truth and answer every question with, "I don't recall," boomed Jerry's lawyer. "Jerry and his gang are like a very oily machine and did not come busting into the store!"

"Is that so? Is that so? Says who?" scolded Scooter.

"Says me," bragged Jerry's defense lawyer.

"OK, I'll rephrase that," replied the prosecutor. "Scooter Hickenbottom, what were you doing in the bookstore when Jerry and his ever loving friends walked very slowly into the book store?"

"I was following Tim Murphy very slowly into the back of the book store and nobody loves Jerry's friends," answered Scooter.

"Did you see Michael Seven Murphy and Hannibal Columbo in a physical fight with Jerry Dickerson and his friends?" asked the prosecutor.

"There was no physical fight," answered Scooter. "Michael hit each one of those rats in the head with this baseball bat and Hannibal gave them the one, two and knocked them out before they could give him the three, four, five, and even the six, seven, eight.

Jerry and his friends may think they are physically tough or just think they are tough. I think they are kinda tough and calloused inside. They certainly aren't noble.

Fellas, I'm sure there is a way we can work this out. If you give me my bat and bring Jerry and his pirates over here, I can demonstrate how it happened."

"Scooter, that idea is very resourceful of you," endorsed the judge.

"Judge, do we have to? Wait a minute. Don't let Scooter do it," pleaded Jerry. "This sucks eggs. If by resourceful, you mean imbecile, you're perfectly correct. Now, Scooter is gettin' ugly and I'm sure he was born that way. May I have one last wish? Can I call the police?"

"If I give you a gun, will that give you some courage?" asked the judge.

"I'm not scared! I just want to run out of here! I want to run out of here as fast as my feet will move. Scooter is really crazy enough to really hit us with that baseball bat!" boomed Jerry. "I don't want to be dead. There is no future in it."

"Jerry just called me a moron. He must have said that, because he likes me," beamed Scooter.

"Roses are red. Violets are blue. You crush his skull, and I will too. Get him Scooter! Get him!" yelled Hannibal.

"Officer," instructed the judge. "Keep that man quiet and your eyes glued to the entrance of the courtroom. Don't let anybody in. Don't let anybody out."

Chapter Fourteen

The Incident of Jerry Pleading Guilty

"Stop it. I can't do this anymore. I just don't have the passion anymore to plead innocent. I've had enough of Scooter," insisted Jerry. "Things are never so bad that they can't be made worse. We'll just leave it at that. Our lawyer recommended that we not have this pointless debate and all of us plead guilty before we came to court.

I know I'm going to regret this more than I do. I changed my mind once and I'm going to do it again, because we're all going to plead guilty to those charges. Now, Scooter doesn't have to demonstrate how we got hit with that ball bat."

"I knew it all of the time. OK, Mr. Jerry Dickerson, do any of your rats, I mean boys have any last words before I sentence you?" asked the judge.

"I'm going to tell you one more time and I know how this looks," insisted Jerry. "I have seen with my own two eyes that there is a real genie that must be coming from the lamp. And I believe he is the new member of the West Side Kids' Detective Agency, who they call Pockets."

Answering Jerry, the judge replies, "We have tried to subpoena that person named Pockets and he could not be found. I heard what you told me, but your mouth was having a major argument with your eyes. Your mouth is saying one thing and your eyes are saying another. Your head is losing.

There are a lot of people in this world that don't amount to a hill of beans. I think you are crazy like Kelly Murphy said or Pockets is just your imagination."

"But judge, just ask the others that here sitting next to me about the existence of Pockets, the genie," pleaded Jerry.

At this hearing, explained the judge, "There is nothing definite about it. There is no genie, no evidence, no see, no talk, no hear, not no genie to be seen nowhere. Now I see.

You and the other members of your gang have something to conceal. You are making it up about the story of the genie. You all pleaded guilty, so it is my wish that all of you will be sentenced to hang until you are dead."

"But judge, I don't think you can do that to us. I think this may sound crazy, because it wouldn't be right," cried Jerry. "Are you sure this is what you want to do? Me and my gang already have the worst of the deal. We were the ones that got beat up with that baseball bat. We were the victims of a hit and run and ended up with terrible headaches.

We didn't do nothing wrong, except what we told you. We didn't even make anything up and we're not even lying about the genie."

"Well, you was beginning to wonder how much your luck can hold out. I made it up about hanging you. I fooled you. I fooled you," laughed the judge. "I probably should fine myself for contempt of court, but I'm not.

People in this town take care of each other. Instead I'm going to sentence you and your boys to six months in the penitentiary, in Fort Washington to serve out the sentence. I'm sure that after six months in jail, you will see the light.

The police van driver is here to immediately take you away. Before you go, can you tell me the whereabouts of Dr. Fine and Charlie, The Chill?"

"I can answer that judge. I am Capt. Columbo, a Davenport Police Detective. Jerry Dickerson told me what kind of car Dr. Fine was driving. The park manager of Round Lake Campground called the

Scott County Sheriff's Department and reported that Dr. Fine and Charlie, The Chill's car was parked at the campground and was found empty and other people were missing. The campers heard a humming sound late that night while they were trying to sleep. A bright light was seen in camping trailers. Some of the campers were robbed.

Another mysterious thing happened at the campground. When a camper woke up, he could see the stars, because somebody stole his tent.

The Sheriff's Department is investigating what happened. The newspapers may be exaggerating what happened, because they announced a warning to the public in the paper. I don't know what kind of monkey business is going on at that campground, but I intend to find out."

"OK, driver, take them away," ordered the judge.

Jerry and his men were then handcuffed and taken out to the police van. After everyone of Jerry's gang was put into the police van, the driver entered the van last.

"I did it again," exclaimed the driver. "I always get in on the passenger side and can't find the steering wheel."

A few minutes later, the driver was finally sitting behind the steering wheel.

"When do we get out of these pumpkin suits?" asked Ace.

Answering Ace, the driver said, "You will be changed into stripped zebra uniforms when you are processed into the Fort Washington Penitentiary."

"Oh great!" boomed Jerry. "As long as I don't have to share a cell with Shorty, because it would be awful! He is a brown nosing yes-man who often falls short of his duties."

"Well here we go. Is everybody buckled up?" asked the driver.

As Hannibal, Scooter, Michael, Betty, Tim and Kelly with the rest of the spectators were looking on, they waved good-bye while they were shaking their heads.

Chapter Fifteen
THE OH HAPPY DAY INCIDENT

"Scooter, you are so wise getting Jerry and his gang to pleads guilty," exclaimed Kelly. "There just ain't nothing a man can do if he believes in himself. I'm never going to forget you."

"Is this a happy day or what? This is a time for celebrating!" yelled Hannibal. "Tim, Michael, girls, Scooter and myself would like for you to come to our detection agency and then after that show you around Davenport."

"Tim and myself have to go back to Burlington," beamed Michael. "Even though we didn't have to testify, it was worth the trip to see Jerry and his friends sentenced to prison. Even though Jerry thinks Scooter is stupid, Scooter really outsmarted Jerry in court."

"It's a gift. Scooter really does have it all," laughed Hannibal. "I think it's time for Scooter and yours truly to head back to our detection agency. Betty, what time do you and Kelly want to meet us at our place of self employment? After you two arrive at our detection agency, Scooter and myself will take you out for breakfast."

"How about eight o'clock tomorrow morning," answered Betty.

"You could give a guy some notice. Then it will be. Here's looking at you cupcake," answered Hannibal as he and Scooter started walking away to get to their agency a few blocks away.

After they walked away where the girls couldn't hear them, Scooter asked Hannibal, "Can I ask you something? Do you think I'm crazy or does Kelly really like me?"

"It's possible that she just might like you. I know that Betty likes me," answered Hannibal. "Why do you ask?"

"I think she is sending me signals that she likes me. When she does that, it leaves a lump in my throat and I am touched and left speechless," insisted Scooter. "I love Kelly for herself and I can't take my eyes off of her. I really want her to be my cup cake.

This act of wholehearted kindness really puts things into perspective. This small act really makes a big difference. If she really likes me, this can be the beginning of a beautiful friendship. What advice can you give to me?"

"The ultimate definition of the concept is that only a fool can receive those kind of signals. If that's the case, the only other choice is crazy," laughed Hannibal. "I really think she believes you are really genuine and that she likes you. I think you should send her a dozen roses."

"Wow! Don't hand me that. You're giving me second thought. It's not funny. I think I know what I'm doing. Twelve roses will be plenty," insisted Scooter. "I'm not sophisticated, rich or good looking. I used to be good looking, but not no more. What would a woman see in a guy like me? I am absolutely baffled."

"You need to be strong and you do have a lot of character in your face," explained Hannibal. "But it takes a lot of late night drinking to put it there. I think you should let the drinking do the talking for you."

"You ask your good buddy for advice," replied Scooter. "And all he has to offer you is to send sunshine up your pants,"

"I'm giving you some friendly advice. I'm only responsible for what I say to you, not what you understand what I said. You're always lost in thought and that is unfamiliar territory to you. As a detective, you should investigate this further just to see how big of a difference this would make," replied Hannibal.

Chapter Sixteen

The Incident of Taking The Girls To Breakfast

Eight o'clock the following morning, Hannibal and Scooter woke up at 6 a.m., in order to get ready for the arrival of Kelly and Betty at the West Side Kids' Detective Agency. The rest of the kids usually get up at eight.

While walking around the house, Hannibal asked Scooter if he wanted to do some stretching exercises with him.

"Sure, it's nice to be limber in case I have to tackle some runner, running away from a criminal act," reckoned Scooter.

"No, I don't want to be limber for that," laughed Hannibal. "I want to loosen up to show the girls our athletic abilities."

"Why? What did you think we were going to do?" questioned Scooter.

"I thought we would play some baseball with the girls, after showing them some areas of Davenport," smiled Hannibal. "Here we go Scooter, stretch this and that. Oh that feels so good. Can you touch your toes?"

"No, but I can touch my head, which I'm thinking, it's time to take a shower!" teased Scooter. "I would really like to have the shower moved up from the basement so we can eliminate the stairs."

"If you want to eliminate the stares, we need to put a shower curtain on the shower," chucked Hannibal.

After taking their showers and putting on smelly stuff, they waited in the living room for the girls to show up.

"Maybe we should call them," suggested Scooter. "They're late. It will sure be nice to see her again. She is a spectacularly likable person, with her bright smile and sense of humor. I always like to spend those golden moments with her."

"That's the way I feel about Betty," smiled Hannibal. "She is an all around kindhearted person and has a charming demeanor about her. She is not a bit naive, because she has a lot of keen savviness."

"We could, but we don't have their cell phone numbers yet. We have the Burlington By The Book phone number. Let's just wait a little while longer," growled a hungry Hannibal.

"This waiting isn't just for me,"proclaimed Scooter. "I could eat a horse."

"Well, make sure you save the hide for baseballs," teased Hannibal.

While Scooter and Hannibal sat in the living room waiting for the girls, The West Side kids began to get up to get ready for the day. As they all begin to gather in the kitchen, still not fully awake, they began to prepare their usual breakfast that they eat every morning.

It was finally 8:30 and the door bell began to ring. Scooter jumped up and went to the door and greeted Kelly and Betty.

Giving Kelly and Betty a high five and a low five, Scooter remarked, "Hey girls, how low can you go? We're so glad to see you. You're late but you made it here just in time to save the life of a horse."

"Kelly's alarm didn't go off and we were late leaving Burlington," replied Betty. "I hope you didn't think we were going to leave you in the lurch."

"If you hadn't come, that would have been a real let down. How was your drive to the detection agency?" asked Hannibal. "For Scooter's sake, I hope you didn't see any buffaloes on your way here."

"The drive was wonderful, but we didn't see any buffalo. How could we save the life of a horse just by showing up at your home?" declared Betty. "The roads were good until we came to Davenport.

The roads in Davenport are just plain hideous. I don't know my way around Davenport, so I had to use my map app to find your home."

"I'm afraid you will have to get used to driving on the crummy roads in Davenport," stated Scooter. "If Friendly Freddy has something to do with it, he would probably wish that the roads were worse than they are."

"Guys, come outside. I have something to show you," insisted a happy Kelly.

Looking out the front door, Scooter beamed as he saw a sports car parked in the street.

"Now I see what you want us to look at!" yelled an excited Scooter. "You bought a new car. My guess is that your car is a 2021 Chevy Camaro. That is really a cool ride you have there.

"You guessed it right. You always say the perfect things," praised Kelly.

"I also have a new Camaro," beamed Betty.

"I didn't know my main muffin had a new car," acknowledged Hannibal. Isn't Betty gorgeous, just like her new car?"

"I knew that," insisted Scooter.

"If everybody is ready to roll, let's all get into the SUV and go for breakfast," instructed Hannibal.

Both detectives immediately went to the driver side of the SUV, while the girls jumped into the back seat.

As the girls were buckling up, Hannibal and Scooter began playing rock, paper, scissors to see who was going to drive. Hannibal won due to his magic.

As Scooter stood there looking at Hannibal, Hannibal asked, "What are you doing?"

"Just thinking," answered Scooter.

"Don't think too hard. That requires a great deal of intelligence which you are short of. It might give you nightmares," chuckled Hannibal.

"Is that so? Is that so? Says who?" stammered Scooter.

"Says me. I'm talking in English and you're listening in moron," alleged Hannibal. "That does sounds like you."

"Oh shut up! There was something wrong with the way you won

the game. Did you win this rock, paper scissors fair?" asked Scooter. Or you was just playing it safe and was going to do it for what? To have it made in the shade by using your magic and making wishes on your own?

Why you Tale of Two Cities. You Oliver Twist. You David Copperfield."

"That's stupid. What are you talking about?" demanded Hannibal.

"I was giving you the Dickens," scolded Scooter. "If you recall, you are not suppose to call me stupid. Now I'm going to put my foot down and wish you back in the lamp."

"Says who?" screamed Hannibal. "Knock it off, you goofball. With all due respect, you are NUTS. I'll show you who is going to be put in the lamp and right now. I'm going to wish that you are trading places with me and now you're the genie and I'm reinstated as the leader of the West Side Kids."

In an instant, a lamp appeared and two puffs of smoke went into the lamp.

"Ulp! What did you do that for? Now we're in the land of oppression and opportunity," gasped Scooter. "How stupid can you be? Now we're both in the lamp."

"Well, that wasn't hard to resist. That was a very understandable mistake. Anybody with an eye could see that coming," babbled Hannibal. "I was going to try and have fun with it. Now that we're both in the lamp, how are we going to get out?"

"Says who?" yelled Scooter.

"Says me," yelled Hannibal right back at Scooter.

"Well, I certainly have had enough. I'm not suppose to be in the lamp. How do I get out?" cried Scooter. "Without all of my bad luck, I would have no luck at all."

"It's not that complicated. I don't want you to feel pressured into doing this. If you don't want to replace Pockets permanently and you want out, you have to follow my rules. I won't embarrass you by mentioning your name. You have to quit being so clumsy, so lazy and most of all, quit doing stupid things," insisted Hannibal. "What's the matter, are you nervous? Aren't you comfortable in this lamp?"

"No! I'm not! " screamed Scooter. "Why me? Why me? Why is it always me? What are we going to do with all that time we're going to throw away, being in this lamp?"

"Who asked you?" challenged Hannibal. "Now hold still while I'll have to try and figure out how to get us both out of the lamp."

"Yes Chief. I just want out of here, so I can get something to eat," begged Scooter.

"Where is Scooter and Hannibal?" asked Kelly. "I thought they were going to take us to get something to eat."

"Kelly, Betty, help! cried Hannibal.

"Where are you?" screamed Betty. "I thought you was going to take us to breakfast."

"Scooter and myself are in the lamp," whined Hannibal. "Let us out."

"You're where?" gasped Betty. "What are you talking about? Are you trying to get out of taking us out to breakfast?"

"Just listen carefully to me and do what I say," begged Hannibal. "There is a lamp on the roof of the SUV. Pick it up and rub it."

"Are you playing a joke on us?" asked Kelly. "I bet Scooter put you up to this."

"It's no joke, I promise you. It's a mighty long story. Just pick up the lamp and rub it," instructed Hannibal.

"Betty, let's just go along with what Hannibal is telling us. The sooner we let him have his joke, the sooner we can go out to eat."

"We will have you out in a minute," laughed Betty.

Betty then picked up the lamp and rubbed it and two puffs of smoke came out of the lamp and within a couple of seconds, Hannibal and Scooter were standing in front of her.

"Greetings, I'm the slave of the lamp," Hannibal began to say. "I'm a magical spirit and you just freed me from my imprisonment of the lamp. Whoever holds the lamp is my master.

To reward you, I will grant you a wish for anything you want and I will get it for you. What do you wish for, gold, diamonds, dancing girls?"

"There is no such things as genies," screamed Betty. "What kind of joke are you trying to pull on Kelly and me? Did Scooter put you up to this?"

"Just wish for something, so I can show you what I can do," asked Hannibal.

"Betty, give me that lamp," demanded Scooter, as he grabbed it out of Betty's hands. "Hannibal, I wish that Betty and Kelly forget about us coming out of the lamp and that you told them you was a genie."

Hannibal then said, "I will grant you your wish, Scooter. Then Betty and Kelly lost their memories of Scooter and him being in the lamp while Scooter hit the pavement running to the passenger side of the SUV. He climbed into the SUV and buckled up.

"Scooter, you're not shotgun. I'm shotgun," ordered Betty. "A man sits next to his girlfriend."

"No you're not," answered Scooter. "I'm shotgun. Hannibal has been my best friend all of our lives before you came along. I am going to sit next to him."

"Scooter, you and Hannibal invited Kelly and me out to eat. So now I'm going to drive to make sure Kelly and me gets something to eat," demanded Betty.

As Scooter began to think about how he had been stuck in the lamp with Hannibal and now they had to hurry to save a horse. Scooter walked over to the shotgun side of the SUV and climbed in. Hannibal then climbed in the back of the SUV with Kelly. Betty then slid behind the wheel, buckled up and started the engine as she began to think,

"Where are we going to eat breakfast? I'm not going to move this vehicle before the decision is made as to where we are going to eat," exclaimed Betty.

"Scooter, I don't know where you want to eat, but I think we should leave the decision up to the girls. Ninety percent of a relationship is figuring out where we want to eat. I don't want to end up eating horse meat. The last time you made the decision where to eat, I was out of commission for 24 hours."

"Ah, you just have a sensitive stomach," insisted Scooter.

"You better believe it, Scoot," challenged Hannibal. "As soon as the girls decide, we can scoot out of here."

"I know where I would like to go to eat," beamed Kelly from

the back seat. "Let's go to the US Feed Restaurant. We have one in Burlington, but I don't know if there is one in Davenport."

"I need to google to see if we have one here in Davenport," replied Hannibal.

"Make sure you're googling the restaurant and not googling Betty," laughed Scooter. "Just hurry it up, so we can eat. OK, step on it, we haven't got all day."

"Don't rush me. Don't rush me. Ah, there it is, on East 53rd Street," assured Hannibal. "OK, we're on our way. Giddy up, let's go, Betty."

Betty then put the car in drive and sped up the street, going north to 53rd Street. On the way to the US Feed Restaurant, they saw a sign at a convenience store that said, "Sorry we're Open. Eat here, get gas and worms. As they finally approached 53rd Street, Betty turned the corner and began driving down 53rd Street where they approached a huge billboard sign advertising the US Feed Restaurant, that was in front of the parking lot.

Chapter Seventeen

The Incident of The US Feed Restaurant

The parking lot was quite full of cars. After Betty pulled in to a spot to park the car, Scooter jumped out of the car first and hurried to the door as if he had forgotten Hannibal and the girls. After Scooter went inside the restaurant, he came to his senses and reserved a table for four.

"Scooter, have you lost your manners because you are so hungry?" scolded Hannibal, as he walked up behind Scooter.

Answering Hannibal, Scooter replied, "I'm sorry Hannibal, ladies. I don't know what got into me, since I'm so hungry. All I was thinking about was making a pig out of myself and what I wanted to put into me. I certainly wasn't planning on eating a horse, when a pig will be much better.

I usually don't go out to eat with a date, because no girl would go out with me. If it counts for something, I did reserve a table for four. I wish the table would be open as quick as I can snap my fingers and our waitress should be here soon, right Hannibal?"

Within a couple of seconds, a waitress asked the two couples to follow her to a nice table for four. After everybody sat down, she handed everybody a menu and asked what they wanted to drink.

Before anyone could answer, Scooter smiled and said, "I'll have the usual."

"How can you have the usual. You have never been here before?" reasoned Hannibal. "Well?"

"I know I have never been here before," replied Scooter. "But after I come back a second time that will be my usual."

"Scooter! knock it off! Waitress, our goal was to get something to eat as soon as possible," assured Hannibal. "The only thing usual about Scooter is that he is usually stupid. If you want to know just how stupid Scooter can get, the possibilities are absolutely unlimited.

If I may order for everybody, bring us each back a large orange juice and a small milk, if that is OK with the girls."

"Hannibal, I love it when you take over," insisted Betty. "Don't you agree Kelly?"

"I sure do," reckoned Kelly. "Sigh. With Scooter, you never know what he is going to say and do next."

"That's what my Uncle Columbo keeps saying about Scooter," laughed Hannibal.

A few minutes later, the waitress came back and set the drinks down on the table while Scooter and Hannibal were telling the girls about their baseball team. The waitress then asked if everybody was ready to order.

"I'll have toast with jelly, and ham," teased Kelly. "From now on that is going to be my usual."

"Make that my usual as well," laughed Betty.

Hannibal was then asked what he wanted to eat.

"I can't make up my mind what my usual is going to be," jested Hannibal. "I know I have it straight in my mind what I want and what I don't want. I know I absolutely don't want horse meat. Too much fat. Let's see, what I think I want. No that's not right. Now I know. I'll have some scrambled eggs, hash browns, toast and a cup of coffee."

"How do you want your coffee?" asked the waitress.

"In a cup," answered Hannibal. "Scooter, you're up."

"Mr. Scooter, before you order, I want you to know we're out of horse meat," explained the cheerful waitress. We do have hay on the menu. It comes with house dressing."

"What is house dressing?" asked Scooter.

"House dressing is shingles on the roof and aluminum siding," laughed the waitress.

"Wait a minute. Let me see the menu. I don't see any hay on the menu," replied a serious Scooter. "What's the matter? Have you been standing too close to the oven?"

"Of course there is hay on the menu. Our customers order it all the time," beamed the waitress. "All the time they say to me, hey get me some of this. Hey get me some of that. The all comes for free with the other food they order. Go ahead and order. Three strikes and you're out."

"Well, I tell you what I want," reassured Scooter. "I'll have a Caesar salad."

"We're out of that," barked the waitress. "Strike one."

"I'm sure you have a Caesar salad," challenged Scooter. "All you have to do is put your house dressing on some lettuce and stab it several times. So how about a plate of," babbled Scooter.

"We're out of plates," alleged the waitress. "Strike two. Do you have another choice? If not, I could give you your order on a paper plate to go and then you can walk out of here."

"Let's see. A hot dog sounds good," reckoned Scooter.

"One hot dog coming up," acknowledged the waitress.

"I said a hot dog sounds good. I didn't say I wanted one. How about a grand slam breakfast?" declared Scooter. "I can take a hint and so I said it before you could tell me you were out of it!

"OK, I'll give you that one. Ball four. Now you're safe. Take your plate," declared the waitress.

"Do you know what a grand slam is, three men on base with a home run? Did you know you can have a grand slam without having three men on base?" asked Scooter.

"NoNoo. No way," jested the waitress.

"Well you can," beamed Scooter. "You have two women's teams playing."

"Fair enough," replied the waitress.

"Now can you tell me what is shorter, first to second or second to third?" smiled Scooter.

"Scooter, you played baseball long enough to know that they are the same distance apart," challenged Hannibal.

"Boy! what a hard head. Wrong again ole chum of mine," Second to third is shorter, because it has a short stop."

While the foursome was waiting for their breakfast to be served, the subject of business careers came up.

"Let's brainstorm about our jobs. Betty, with all due respect, what is your job? We never see you doing anything," beamed Scooter. "They say that work can take your mind off of your problems."

"It looks like you're on me. I appreciate your concern, but there is no way to worry. I'm sure there is nothing to worry about," reassured Betty. "I have aspirations working for the Burlington Water Company. Right now, I am the assistant to the manager of water quality. I expect in a couple of years, I will move up to the manager position."

"This is heavy stuff you're telling us," reassured Scooter.

"Kelly, what are you planning to do after helping your brother, Chris, in his book store," quizzed Scooter. "Your brother Chris is a nice guy. He's already in my book and I do a lot of reading."

"I'm interested in managing a library or a museum," smiled Kelly.

"With the success you had in college, you should be an easy pick for those jobs," reckoned Scooter as he took some tobacco and cigarette paper out of his pocket.

"What are you doing there?" demanded Hannibal. "You don't smoke."

"I know exactly what I'm doing. Maybe not exactly," replied Scooter. "I just like to roll my own cigarettes."

As the waitress returned and acknowledged to everyone by saying, "Hi, I'm back," she saw Scooter sitting there rolling a cigarette.

"I've always wanted to be a cowboy," Scooter continued to say. "This is something I have to do. I just wear these cowboy boots to confuse people."

"Well, if you're hungry stranger, I can rustle you up some grub," chuckled the waitress. "This is a no smoking restaurant. You have to get rid of that cigarette before I can give you your beans and coffee, stranger."

"I can live with that gal," teased Scooter.

The breakfast was served and a period of companionable silence proceeded while everyone enjoyed their meal. The silence was broken when Hannibal heard a noise coming from Scooter while he was chewing the ham. Kelly and Betty did not say anything, because they were trying to be polite. Hannibal wasn't so polite and lost his patience.

"Scooter, be quiet while chewing your ham. You act like you're chewing a horse," scolded Hannibal.

"No! I can't be quiet. I have a condition with my jaw joint that pops when I chew thicker foods, like the ham," admitted Scooter. "Sometimes my jaw hurts for a day, but then the pain goes away."

"I'm sorry to hear that buddy of mine," sighed Hannibal. "I didn't really know that."

"I knew that," reckoned Scooter.

"Then why didn't you go see a dentist about that?" scolded Hannibal.

"OK. I'm going," promised Scooter.

While the four of them were finishing their meals, Scooter asked Kelly about her new 2021 Chevy Camaro.

"Why did you decide on the copper color?" smiled Scooter.

"It reminds me of lots of shiny pennies and the pennies I used to buy it with. Grandma always gave me pennies when I did a chore for her. I used part of the lottery money I was given to help get back the winning lottery ticket to give to Michael, alias Doctor Zodiac," explained Kelly.

"I went with Kelly and bought a yellow 2021 Chevy Camaro," beamed Betty. "That's not all. We plan to buy our own house together and share the cost to live there. The decision will be coming soon!"

"Do you know what Chris and Michael are going to spend with their millions?" replied Hannibal."

"No, we don't know what they are going to do with their money," replied Kelly.

"We haven't decided what we are going to do with our two million dollars yet," exclaimed Scooter. "I'm sure we will be upgrading our detective agency, to have all of the equipment to be the best detectives in Davenport."

"That's really cool," yelled Kelly and Betty at the same time.

"What car doesn't seem to go anywhere?" chuckled Scooter. "A stationary wagon or Kelly's car parked on the street by the West Side Kids' Detective Agency. It will be my treat to pay the bill for the food and leave the tip on the table. What is the tally on these little snacks?"

"Without seeing the receipt, how do you know how much the tip will be?" replied Hannibal.

"Well, I do have a tip for the waitress of my own," chuckled Scooter.

"Don't even think of saying it in front of the girls before you say something you're not suppose to, you pudding head," challenged Hannibal.

"I won't do that, because I always avoid the language and the nudity and the violence and everything. I have enough of that at the agency.

Now let's see, there must be at least four of us. That's how many that came with us." assessed Scooter. "Wait, I've got it. If four more people came in with us, that is six people altogether. What happened to the other two?" asked Scooter. "Now, I'm stuck with the answer."

"You knucklehead. It looks like I have a lot of work to do with you, to figure this out" insisted Hannibal.

"Now I have the answer," coughed Scooter. "Since the other two are missing in action, that leaves Kelly, Betty, you and I left. So the tip has to be it at least $4.00.

"Na, na, na. All wrong," challenged Hannibal. "I have a major bulletin for you. You need to figure at least 10 to 15 per cent of the total cost and add a few dollars more, depending on the cost of the meals."

"What else!" replied a confused Scooter. "I don't have a calculator with me."

"I'll show you how my way is so simple," reassured Hannibal. "Let's go up to the cashier with the receipt and I will show you how it works. After we get that figured out, everything will be Humpty Dumpty."

"OK kid, I'll be right behind you, in a jiffy," volunteered Scooter. "Girls, you wait here and see if the other two come back."

A few minutes later, Hannibal and Scooter came back to the girls with the estimated tip. Hannibal then paid the bill with the West Side Kids' Detective Agency debit card.

After the bill was paid, the waitress said to Scooter, "I'm not feeling very good you poor, pathetic, strange little fellow."

"Do you have a temperature?" asked Scooter.

"No, I think I'm in love," replied the waitress. "When I was a young girl, my father suggested that I have plastic surgery."

"When are you going to have it?" asked Scooter.

"I already had it. You get what you see and you saw what you'll get," answered the waitress. "Why do you have to go? Can I go with you?"

"One thing is for sure gal, if we get married, our daughter isn't going to be in any beauty contests," reckoned Scooter. "I'm not big on good by's gal. But I have a girlfriend and we ride alone.

Gal, before I go, I want to give you this harmonica. It belonged to Billy, The Kid. He didn't play the harmonica, but I think the man he killed did."

After the four of them began to leave, the waitress, smiled and asked, "Who was that cute little guy?"

The gang gathered at the exit door and talked about going shopping on Elmore Avenue. Scooter wanted to go to the casino and gamble. Hannibal looked at Scooter and shook his head no and said, "We're not going to go to the casino. The girls would prefer to shop."

Chapter Eighteen
THE WHAT'S THE CATCH INCIDENT

After shopping for an hour, Hannibal and Scooter ended up buying Betty and Kelly bracelets. Still not hungry, they decided to go to the world's largest truck stop on Highway Interstate 80, by Walcott. On the way there, Hannibal and Scooter decided to make a detour and drive to West High School, where they graduated.

After pulling into the parking lot at West High School, Scooter began to tell the girls about where the coaches assembled the best baseball team to ever play at the school. Scooter went on to say that the team is still together, today. "They are The West Side Kids who bought the detective agency after their experiences in college.

With the help of Capt. Columbo, Hannibal's uncle, we passed the requirements to become detectives to help the Davenport Police Department and the city's population. Some of the people in the police department hate detectives. That is a different story with Hannibal's uncle and Rex Tarillo."

"Wow, that's really impressive," beamed Kelly.

"Now that we're here, do you want to play catch?" offered Hannibal. "We have balls, gloves and bats in the car."

"No, you might hurt us with your fastball," exclaimed Betty.

"Oh stubborn, eh?" laughed Scooter. "Here take a glove."

Holding a softball in his hand, Scooter threw it to Kelly and bellowed, "Here Kelly, I have to get rid of this."

Being afraid of getting hit with the ball, Kelly moved to the side of the throw. The ball went past Kelly into the parking lot and rolled underneath a car.

"Scooter, did you throw a softball or baseball to Kelly? You see what you did," roared Hannibal.

"Did you see where the ball went?" asked Scooter. "Where do I find it?"

"That's your job, dummy," yelled Hannibal. "You knew Kelly was afraid to play catch, yet you decided to be stupid by throwing the ball to her."

"Don't go anywhere Kelly. I'll be right back." Then Scooter said to himself," Now if I was a baseball, where would I go? Wait a minute. I'll find it or else. I'll find it if it kills me.

After looking around the cars in the parking lot, Scooter finally sees the ball underneath a car.

Thinking to himself, Scooter says," I better crawl under the car quietly to get the ball. I don't want the owner of this car to see me."

"Scooter, where are you? Are you still here?" yelled Hannibal.

"No, I just left," answered Scooter.

After picking up the baseball, Scooter crawled back out from under the car and walked back to Hannibal and the girls.

Showing the baseball to Hannibal and the girls, Scooter remarked,"No wonder this baseball ain't any good. They're clogged up with horse hair."

Chapter Nineteen
The Truck Stop Mystery Incident

"I think we better leave for the truck stop now," instructed Hannibal. The game is postponed due to stupidity and it's time to continue our trip to the truck stop."

After fifteen minutes of driving, Hannibal pulled into the parking lot of Grand- Paws Eatery. The restaurant was very busy, because people were visiting the I-80 Truckers' Jamboree, just north of Walcott.

It was shortly afternoon and none of the four were hungry after eating their large breakfast at The US Feed Restaurant.

"The name of this restaurant is really weird," boomed Scooter. "Let's go in and see why it is named that way."

After you, you cute little guy," laughed Hannibal. "Now that we are here, let's find a table and order some ice cream."

"You know, you are, what you eat," laughed Betty.

"What I eat allows me to live long enough to like myself," bragged Scooter. "When I accept myself as I am, then I can change."

"That's nice, which is being better than being better," added Kelly, with a giggle.

After looking around the restaurant, the four found a table with a view of the I-80 traffic.

After sitting down at the table, Betty said to Hannibal, "Everybody knows that apples have skin on the outside. Did you know that apples can have skin on the inside?"

"What are you talking about?" demanded Hannibal. "Apples don't have skin on the inside? Scooter, did you ever hear of apples having skin on the inside?"

"I'll bet you $5.00 that I have apples with the skin on the inside," challenged Betty.

"You're on. I'll take that bet," replied a serious Hannibal as he began to look out the window at all the truck traffic.

"My apples have skin on the inside," laughed Betty as she grabbed the $5.00 out of Hannibal's hand. "They are under the crust of my apple pies. I'll flip you double or nothing if you want to get your money back. Do you have a quarter?"

Hannibal then reached into his pocket, to get a quarter and handed it to Betty. Betty flipped the quarter and asked Kelly to call it. Kelly called in a muffled voice. Betty then showed Kelly the quarter after she flipped it and asked her if what she called came up.

In a muffled voice, Kelly answered yes.

"Hannibal, you lose again," laughed Betty as Hannibal began to look out the window again, watching the traffic.

Hannibal spent a long time watching the traffic and forgot about everyone else and not realizing Betty had asked him a question.

"Is there something wrong? What have you been looking at?" asked Betty. "I have been trying to get your attention to find out what flavor of ice cream you are going to order? You're sitting there in thought like the parade of life is passing you by."

Looking at Betty, Hannibal grinned and said, "Right now, I'm giving you my attention. I see a group of guys wearing baseball caps, two tables over looking at the traffic and drinking coffee. I wonder if they are on a baseball team. Hold that thought. Scooter and myself will be right back."

Hannibal and Scooter excused themselves from the ladies and walked over to the men wearing the baseball caps.

"Hi, I'm Scooter and this is my friend Hannibal and those ladies sitting over at that table is Kelly and Betty," beamed Scooter. "Hannibal and myself couldn't help notice that you are wearing baseball caps."

"I just thought we would stop by because we were curious. We came over to find out if you were on a baseball team," explained Hannibal.

The man facing away from the window replied," Hi, my name is Larry, this is my brother Jerry and this is my other twin brother Jerry. Sitting across from me is Harry. To answer your question, no. We are members of the Walcott American Legion."

"Are you the group that keeps minutes and wastes the hours," asked Scooter.

"Don't pay any attention to Scooter," declared Hannibal. "His brain is special and starts working when he gets up for the day and doesn't stop until he has to learn something,"explained Hannibal. "Scooter and myself was on a baseball team while we were in high school. You can lead Scooter to practice, but you can't make him think. Our baseball team won the state championship every year we were in high school."

In unison, the four Walcott American Legion men replied, "Congratulations."

"How long ago was that you were in high school," asked Larry. "You don't look past college years.",

"It was eight years ago that we graduated from high school," explained Hannibal. "Everybody on the team had nicknames then and we kept them to this very day.

As Scooter told you who we was, I will explain our names again to you. I'm Hannibal and this is Scooter. Then the rest of the gang's nicknames are Who, What, I Don't Know, Because, Smiley, You Don't Say, I'm Not Sure and Whatever."

"The American Legion is also a team of players," assured Larry. "As a country wide organization, we advise congress representatives on behalf of all military and personnel for their earned benefits. We also take part in supporting community activities and educating our youth in Americanism and Patriotism."

"It sounds like a very good team to me," exclaimed Scooter.

"I hope we meet again to help the community," replied Harry.

"Have you noticed a lot more truck traffic on I-80?" quizzed Hannibal as he looked out the window. "Those trucks appear to have special large equipment on them. I know they don't look like parts to a wind turbine."

"I am here at the I-80 truck stop often," Larry commented. "I'm not much of a chatterer, but I have also noticed it and I don't understand it. There has been a lot of construction going on near the Davenport Airport."

"Thanks for the tip. I should have figured that out. Now it's starting to make sense," declared Hannibal.

"I also come to the truck stop, a lot," added Jerry. "Me and my twin brother Jerry fortunately have understanding wives. When we come home from the casino, they never ask us any questions. We just tell them that we just ate a $380.00 hamburger there at the casino's restaurant.

One time my brother Jerry came home late from the casino and his wife asked him what time he came home. He told her that he would be more than happy to tell her what time he came home."

"That's right," confessed Jerry. "I would have told her, but I couldn't, because I lost my watch in a poker game."

"What do you do for a living?" asked Harry.

"Scooter and myself are private investigators," answered Hannibal.

"What do you do for these people?" asked Larry.

"Nothing. What do they ever do for us?" laughed Scooter. "Our clients aren't going to go anywhere. I also like to spend my time working with wood. I make furniture that falls apart."

"OK, wise guy. Just what do you know about being private investigators? Have you got any experience or do you just specialize in the mundane?" barked Larry.

"We graduated in the highest of our class," replied Scooter.

"Some class," groaned Harry. "Pardon me cutie pie, if I laugh."

"I've got some great news for you," insisted Scooter. "We're going to get better."

"Scooter and myself as private investigators help the public solve controversial issues," explained Hannibal. "We give our lives to duty and humanity."

"Where is your detective agency located?" asked Larry.

Taking a pen and a piece of paper out of his pocket, Hannibal started to draw a map with a line right across the paper. Then he drew another line two inches above the first line.

"That's not right," exclaimed Scooter. "Give me that pen."

Scooter then took the pen and drew a line down the piece of paper and then another one two inches over.

"Let me see that piece of paper," demanded Harry. "Jerry, take a look at this piece of paper.

Scooter then handed the paper and pen to Harry. Harry handed the piece of paper and pen to Jerry and Jerry proceeded in playing tic tac toe with Jerry.

"Whoa, look at the time?' asked Hannibal. "Scooter, what does your watch say?"

"It doesn't say anything. You have to look at it," answered Scooter.

"Experience is what you have after you've forgotten where you left your girlfriends. We have to git back to the ladies before they think we ditched them," reckoned Hannibal. "Scooter, I came to a decision and we have to git. Are you ready to go?"

"I'll do it when I'm ready," answered Scooter.

Raising his fist, Hannibal asked again, "You goofball. Are you ready to go now or do I have to crack the whip?"

"Why certainly I'm ready!" growled Scooter. "You don't have to be in a snit."

"Say good bye, you idiot," ordered Hannibal.

Looking at the men from the American Legion Scooter said, "Good-bye you idiots."

"Men, don't pay any attention to Scooter. I'm going to learn him his manners when we git back to our table. Enjoy your meal and maybe we will see you again," reckoned Hannibal.

As Scooter and Hannibal walked back to the table, they continued wondering about the unusual traffic.

Returning to the table, Hannibal saw Betty sitting at the table with a frown.

"Now here we are," laughed Hannibal. "Can I get some punch for my Judy?"

"Welcome back boys!" boomed Betty. "You still here? What's the idea of taking so long? Let's order some ice cream now!

OK? Kelly told me you would try to pull something like this. What ever happened to the laws of nature? I just don't understand you. I told Kelly that when you came back, we shouldn't let you provoke us or give you the time of the day, because sometimes you're as incorrigible as Scooter."

"Betty, don't be a hot head. A good girlfriend always forgives her boyfriend when she's wrong. Just the look on your face makes me nervous," exclaimed Hannibal. "I'm going to jump into this one. What do you want? Can we talk this over?"

Betty just sat there in silence, chewing her gum, looking at Hannibal.

"It's been nice talking to you. I'm going to stick my head way under the dirt. I'm going all the way with this one. What do you want?" asked Hannibal.

"I just want to powder my nose," sobbed Betty.

"I hope it's blasting powder!" exclaimed Hannibal.

"Don't yell at me!" screamed Betty.

"I'm sorry. Just forgive me. Those words just fell out of my mouth. I'm never going to do it again," promised Hannibal as he glanced out the window, watching the trucks go by. "I know I can be a pain sometime. I'm scum and a low life. Please don't be mad. I'm your friend. I care about you. You're a nice person. How do you become nice?"

"That is the most insensitive thing you can say to me, that you want to be a nice person? In your wildest imagination and I doubt if you even have one. Maybe you want to be a nice person, because that is all the rage," cried Betty. "Did you ever think of taking your vacation in the Bermuda Triangle?"

"Oh! ungrateful, eh? This is silly. I seriously doubt that I didn't start this one. I know you're an angry woman and I have no idea why you're angry," complained Hannibal. "What do you say? Will you give me a break? I said I'm sorry. Do you want a signed confession?"

"What were you doing over there?" sobbed Betty. Why do you keep looking out the window? You never look at me that way."

"It's a darn shame. You really don't know what's going on, do you?

Can we talk?" asked Hannibal as Scooter sat down on the chair next to him, accidentally hitting him.

Hannibal then raised his fist as if he was going to hit Scooter and said, "Why you imbecile. If they declare seasons on pelicans, you better duck."

Seeing this Scooter picked up a pair of empty glasses setting on the table and put them in front of his eyes.

"Don't you raise your hand to me. You can't hit a man with glasses," proclaimed Scooter. "Watch it. There are ladies present. If you hit me, it will give me a pounding headache."

"I would like to give you a pounding headache," exclaimed Hannibal. "I'm going to either do that or tie a knot in your neck. Then I'm going to do something drastic."

"What's that?" challenged Scooter.

"I'm not going to let you go to camp this summer," declared Hannibal.

Hannibal then put his hands up in front of Scooter like he wanted to play patty cake. Seeing this, Scooter set the glasses down on the table and put his hands up in front of him. Hannibal then saw his chance and slapped Scooter in the face.

"When I saw Scooter put those glasses in front of his eyes, it made me realize that I never told you that I wear contacts," exclaimed Betty. "I can't see without my glasses and because of that, I fell down a whole flight of stairs."

"Did you get hurt?" asked Hannibal.

"No, I didn't," answered Betty. "Luckily, I landed on Kelly's brother, Chris."

"I can't believe a strong man is sitting by my side," exclaimed Kelly.

"Why, did somebody else come in?" asked Scooter.

"Now Betty, I want to finish explaining to you what is going on," smiled Hannibal. "It's a stupid lucky break and I can explain everything. I'm getting ahead of myself and I know it sounds crazy and I can't prove it."

"I just don't understand you," exclaimed Betty. "I'm confused."

"Everybody gets confused. You can't write the scenes and direct the action of life," declared Hannibal. "Right now, I have my reasons and all I have to give you is my opinion. These men, Scooter and myself were talking to, are from the Walcott American Legion and they are not on a ball team.

Will you make up your mind about something? I came bearing news. It's not what you think. As detectives, I think we have a problem. It's a different kind of problem and it's a little scary. I don't think that's a coincidence and it's something I have to work out. Something suspicious and strange has been going on around here.

There has been a lot more truck traffic on I-80. It seems to be very unusual traffic. Those trucks on I-80 appear to have special equipment on them and they seem to be going near the Davenport Airport."

"How exciting. Maybe we should get excited more often. But what does that mean to me?" asked Betty.

"I was temporary out of my head," exclaimed Hannibal. "You're a very pretty girl and every time I see that cute little button nose of yours, I feel better. Are you going to listen to me, or exercise your mouth?"

"I believe you," promised Betty. "I just happen to trust you and I can see you are telling the truth, because with your kindness and decency, you always tell the truth."

"That's it and you're not upset?" acknowledged Hannibal.

"Yeah, that's it," reassured Betty.

"Now, what kind of ice cream do you want?" asked Hannibal.

"I've been hungry for chocolate ice cream," beamed Betty.

Whoa! You just read my palate," alleged Hannibal "I think that's what I'm going to have is chocolate ice cream and party hearty."

As they sat there, eating their ice cream, Hannibal casually, continued to look out the window.

After eating their favorite ice cream, Kelly smiled and wondered, "Why did the owners name this restaurant Grand-Paws Eatery?"

Offering an explanation, Hannibal pointed to the pictures on the walls and said, "These are pictures of famous and loved dogs. There is a picture of Rinty Tinty Tinty. The one next to it is Princess and the one next to that is Lady and the Scamp. There are other pictures on the walls of movie dog stars."

"Oh, goodie gosh. That's so wonderful. Those are cute pictures. Now I understand," reasoned Kelly.

"I have a question," laughed Scooter. "If a group of bananas is called a hand and a single banana is called a finger and somebody cuts you off in traffic, do you give him the banana?"

"Did you know that in the Philippines, bananas are used to make ketchup," replied Kelly.

Still concerned about the strange traffic. Scooter suggested, "We have responsibilities as detectives and need to find out what's going on with the strange traffic. I think we should do some poking around and find out where these trucks are going."

"If everybody is in agreement, I reckon I should pay the bill so we can leave the restaurant and follow those trucks," said Hannibal.

Chapter Twenty

The Incident of The Investigating Detectives

After everybody got into the SUV and Hannibal sat behind the wheel, "Betty said, "Isn't this exciting, Kelly? Now we're going to find out what detectives do."

"It's just a passing thought. I don't know what to do. Maybe we should follow some trucks carrying hidden, large loads that look suspicious," suggested Scooter. "I think they may be going to the airport."

"I have a better idea that's coming right up in my head. I think we should start in a different direction," replied Hannibal. "Since we're here at the truck stop and they are having a Truckers' Jamboree, the four of us should get out of the SUV and check out the trucks here. If anybody asks, Scooter and myself are truck drivers and are showing you girls all the trucks here at the Truckers' Jamboree."

The four of them then got out of the SUV and started to walk toward the trucks parked on the other side of the Grand-Paws Eatery Restaurant. After taking a few minutes looking for suspicious trucks, Hannibal came up with a plan.

"OK, gang. Here's what I think we should do," instructed Hannibal. "This truck we're standing next to looks like a suspicious truck. Since I don't see anyone around, now, here's our chance. Scooter, go around the back of the truck and climb up under the tarp to see what this truck is hauling.

There is nothing to be afraid of. Hurry and get in the back right now. If anybody comes, we will start singing Yankee Doodle. Then you get out of the back of the truck in a hurry."

Scooter then went to the back of the truck and crawled under the tarp when four men started to walk to the truck.

"OK girls. Ah one, ah two ah three, Yankee Doodle went to town riding on a pony."

"Hey! What in tar nation is going on here? Who are you people? What are you doing here messing around our trucks?" screamed one of the truckers.

"Hi. I'm Hannibal. This is Kelly. This is Betty and standing behind us is Scooter," answered a nervous Hannibal.

"All my friends call me Scooter," bragged Scooter.

"You don't say? What do your enemies call you?" asked the trucker.

"He did say," gasped Hannibal.

"You sound like a merry one," declared the trucker.

"Do you mind if we look around? I bet you won't believe this. Scooter and myself drive the big rigs our own selves," alleged Hannibal. "We came to the Truckers' Jamboree to show our main muffins the different kind of trucks there are."

"Wait a minute! I'm not falling for that one! You got a bit of a problem Mac. I'm almost as stupid as you are if I let you try to bait me!" shouted the trucker.

"Whatever turns you on," growled Hannibal.

"You're in a lot of trouble. We're going to keep an eye on you, so get out of here, right now," bellowed the truck driver. "You stay away from our trucks or we're going to have ourselves a real ball. We're going to cut your life in half. I hope you don't have any other plans today. Because we're going to toss you in the air and when you come down, the four of us are going to beat you to a pulp and it isn't going to hurt at all!

Do you understand me? We are going to take your main muffins with us because they got a good look at you and decided to go with us!"

"You haven't got nothin' but a big mouth," roared Hannibal.

"What did you say?" screamed the truck driver.

"You heard me, rum dumb. You would have trouble messing up a bed," boomed Hannibal.

"I'm going to come down on you so hard, that you will have to reach up to tie your shoes," yelled the truck driver.

"You're getting very tiresome and you qualify for a very smart mouth," proclaimed Hannibal.

"Let's go Hannibal. It looks like we're in a tough spot," exclaimed Scooter.

"It's going to take brains to get out of here," replied Hannibal.

"That's why I said. We're in a tough spot," cried Scooter.

"Well, that is just dandy. But what the hey?" exclaimed Hannibal. "Who wants to go out and paint the roses when you can get your head blown off in an alley?"

"Hannibal, I'm scared," whispered Betty.

"So am I," whispered Kelly.

"I don't mind telling you, I'm starting to sweat," urged Scooter. "I have to go home. I forgot something. I forgot to stay there."

Turning to Scooter, Kelly and Betty, Hannibal whispered, "Nothin' scares me. We're getting no place fast. Be tricky. Be Tough. Be a tiger."

"Hannibal, this is no place for a weak stomach and I want to get out of here," demanded Scooter.

"Scooter, quit your squawking. We'll be out of here in a minute. I want to get the girls where they will be safe," replied Hannibal. "I'm the boss. So do what you are told and you're going to be OK."

"OK, Chief. I'll take your orders," cried a scared Scooter.

"How about talkin' this over?" asked Hannibal to the truck drivers.

"You have sixty seconds to leave," instructed the truck driver. "If you don't, leave, I'll get mine and you'll get yours. When we're done with you, you're going to howl like a hound."

"You haven't heard the last of this. That's what I call besmirched gratitude. Even when I go to war, I get no peace," scolded Hannibal. "Whoa! Look at the time. We're having more fun than a frog in a plate of hot water. Now is the time that we have to leave. Now gang, let's get out of here. Good-bye. Have a nice day," yelled Hannibal to the truckers, as he ushered the girls back to the SUV.

After they got back into the SUV, with Hannibal again behind the wheel, Hannibal, proclaimed, "It's all over gang. We certainly scrambled their eggs, because we fooled them. Scooter, did you see anything suspicious when you climbed in the truck? Do you know what was in there?"

"No Chief. I did what you told me to do. It was hot and too dark under the tarp for me to see anything. I wasn't in there long enough to see anything, thanks to Yankee Doodle," replied Scooter.

"There goes a suspicious truck going east on I-80. Let's follow it and find out where it's goin'," declared Hannibal.

Hannibal then started the engine and drove onto the interstate in cruise, following the suspicious 18 wheeler one half mile behind. One truck took the I-280 exit and another truck kept traveling east.

"Let's follow the truck going east, to Davenport," insisted Scooter. "Look, he's taking the exit to Division Street."

After taking the exit, the truck began to travel north toward the new construction site by the soccer fields. Following the truck further, the gang saw the huge truck turn into a warehouse, big enough to cover three football fields.

"I reckon this must be the place," exclaimed Hannibal. "What do you think Scooter?"

"If there is no place around this place, this must be the place, I reckon this must be the place," proclaimed Scooter. "I'm glad you're with me, so I don't get lost by myself.

"Hannibal, I need your advice. What do you suggest?" asked Scooter. "We need to investigate. Do you think we ought to follow the truck into the warehouse? We may get the information that these are spies. I can smell a spy a mile away. Let's go. I'm ready with the camera. I can hardly wait to get in the warehouse."

"What a creepy looking joint, Scooter, Under the circumstances, what have we got to worry about? I want you to get something straight," declared Hannibal. "This is getting better and better. We have a problem and it's getting better and better than that. This could be a tough game, because if anybody finds out we're here, it's just a head scratchier. It could be too dangerous, because the girls are with us. We need to get the information, provided we can get back.

This is serious. It would be better if we wait. Right now if we go in there, we would be acting like a big dumb buffalo and it would be the same as having a grenade in a wedding cake.

I'm sure we're going to get to the bottom of this. We're detectives, we better sit on this and see where it goes. Don't worry. We'll take care of everything. As a precaution, I think it's absolutely necessary to get the Davenport Police Department involved with us at a better time. We will have to convince them that there is a cause for an investigation into the warehouse."

"I'm glad you thought of that," reassured Scooter.

"It would be cool to see your hair stick straight up, because you are scared," laughed Hannibal.

"We're not scared," laughed Kelly. "Our hair isn't sticking straight up, yet. Let's get out of here before that happens. Betty and myself have to get back to Burlington to get ready to go to work tomorrow. I should have said, Betty and I. Not Betty and myself. I think Scooter is a bad influence on my talking not so good and I love it."

"OK. We'll take you back to your no where, cool Camaro," reassured Hannibal.

"It's mid afternoon and you have a one and a half to two hours drive home."

The drive back to the West Side Kids' Detective Agency was uneventful. It seemed like everyone was reflecting on the events of the day in a companionable way. After they got back to the agency, Kelly and Betty got into their cars.

"Oh dear. No keys," alleged Betty as she was looking in her purse. "Oh! Here they are. I guess I'm out of it from what happened today."

"It was a wonderful day, because we enjoyed spending the day with you girls," beamed Hannibal. "Good bye Betty, I hope to see you soon."

Walking up to Kelly, Scooter smiled and said, "Ditto. Good bye until we meet again, my main muffin."

As the girls drove away, Scooter said to Hannibal, "I still think something is fishy and secretive about the warehouse and I bet more trucks are delivering unknown and dangerous things."

"There aren't too many times I agree with you Scooter, but I believe you are right," reassured Hannibal. "We need to tell the authorities of our suspicious, strange and weird things that are happening."

Scooter, with a brick, thinking about the day's events.

Chapter Twenty-One

The Incident of Uncle Columbo and Rex Tarillo

The next morning, Hannibal and Scooter were eager to visit with Capt. Columbo, Hannibal's uncle. The other West Side Kids were busy working for other clients. They were spending their time looking for evidence in insurance fraud and a "Ghost Gun" case. Shootings were going on most days of the week in the Quad Cities.

"Good morning, Uncle Columbo," greeted Hannibal, who was standing in front of the Davenport Police Department reception window. "I would like to have a couple of words with you."

"What can you say in two words?" Hannibal.

"Scooter, I'm trying to tell Uncle Columbo what we know," scolded Hannibal.

"Do we know something?" asked Scooter.

"Scooter, you know that you and myself came to talk to Uncle Columbo and Sgt. Tarillo about a suspicious warehouse near the airport, north of Davenport?"

"What did you say?" nephew?" asked Uncle Columbo. "I had some other things on my mind and I wasn't paying any attention."

"That's OK," laughed Scooter. "We always have a cash flow problem and never have enough money to pay attention."

"It's important that we speak to you right away," insisted Hannibal.

"Yes, of course, nephew," answered Uncle Columbo. "Let's go back to the conference room. I will page Sgt. Tarillo to meet us there."

After everybody met in the conference room and sat down at a table, Scooter began to make his case to the two detectives.

"We're here on business," explained Scooter. "Hannibal and me was on a date with Betty and Kelly."

"Are your girlfriends blonds or brunettes?" asked Uncle Columbo.

"I can't say. Everyone says they are very light headed," answered Scooter. "Hannibal and me saw some commercial and military trucks traveling east from the I-80 Truck Stop's Grand-Paws Eatery."

"Other than that, how is it going nephew?" asked Uncle Columbo.

"I can't complain," replied Hannibal.

"That's good," reassured Uncle Columbo.

"No, it's not," admitted Hannibal.

"Do you want to complain?" asked Uncle Columbo.

"You know what I want," maintained Hannibal.

"What's your story? What do you want?" asked Sgt. Tarillo. "Why does the truck activity cause your concern?"

"It's not only our business to prevent a crime. It's everyone's business to prevent a crime. That's what I want," explained Hannibal. "It's a wicked world out there. There are some clever men, who have turned their brains to crime and we need to find out who is responsible."

"What do you mean?" asked Uncle Columbo. "What makes you say that?"

"We didn't know who else we could turn to," answered Scooter. "It's very hard to put into words. I think Hannibal will agree with me that there is a gut feeling of a terrible despicable crime, because something strange and dangerous activity is going on in that warehouse. We have to find out, so we can control these unruly elements."

"What do you mean? That's wild. That's way out," assessed Sgt. Tarillo. "Did you think our hearts were going to bleed for you by telling us this story?"

"You shouldn't have done that. What was you doing following a truck to the warehouse?" asked Uncle Columbo. You just shouldn't have done that."

"We was just scouting around. Why, was anything missing?" challenged Scooter.

"Scooter, I would like to help, but you know that you have a reputation of being far out with your hunches. I know you can't believe everything you see and hear, but you like to repeat it anyway. What makes you think this is different?" asked Uncle Columbo. "When we listen to you, we get plowed under, every time. If you don't like my opinion, you can ask my bartender what he thinks."

"I think we should send Scooter and Hannibal over to the Sheriff's Department to tell them their story," suggested Sgt. Tarillo.

"That's a profound thought. But why should we do that?" asked Uncle Columbo. "What have they ever done to us?"

"Why do you always bawl me out when I come to tell you things like this?" asked Scooter. "I've got feelings too. I work hard and you're always picking on me. You don't have a consideration for me."

"That's because Sgt. Tarillo and I always think you make things up as to what you said was right," answered Uncle Columbo.

"Wait a minute. What are you laughing at?" insisted Scooter. "I don't like the way you two are working together. Don't make me get short with you."

"I can remember when I was a chemistry instructor at The University of Davenport, you took a class in logic and the instructor failed the class," laughed Sgt. Tarillo. And every time you handed in you're homework to me, you spelled your name wrong. We're the detectives. Now say that you are sorry."

"OK. I'm sorry that you are detectives," proclaimed Scooter. "What are you doing, Sgt. Tarillo?"

"I'm taking my blood pressure," declared Sgt. Tarillo. "I'm just trying to stay calm."

"Scooter, you can say, whatever you want to say," exclaimed Hannibal "You can go through me and I'll tell em what you want to say, because you and I are buddies. I'm not going to talk too much, so say whatever you want to say. We will always be friends. It is alright with me."

"Well, you tell those two that I know, that you understand it all wrong. Nobody pays attention to the almost there guy and I'm not really surprised. This is bad, because this is all wrong," exclaimed Scooter. "What's bothering you, besides me?"

"Scooter told me to tell you, Sgt. Tarillo and Uncle Columbo, that you understand it all wrong," acknowledged Hannibal. "Nobody pays attention to the almost there guy and I'm not really surprised. This is bad, because this is all wrong. What's bothering you, besides me?"

"I heard him. I know all that, but I'm confused," said Uncle Columbo.

"You can't mean it. What's wrong with it? Why is everything I do is no good? I think the problem is that we have a generation gap," alleged Scooter. "There is nothing I can ever do to make you believe me. It isn't what you think it is. You're always jumping to conclusions."

"Stupidity is not a crime. I'm glad you're not the very brains of the detective agency, even though you are their new leader," laughed Uncle Columbo. "If we solve this crime, it will be a miracle. I think you're barking up the wrong tree."

"If we bark up the wrong tree, someone in the right tree might come down," reasoned Hannibal. "When opportunity knocks and we don't see it coming, we won't be prepared for it."

"You never give up, do you?" asked Sgt. Tarillo.

"No we don't," reasoned Hannibal. "That's how we make our living."

"Will you quit being so stubborn and listen to us? There has got to be a way to solve this crime. They are hiding their crime in the warehouse," insisted Scooter. "We followed a truck to the warehouse near the Davenport Airport. When the large door was opened, the truck we followed, just went into the warehouse and disappeared. They say that a criminal always returns to the scene of the crime. That must be true, because these trucks keep coming back."

"I suppose you think this is like they're in charge of the underground and this is an inside job, because they are hiding their crime inside the warehouse," laughed Rex.

"What have they been building, sewers?" asked Scooter.

"Hey fellows, look. I can only inform you, that for two years there have been large trucks going into that warehouse," explained Uncle Columbo.

"No Scooter. Government vehicles, also have been traveling north on Division Street. We have not been real concerned about this."

"Well, now is the time to be concerned and you're making a bad mistake. I think you're blind. You don't even see what's going on here. Those government vehicles could be a perfect alibi. We need to find out right away," exclaimed Scooter. "Our country could be in danger. These people in that warehouse could be a terrorist organization that wants to take over the airport and Eastern Iowa."

"The trucks looked like they were carrying parts of weapons of war," added Hannibal.

"Really! OK, okay. Maybe you're right. Since both of you are that concerned, you convinced me at this time," admitted Sgt. Tarillo. "You really have a knack for negotiating. I will begin to look into this more closely."

"Since we brought this to your attention, we want to come along," begged Scooter.

"Because I have been trained to be a detective, I want to follow through with my suspicions and come along to see if I was right," insisted Hannibal.

"Alright, just for your plain old satisfaction, you silly boys want to come along, maybe we can save a life," acknowledged Sgt. Tarillo.

"If you two are coming with us, we need a plan," declared Uncle Columbo. "The only advantage they have, they know what it is in the warehouse. If this turns out to be one of Scooter's far out hunches and you are wrong about this whole thing, we will have to do a lot of explaining and cooperate with the higher ups."

"If I'm wrong, you're going to blame me and I get drunk on water. With our influence, you will be remembered as a couple of guys from the higher ups," laughed Scooter. "That's how influence works. One hand washes the other."

"If this is the army, we're not going to mess around with them even though as civilians we outrank the lieutenants and the colonels," insisted Sgt. Tarillo.

"I think we should out flank em with the pizza movement," declared Hannibal.

"We're going to do things our way or we're out. To start with,

I think we should go in Hannibal's SUV and park it at the soccer fields, right across the street from the warehouse," explained Uncle Columbo. "At 2200 hours at night, we will sneak across the street and slip into the warehouse, immediately following a truck for cover. Rex and I will be wearing black uniforms and we will carry flashlights and have an earpiece for communication. Only Rex and I will carry a handgun and a taser."

"Can we whisper like cops and say roger, copy that, over and out?" questioned Scooter. "I will be bringing my brick."

"That's what we were planning on. That doesn't surprise me that you asked. As you wish," sighed Sgt. Tarillo.

"Oh boy! This is my lucky day," yelled a happy Scooter.

"Are there any other questions?" asked Uncle Columbo.

"Are you always this well prepared?" asked Hannibal.

"Yes, we have to be prepared for anything that comes up," answered Uncle Columbo. "If there aren't any more questions, Rex and I will come over to the agency at 9 p. m."

"Copy that," replied an excited Scooter. "Hannibal and me will be ready like black knights."

"OK. Go to the supply room," instructed Uncle Columbo. "Take this request with my signature on it and get the things you will need for this adventure."

After Hannibal and Scooter went back to the detective agency, it was very quiet. Most of the West Side Kids were out on different assignments, working for their clients. I Don't Know and You Don't Say were reading detective stories, to learn how to act like intelligent detectives.

"Boys, do you know where the others are?" asked Hannibal.

"I don't know," admitted I Don't Know.

"We need a better system to keep track of our guys," proposed You Don't Say. "Everyone has a cell phone, but they have to use them to inform us where they are and what they are doing."

"You are right," replied Hannibal. "As detectives, we should be able to solve that very soon, with our two million dollars. Scooter and myself will arrange a meeting to discuss that problem. Will you relay the message to the others and call them in case Scooter and myself have to leave before they get back? At nine o'clock we are going on an adventure with Uncle Columbo and Sgt. Tarillo."

Looking at the time, Hannibal saw that it was finally nine o' clock.

"Scooter, look out the window and see if they're here yet?" asked Hannibal.

"They're here. I can see the black and white parked on the street," declared Scooter.

"Well, Daniel Bonehead, don't forget to put on your work boots," laughed Hannibal. "Oh yeh. Wear your two brick holster belt, Two Brick Scooter. Stick to your guns, even if they are empty."

"I can't. I've got a weak back," replied Scooter.

"How long have you had a weak back?" asked Hannibal.

"About a week back," answered Scooter."

"You got it, I will wear my brick belt, No Brick Hannibal. Let's play rock, paper, scissors to see who will get to sit behind Uncle Columbo, who will be sitting in the driver's seat."

This time Scooter won and climbed into the SUV behind Uncle Columbo.

"If everybody is in, buckle up," instructed Uncle Columbo. "It would be against the law not to buckle up. It's for your safety and I would have to write you out a ticket, if you don't."

"So let us live, because if we die, the undertaker will be sorry," exclaimed Scooter. "If I'm going to get my throat cut, I want to see what happens."

"Wow! That's heavy!" responded Sgt. Tarillo. "To live tonight, stay out of my way."

"What do you get if you mix The Lone Ranger with an insect?" asked Scooter. The Masked quito!"

"Don't pay any attention to Scooter. Don't scramble his brains anymore than they are," laughed Hannibal. "He gets that way when he's nervous and scared and he might change his mind going into the warehouse, after we git there."

Chapter Twenty-Two

THE DETECTIVES ON A
MISSION INCIDENT

The group finally arrived at the soccer fields, before ten o'clock. The soccer fields were empty and the lights were off. The foursome waited until ten o'clock to exit the SUV.

Uncle Columbo whispered, "Stay low men, until we get to the side of the warehouse. We will be going in, anytime now."

"Do you hear that?" whispered Scooter. "It sounds like someone is calling for Who?"

"It's just a Hoot Owl in the trees, here at the soccer fields," whispered Uncle Columbo.

After a few minutes, the fearless foursome see a truck's headlights coming toward the entrance of the property and watched it turning toward the warehouse. Next the foursome heard the noise of of the giant door opening up for the truck to enter.

"Let's follow the truck into the warehouse while the door is still open," instructed Sgt. Tarillo. "After we get in, we'll have to figure out what to do next."

The four detectives quickly scrambled behind the truck and ran to cover behind the pallets of huge boxes. After reading the word ammunition on the boxes, Hannibal had to cover Scooter's mouth, before he let out a scream, because he was shaking all over.

"Scooter, settle down. You're kind of jumpy and you're flipping out," scolded Hannibal.

"There is something I forgot to tell you. I'm a coward with flat feet," whispered Scooter.

"I knew it all of the time. You have more of a flat head," whispered Hannibal. "I would like to replace you with a good watchdog."

"Scooter, I know how you feel. I know you run scared and you might change your mind," whispered Uncle Columbo. "You have to stay calm and be quiet. You keep your mouth buttoned up. For our own safety, I need to make you understand, they have eyes everywhere. They might even have a night watchman. It looks like another door is opening for the truck and its going into a tunnel."

"Where do you think it's going?" asked Scooter.

"OK. That's better. It looks like we're moving into bigger and bigger areas. Well, let's follow the truck and find out," answered Rex. "I'm going in, but not too close."

"I'm also going in," declared Uncle Columbo.

"I'm right behind you, Uncle Columbo. I'm going in," whispered Hannibal.

"If you're all going in, there is only one thing I can say," whispered Scooter. "Good-bye."

"Scooter, come on. Just keep quiet and your nose to the ground stone," ordered Hannibal. "Just follow me."

"What else?" whispered Scooter.

The fearsome foursome then moved like combat fighters moving across the terrain. As they moved into a lighter chamber, underground, the truck stopped and the fearless four stopped.

They saw many soldiers and civilians moving around the chamber, getting ready with forklifts to unload the truck.

"That looks like a huge kitchen, like a laboratory over there," whispered Scooter. "What's that huge roller coaster thing doing over there?"

In a soft voice, Uncle Columbo replied, "It appears to be parts of a launching device. Look at that! Those parts may be a weapon, like a missile."

Nodding his head, Scooter replied, "I told you so. This was my gut feeling of major concern. Not one of my far out hunches."

"There are soldiers on guard here," whispered Rex. "So be quiet and careful while we are snooping around for evidence of wrong doing."

"Roger that," whispered Hannibal.

The fearless foursome then began to use all kinds of objects to hide behind and then they stopped in front of a doorway.

"Let's see where this leads us too," whispered Hannibal.

After opening up the door, they went up several flights of stairs to another door and stopped.

"Scooter, since you're in front of us, you open up the door," instructed Hannibal.

Thinking that sometimes silence speaks volumes of bravery, Scooter opened the door with his eyes closed.

As Scooter opened the door, the four brave detectives came face to face with a strong looking soldier, dressed in a combat uniform, aiming a dangerous, killing rifle at them and asked, "Who's there? How did you get in here?"

"Termites," answered Scooter.

"Haven't I seen you guys somewhere before? You better start talking, because you may be in big trouble. I want to know who you're working for and what you're doing here.

What have I got to lose? I'm not going to say I'm sorry, because I won. If I kill you, it will look like I was doing my job. Now, that you're here, you may be causing us a lot of problems and because of that you come along with me."

"No thanks," challenged Hannibal. "I'll vouch for my three friends. They're OK."

"I'll vouch for my three friends," insisted Scooter. "What do you say, Rex?"

"I will also vouch for everybody," declared Rex.

"You can trust these people. I'll vouch for them," Uncle Columbo said to the soldier.

"Are you crazy? You are all crazy people. Just what on earth do you think you're trying to pull on me?" asked the soldier. "What's the matter with you? What's the idea?"

"May I say something? Are you ready for this?" asked Hannibal. "This isn't what we had in mind. We're just a couple of guys here to help you with your problems. We're not afraid to jump in and get our hands dirty. We're trying to deal our way up. Do you know what I mean?"

"Oh, wise guys, huh? What are you trying to do, hustle me?" asked the soldier. "Have you got any specific information for me? Give me your names and I will check you out. Anyone who isn't up to snuff and isn't ready for me to rip them to shreds better leave now if they know what's good for them."

"Don't do that! Don't point that rifle at us!" screamed Scooter. "I said, don't do that! I've had it with you!"

"What do you want?" asked the soldier.

"What else? What do you think we want?" asked a nervous, fearless Scooter. "We want to find our way out of here. Maybe I asked for it, but you're going to get it. If you don't put that rifle down, I'm going to club your head down to your knees. There is just one thing holding me back, me."

"If that guy smiled, his face would fall off," roared Hannibal.

"As things weren't looking good for the four fearless detectives, Sgt. Tarillo asked, "Now what are we going to do? It looks like we're in more turmoil than we can handle. Things aren't looking so good for us and this is going to ruin everything."

After considering the seriousness of the situation, Hannibal spoke surprisingly by matter-of-factually. "Over here, you big jerk. Just pucker up and blow right out of here. If you're constantly going to put me under pressure, you're going to turn me into a dragon. It's not who I am. It was like I was in a bottle and the lid was closed."

Immediately, Scooter was left crushed by what happened and felt the sudden urge to say to the solider, "You better watch it or I'm going to find your off switch! This is a message I don't want you to forget!" and then Scooter dropped one of his bricks on the soldier's foot and the soldier dropped his rifle and began to hop up and down on one foot.

"I got him!" yelled Scooter "I got him!"and then Scooter wished for Hannibal to disable the soldier and wipe his mind out of this encounter.

"Something just happened, but I don't know what it was?" yelled Uncle Columbo. "Don't think about it! Ready men! We now have a marathon to run and it's right in front of us. On your mark! Scooter pick up your brick and let's go! Head for the hills! Let's get out of here and now!"

Turning around, they ran down the stairs, with Scooter in the lead and ran faster than rabbits going from full speed to a dead calm in a few heartbeats, to the parked SUV in the soccer field parking lot.

Hearing the Hoot Owl go Who, Scooter, asked the owl, "Why do you keep calling out Who when you know it's just us?"

"I'm sorry," said the owl. "Scooter, Scooter, Scooter."

"Be quiet, we're hiding," demanded Scooter. "I have a perfect record of not being found. So be quiet."

After that, everybody climbed in the SUV and waited for their hearts to beat a normal rhythm again. As the fearless foursome sat there in a companionable silence, they listened to the Hoot Owl calling out for Scooter and wondered how dreary of a story that just happened to them. As they sat there thinking about it, they couldn't understand why.

Scooter then broke the silence by saying, "Well, wasn't that special? Wait a minute. I thought the possibility, that there were terrorists in the warehouse. We didn't know for sure until we went into the warehouse. Now I believe we found out the secret that they kept for several years and we hit the jackpot."

Sgt. Tarillo, then gulped and said, "Of course. Boy, that was a narrow escape. We never knew what we were going to find out until we went into that warehouse. It's about time that we found out. This whole thing is starting to sound a little odd. It's going to be hard to get the government to talk to us, as bad as it is.

Now that we're working on it and have a line on them, the government has some explaining to do about the warehouse to Capt. Columbo and myself.

Scooter, Hannibal, I have something I want to say to you. It's incredible, because you heard it from me. I want to thank you for bringing this to our attention."

"Uncle Columbo, I know this is a delicate question for you to answer," reckoned Hannibal. "Look at you. I see your hands shaking and you don't look like you're in any shape to drive."

"I'll be OK in a minute, nephew," answered Uncle Columbo.

Uncle Columbo than began to search with his eyes to the other three of the fearless foursome and asked if everyone was fine."

"No one is after us that I'm aware of," replied Scooter with a sigh of relief. "I think we're all going to be alright."

The ride home was full of consideration about the late night adventures.

"What we saw, supports the terrorist theory I had," sighed Scooter. "Now you know this wasn't what you called one of my far out hunches. Aren't you glad you listened to me? It's a good thing you wanted to work with Hannibal and myself, because our relationships with each other is the best weapon we have."

"Scooter, I'm sorry to put you in this position, but I want to be frank with you. We must keep this a secret," explained Uncle Columbo. "You did the right thing coming to us. I think your hunch was right and it paid off. After what we witnessed, this gives us a clear field to talk to the government. We may have to use a steady approach to solving this mystery.

After hearing what the government has to say, the facts may still have to be a secret from the public. It looks like they were setting up a mission operation control center."

Scooter then nervously responded," Why does the turkey want to cross the road? To prove he's not a chicken," laughed Scooter. "If a train is going at 120 miles an hour, how do you find out the name of the engineer?"

"I don't know," answered Uncle Columbo.

"I asked him," laughed Scooter.

"Scooter, will you listen to yourself?" asked Hannibal. "You're really starting to sound like a jerk."

Several minutes later, the gang pulled up to the detective agency. After getting out of the SUV and saying good-bye to Uncle Columbo and Rex, Hannibal and Scooter agreed that a need for protection and security of the detective agency was crucial. The planning should be now.

Chapter Twenty-Three

THE INCIDENT OF THE MEETING

After a frightening night with Uncle Columbo and Rex Tarillo, Hannibal and Scooter woke up with the rest of the West Side Kid Detectives and explained to them that after breakfast, there would be a meeting of urgency to inform the gang about their next plans to improve and protect the detective agency.

Because Uncle Columbo wanted it to be a secret for now, Hannibal and Scooter couldn't tell them what they encountered last night.

As the meeting began, Hannibal asked Scooter," Where have you been? Why are you sneaking around the house? Why did you lock your door to your bedroom? What is going on with you? When you came back, I could here you way down the hallway. Are you too nervous to start the meeting?"

"I'm sorry I'm late Hannibal. I just got trapped on the phone," explained Scooter. "Some people are hard to get rid of."

"What's the matter with me? Why can't I believe you?" proposed Hannibal. "Maybe I can help you. It won't hurt to talk about it."

"Because you believe the worst in me all of the time. You're really up tight and besides anything I say before I have my coffee can't be used against me," challenged Scooter. "Don't you ever give up?"

"I never give up. That's how we make our living, as detectives," reassured Hannibal.

"Let's see if I can get you to make any sense out of this," explained

Scooter. "Try not to worry. Everything is going to work out. I need your help and the help of everybody.

I want to begin the meeting by talking about the improvements that would allow our detective agency to be a top rated modern detective agency.

Boy, have I got some sensational ideas. I think the first thing we need to purchase is a security system for our home, which we consider our beloved West Side Kids' Detective Agency," suggested Scooter. "The security system will help prevent outlaws and thieves to break into our home. That's why I was hiding in my bedroom when I decided to take the call. I wanted to use this for an example about needing a security system."

In approval, everybody nodded their heads.

Hearing Scooter talk, Hannibal thought to himself, "Not bad. Not bad. I'm going to keep an eye on Scooter even if it's the only idea he has and I don't think much of it. I'm not going to interrupt Scooter doing something that I believed he could never do."

"I think we should buy the best cameras and alarm systems that we can get," Scooter went on to say. "We should install those cameras outside of our house and position them to cover the property. This way, we can see any person coming to our home. There are also door bell cameras we can buy to cover the front and back doors.

Along with this system, we will need sophisticated computers to see the action outside and inside the house."

"Are you ready for this?" asked You Don't Say. "How about for security purposes we buy a special dog that barks at strangers and attacks upon command, to catch the offender?"

"That's a good idea, You Don't Say," reasoned Hannibal.

"I think we should go to that new place on State Street," exclaimed Because. "They have a dog with freckles that I would like to get."

"I don't think so," replied What. "I think we should ask Hannibal's Uncle about the advice we need to buy that special dog."

"Now that we have security taken care of, the next problem I want to communicate with you is about communications," chuckled Scooter. "Everyone has a cell phone, right? Now that I think about it, maybe we should get one for our new security hound."

Mutts to you Scooter. You have to be kidding. That's pretty stupid. You're really something else," scolded Hannibal. "We're suppose to be talking about something to rely on in case the power goes off. How can a security dog use a cell phone?"

"Says who? What's it to you? If we're buying a special trained dog, I think with special training, he will learn how to use it," explained Scooter.

"I don't think so Scooter. He won't be making any phone calls on any cell phone," laughed Hannibal. "You know? I think you're out of your head as usual."

"I know. I know what we should do," suggested I don't Know. "First you thought I was going to say I don't know. But, surprise, surprise, surprise. I do know. I think Scooter should quit whining and being a nuisance about getting our very special trained dog a cell phone and that we spend our money on a Ham Radio, equipped with several long lasting batteries."

"Wait a minute," replied a confused Scooter. "You're telling me that we can't get our trained mutt a cell phone. That a pig giving us the word is better. I think we would have better communications with a buffalo."

"No, no Scooter. Boy are you confused. I think your nickname should have been I Don't Know," laughed I Don't Know. "I'm talking about a radio operated by batteries. It can be run by car batteries and other forms of 12 volt DC electricity. You can talk into it and it can talk back."

"Well it better not talk back to me or I'll have our specially trained dog attack it," insisted Scooter. "How long is a short wave?"

"That's cute Scooter. Really cute," chuckled Hannibal. "I always knew you were an idiot and I would like to present you with a ribbon. I'm going to have to write down the stupid things you say and put them in a book. What we need is a volunteer to operate and get a license to be a Ham Operator. He will need a call sign to communicate with other Ham Operators and the authorities. It works great in times of international and national responses to disasters."

"That's a great idea about getting a Ham Radio," declared Because. "Because the detective business is kind of slow right now, I will have the time to study to learn the system. Because I can, I want to be licensed to run the Ham Radio. With this equipment, we will be coming into our own kind of agency. It will give us a level of experience and professionalism that will be head and shoulders above any other agency."

"That's awesome, Because. Thanks for volunteering to be a ham."acknowledged Scooter. "I think we also need two large 64 inch TVs to keep up with the news, locally and around the country. We already get the Davenport Quest newspaper when we remember to pay our bill. While we are at it, let's get a 42 inch TV for entertainment in the finished basement."

"We don't have a finished basement," declared What.

"Yes, I know. I know. I plan to finish it myself after I make some awesome bricks with my chemistry set that I have in the basement to finish the basement," reassured Scooter. "Now that you understand this conversation, I think I finished what I have to say about that."

Scooter then continued to lead the meeting by saying, "Now, let's talk about transportation. Since the agency has ten people, we will need more than one vehicle to get parking tickets on the street. Now that we have two million dollars, we can afford to buy a Ford, like two Ford Explorers. I think we should explore those options."

"Scooter, I think you're right. That's a great idea. I think we're getting somewhere fast. At least that's a better idea than losing our money at the casino," laughed Smiley. "Sometimes we need to go places as a group and without any more cars, we will be going no place fast. There are times we need more cars for individual purposes and time to work for our clients. With more vehicles, we can go where we're called a lot faster."

"I knew that," reasoned I'm Not Sure.

"No you didn't. I'm sure you didn't know that," replied Smiley. "I thought if I explained this to everybody, you would also know that."

"I want to keep the 2010 Dodge SUV," insisted Hannibal. "We need to git rid of Scooter's falling apart Ford Taurus. Even Friendly Freddy thinks it's unfix-able."

"Since this meeting began, we have talked about security, a special trained dog, a Ham Radio, computers, TVS and cars," said Scooter as he summarized what was talked about. "Let's see. What did I forget? I know. I have a strong finish. Some people won't advertise what they want over the phone. We need something to record every phone call that comes to the agency and also get licensed for hand guns. Well, that does it. I think I covered it all."

"Now I think I am going to decide who is going to work together, to get what we need," declared Scooter. "Since I'm the boss, Hannibal, who is a genius of genies and myself will be checking out the security and the vehicles we need. We definitely won't be going to Friendly Freddie's to get what we need, because the last time when Hannibal and myself saw Friendly Freddie, he wasn't friendly.

Who and What will be looking into getting a dog, that can be specially trained to lick all of our stamps and envelopes for us. Right now, they are working on a case that a Davenport, airport security officer hired them for. He hired them to look for his missing wife. While they are at it, maybe they can also train the dog to find the missing wife.

Smiley and You Don't Say will be shopping for computers. They were hired to find out who murdered a woman, who the police believe committed suicide. The computers should help them solve that case.

I'm Not Sure and What will be trying to gamble on finding good prices on TVs. A compulsive gambler who is running away from loan sharks has hired them to protect him and expose the loan sharks.

Because business is slow, Because and I don't Know will look into a ham operator system that you can talk into. Since business is slow, the only case they have to work on is a case of beer.

"Are there any questions?" asked Scooter.

"Who will get to use the SUV first?" asked Who.

"Who and What, this is your big moment. Let's initiate the plan right away and get the ball rolling," instructed Scooter. "You take the SUV first. As soon as you get that special dog, you can find that missing wife. OK, let's do it."

"Come on What," ordered Who. "It's all beginning to add up. Let's get out of here. We've got work to do."

"Scooter, I thought this ax was a little bit too big for you to grind and it turns out that you were sensational. With great powers comes great responsibilities," reassured Hannibal. "This is no joke. You are too much. That was some play."

Chapter Twenty-Four
THE INCIDENT OF DOBERMAN GUARD DOGS

Fifteen minutes later, Who and What were talking to Capt. Columbo at the police station.

"Since our police department has a canine unit, I can suggest the best kind of dog to get for your home security," explained Capt. Columbo. "I won't say the German Shepard would be your first choice, because the Davenport Police Department is training most of those dogs.

What I would recommend to you is the Doberman Pins her. They are also noted for being guard dogs. The Doberman Pins hers are obedient and they can learn fast. They are also known for their intelligence, loyalty and protective nature. They are also gentle to family members."

"The first thing to order is potty training," laughed Who. "If we can train Scooter, we can train the Doberman."

"I'm sure the Doberman will already be trained in that matter," jested Capt. Columbo. "When you look for one, find one at least six months old. Their puppy behavior will change between six to twelve months of age."

"How hard are Dobermans to train to attack?" asked Who.

"Some will protect you and some won't. These animals are always eager to please their masters," reassured Capt. Columbo. "To train them, you may have to put them in a position where they will want to attack you. To do that, try tapping them on the face with a glove on your arm.

A well trained dog will make no attempt to share your lunch. He will just make you so guilty, that you cannot enjoy it. If you think dogs can't count, try putting three treats in your pocket and then only give them two."

"Will it be better to get a male or a female?" asked What.

"Males are the best kind to get for what you want," explained Capt. Columbo. "They are likely to bond with a whole family. Females focus more on guarding and protecting one specific person that they bonded with.

Dobermans are very good at protecting a large piece of property. They are extremely fast and are able to reach an intruder in a short amount of time."

"Where is the best place to buy a Doberman?" asked What.

"I would check The Dog Oasis on West Thirty-fifth Street first," replied Capt. Columbo. "I was there last week, looking for another German Shepard and I saw several Dobermans at The Dog Oasis."

"Thanks Captain for telling us what we need to know," acknowledged What. "After we get a Doberman, we won't have to train Scooter to attack people."

Who and What then left the police station and climbed into the SUV and left for The Dog Oasis on West Thirty-fifth Street. When they arrived, they saw a facility made of red bricks, with yellow trimmed windows. A large fence was on the front lawn. After finding a parking place for the Dodge SUV, Who and What got out of the SUV and began to walk into the building.

"Look at all of those red bricks on the building," exclaimed What.

"What did you say, What?" asked Who.

"I said, look at all those red bricks on the building. Scooter would certainly like this place," declared What. "I wonder if Dobermans come in red hair, like those bricks."

As Who and What entered the building, they eyed a red haired, middle aged woman in a checkered red and white dress. The name tag said Gloria.

Between the color of the building and Gloria, Scooter has got to like this place," laughed Who.

"May I help you young men?" asked Gloria.

Both Who and What were happy that she said it with respect.

What answered and said, "My name is What and this is my friend and associate, Who. We were referred to your Oasis by Capt. Columbo, of the Davenport Police Department. We have our own private detective agency and are looking for a guard dog, specifically, a Doberman Pins her."

"What? Who did you say you were?" asked Gloria.

"That's our names," replied Who.

"Who's names?" asked Gloria.

"What is my name," declared What.

"What is your name," asked a confused Gloria.

"That's right and this is Who," explained What.

"That's what I'm trying to find out. What are your names?" gasped Gloria.

"You know our names as well as we do," alleged What. "He's Who and I'm What."

"Whoever you are, what are you looking for?" exclaimed Gloria. "If you're looking for Dobermans, you are in luck. We have three Dobermans left. If you want me to show them to you, follow me to the kennels."

"Lead the way Gloria," insisted Who.

As Gloria led the way, they walked through the back doorway and down a hall, to a large open room with several kennels. Three Dobermans were in the middle of a line of kennels, with each separated in each kennel.

Who and What noticed that all of the dogs looked happy and well taken care of. As What and Who approached the kennels of each Doberman and placed a closed hand to the wire, the dogs licked their hands as all three dogs were eager to have a home outside of the Oasis.

"There is no psychiatrist in the world like a puppy licking your face," exclaimed Gloria. "Dobermans have a way of finding people who need them. Their aim in life is to give you their heart. A Doberman would be perfect for your detective agency. If they could talk, they would keep your secrets safe. On the other hand, if a cat could talk, it would blab out all of your secrets. Then your Doberman would have to eat it."

"You're really a funny lady," laughed Who.

"Who, I think we should get a dog with short hair that sheds very little," clarified What. "I don't want to have to vacuum the house every day."

"The Doberman meets the requirements of being obedient, loyal, trainable and protective of their owners. They are cautious of strangers," explained Gloria. "When you take your Doberman in a car, they will bark to protect you, by barking at nothing right in your ears. You can say anything stupid to a Doberman and he will give you a look that says, boy you're right on. I never would have thought of that. You can't go wrong with owning a Doberman."

"I think that's the dog for us," reckoned Who. "That's the dog for Scooter. He can talk to the dog about all the stupid things he wants to say and the dog won't call him stupid. Then we can save money by not sending him to a psychiatrist. Then it's possible we won't, because we'll have to send the dog in his place. What, what one should we buy?"

"Let's take home the black and rust colored one," declared What. "I think he just smiled at us."

"Are all the shots taken care of?" asked Who.

"Yes, he not only had his shots, but he's also been neutered," declared Gloria.

"Ouch! That dog frowns and growls," laughed What and Who.

"Hey, don't talk about neutering in front of the dog," suggested Gloria.

"OK," replied What. "I think that dog is starting to train us. Maybe we can train the dog to train Scooter. Let's go up to your front desk to settle the deal."

"No problem. If you think that dog is still right for you, follow me and we'll seal the deal," insisted Gloria.

After they arrived at the front desk, Gloria stated, "You're in luck. Today I have a good deal for you. With your Doberman, I will include the leash, the food bowl, the kennel and one months supply of the Doberman's favorite food."

"What do Dobermans like to eat, cats?' asked Who.

"No," laughed Gloria, "Their new owners. As I was saying, I am also going to supply you with proof of ownership and vaccination records for $600.

"Can you promise me that our Doberman will bark at strangers and like us?" asked Who. "I mean he will not eat us or the other members of the West Side Kids' Detective Agency?"

"That depends on you and your friends," replied Gloria. "Your goal through the process of training him should not to be making your job and your life more difficult. The possibly that will affect his behavior to achieve the outcome of what you want is to be kind to him and show him love and he will be kind and show you love back. Then he will be the best friend you have."

"What do you think?" asked Who.

"What? Are you talking to me?' asked What.

"No, I was lonely and I was talking to Gloria. Of course I was talking to you," answered Who. "Where were you when I asked you the question? Was you begging Gloria to let you out, so you could go to the potty?"

"No, I was envisioning you being chased by the Doberman," laughed What.

"OK okay," smiled Who. "Do you think the black and rust colored one who smiled at us and licked our hands would be the best choice to take home to the detective agency to protect us?"

"In one word, I think so," chimed What.

"That's not one word," said a frustrated Who.

"I knew that," laughed What.

"I know you knew that, you imbecile," challenged Who, as he handed the West Side Kids' Detective agency's debit card to Gloria.

Hearing the tension in Who's voice, the Doberman began to bark at Who to protect What, while Gloria was processing the charges.

As Gloria gave the debit card back to Who, she said, "This is a smart dog. You have to watch what you say in front of him, unless you want your hand bit off."

"I'll wait while you put the leash on the dog," proposed Gloria.

"No, I'll wait while you put the leash on the dog," approved Who. "What kind of fool do you take me for?"

"Why, is there more than one kind?" laughed What.

"Gloria would you put the leash on the dog while What and myself put the back seats down on the SUV?" asked Who. "After we get that done, we will come back to get the kennel, his food bowl, his favorite food and the paperwork."

Five minutes later, What and Who went back into The Oasis to get the Doberman and supplies to take back out into the SUV.

"Enjoy the ride home, honey," responded Gloria, as What grabbed the leash with the dog on the other end of it, while Who took the supplies out to the SUV.

The Doberman was very cooperative and looked like he had a smile on his face as What led the Doberman out to the SUV and put him into the SUV.

The drive home to the detective agency was uneventful. The Doberman made sounds like he was happy watching the buildings and cars go by.

When What and Who arrived at the agency, the job of getting the smiling Doberman out of the SUV wasn't easy. Who finally held onto the leash and wheedled him out of the SUV, by giving him little bits of his favorite food.

As they were taking the Doberman into their home, What laughed and asked, "What happens to a dog that keeps eating off of the table?"

"I don't know. You keep eating off of the table. What happens to you?" laughed Who.

"This is a joke about a dog, not me.," declared What "If a dog eats off of a table, he gets splinters in his mouth."

"Ha, ha, What," laughed Who, as he opened up the front door to the agency. "This isn't going to happen to our dog, because we have a metal table."

Who then guided the Doberman through the door into the main lobby, where the rest of the agents welcomed them. As What and Who approached the gang, they introduced the Doberman to them. The Doberman who was standing in front of the boys, began tapping the floor with his paws and looked like he had a smile or snarl. None of the boys could tell which it was.

Who then said to the young detectives, "Let's give our Doberman a name. His ancestors came from Germany and he is a neutered male."

At the sound of the word neutered, the Doberman started growling and barking as if to say, "Who, will you leave me alone. Just who do you think you are, anyway?"

"I think we should name him Bruno," suggested Because.

"I'm not sure, but I think Haus would make a better name for him, since his ancestors came from Germany," clarified I'm Not Sure.

"I don't know what it sounds like to you. But when I hear Haus, it would sound like a horse," laughed I Don't Know. "In my opinion, we should call our dog, Stella. By the look of him, you can't tell if he is a male or female."

"If you're an intruder and he is chasing you, you're not going to care who he is," jested Because. "You just going to run."

"I like his smile," added Smiley. "His smile is full of teeth and gums. When he smiles, his ears are straight up."

"You don't say?" chuckled You Don't Say. "I think Stella is a great name for him, although it's not proper. But I think it will give him character. I think we can live with that and train Stella to answer to that. If Stella could talk, I wonder what Stella would name us? Besides, what's in a name?"

"What do you think is in a name?" smiled What, as the Doberman began to bark he was thinking, "Who are these people? They all have stupid nicknames and now they are going to give me the name Stella. I just want to go back to the Oasis right now."

"I think since Who and myself are in charge of getting Stella trained, Who should begin by escorting Stella around this large house, so he can get used to his new surroundings," exclaimed What. "Then Who can take Stella outside to the fenced back yard. Now that we have found a security guard dog, I Don't Know and Because, here are the keys. Now it's your turn to use the SUV to shop for a Ham Radio Operator System."

Chapter Twenty-Five
The Buying of The Ham Operator System Incident

Without argument, Because pressured I Don't Know to be the shotgun passenger.

After Because started the engine of the SUV, he googled directions to a communications store, called Hamsons Your Wave Teck on East Belmont Avenue, in Davenport. As they pulled into the parking lot, the store reminded them of a large Morton Building.

After killing the SUV engine, Because and I Don't Know walked up to the front entrance door to a large open bay with all kinds of communication systems. The building was cooled by a large AC unit. As they stood there, looking around, a salesman came up to them and asked what he could do for them.

The salesman looked like he had just finished eating his lunch, because he had some dark food caught between his lower front teeth and a yellow stain on his white long sleeved shirt.

I Don't Know and Because introduced themselves with their nicknames. The salesman's name was Marty and he was not surprised at them having nicknames.

"I have a friend with a nickname called Froggy," explained Marty. "He was given that nickname because he was always jumpy. He must be taking a lot of energetic medications and he frequently has a large cup of coffee in his hands."

"I didn't know that," replied I Don't Know.

"Well, I knew that," declared Marty.

"Anyways," reassured Because. "We are here to find a Ham Radio Operator System for our West Side Kids' Detective Agency. Here is our business card in case you need our help.

"OK, thanks, replied Marty. "I have several Ham Operator Systems here, because you never know when all communication systems will black out."

"That's what we want to be ready for if that time comes where we will need it at our agency," added I Don't Know.

Marty then continued to explain," I suppose that you know that it is required when you use a Ham Radio, that you have to register, pass a test, get a license and have a call sign.

"Yes, we know that," stated I Don't Know. I just don't know why we have to have a sign on the building."

"The sign is a group of letters or numbers to identify you on the radio," smiled Marty.

"Eh-yup, we know that," explained Because. "I Don't Know was just being a ham and teasing you. He will tease the pants off of you, if you will let him"

"OK, then walk over there and check out the kind of Ham Radio you want," directed Marty. "Then let me know which one you want to buy."

After investigating the different choices, Because and I Don't Know decided to buy a brown set of equipment. The price tag said $1,200.

"Because, did you get the debit card from Who," asked I Don't Know.

"Never fear. The card is here," laughed Because as he motioned for Marty to come over to them.

After Marty's arrival, Because demanded to have two 12 volt batteries included in the price.

"We don't get many people asking for a Ham Radio Operator System. They must take electric power for granted," explained Marty.

"So yes, I can give you the two 12 volt batteries included in the $1,200 price. How are you going to pay for this?"

"We're going to use the detective agencies debit card to process the transaction," answered Because. "And we will load the SUV."

After saying farewell to Marty, I Don't Know and Because took their purchase out to the SUV and loaded it in the back. The two detectives then climbed into the SUV. Because fired up the engine and drove back to the West Side Kids' Detective Agency. After fifteen minutes of city traffic, arrived back at the agency.

As Because and I Don't Know tried to enter the house, they were trapped inside of the door, by Stella, the Doberman Pins her, with Who holding tight onto the leash. Immediately, the two detectives found out that the smile turned into a ferocious sharp teeth growl, not to mention the loud thunder of barking."

"I think that dog is mentally disturbed!" yelled Because. "What's disturbing him?"

"You two are. You weren't around long enough to pet Stella," laughed Who. "Come on, you dummies. Why don't you be more careful? Unless you want to lose a hand, reach out with your hands closed for him to smell you."

"Ya, right! screamed I Don't Know. "I won't do that until he stops showing me his sharp teeth."

"Now calm down Stella," pleaded Who. "They're our friends."

After a minute of Who petting Stella, Because and I Don't Know slowly lowered their closed hands for Stella to smell and eventually allowed the two over to pet him and calm him down.

"You will be buddies with Stella in no time," reassured Who. "Before it's time to eat, I think you should take Stella outside and play fetch the ball."

After everybody was done eating and getting acquainted with Stella, Hannibal requested to I'm Not Sure and Whatever to take their turn with the SUV next and go purchase the TVs they were assigned to buy, so they can utilize them tonight.

Before I'm Not Sure and Whatever left the agency, I Don't Know and Because unloaded the SUV and took the Ham Radio Operator System with the batteries in an empty room, in back of the house.

Chapter Twenty-Six

The Incident of The
Detectives And The Girl

Before I'm Not Sure and Whatever left, it was agreed to have Whatever drive the SUV. Before they left the agency, they read through an advertisement flier and found a sale of TVs at TV R-us store.

After Whatever started the engine, he put the SUV in drive and headed north on Gaines Street from 6th Street to Elmore Street. When they arrived, there were many people walking into the store.

"We better hurry and get in the store right away or there may not be any TVs left," maintained I'm Not Sure. "It's the 64 inch and 42 inch TVs I think we better get and we better do it in a hurry."

"Let's follow the crowd," requested Whatever.

"Right! Of course we should follow the crowd. Then maybe the crowd will help us carry out TVs out to the SUV," exclaimed I'm Not Sure. "Whatever, run! We need to get there before the crowd gets there!"

After brushing by several shoppers, Whatever and I'm Not Sure found the TVs they were looking for along the far wall of the store. After finding the TVs, I'm Not Sure begged for attention of one of the many employees on the floor to talk about the superior operation of the TVs. Each TV had multiple functions, with 1080 pic HD.

"These TVs are perfect for us," exclaimed Whatever. "They will be a nice fit to get the entertainment and information we need for our home and business. We need to make sure we get the electric cords and adapters for the functions of the TVs to hook up the DVD, computer and games."

"I'm not sure what to get. I don't even know what a 1080 pic HD is. So Whatever, you pick out what you think we need and I'll agree to it," reasoned I'm Not Sure as his attention and eyes were directed toward a young woman who looked like she was in her twenties, with long brunette hair that was put into a ponytail. She had a perfect tan complexion and was wearing a light blue sleeveless dress.

"If we had Stella here with his sharp teeth, we could get rid of the crowd in a hurry, so we could get waited on," I'm Not Sure continued to say. "Hey lady, bring your eyes over here and pay attention!"

Hearing I'm Not Sure, the young woman walked over to I"m Not Sure to see what he wanted.

"Now my friend, Whatever, we can expect some action," beamed, I'm Not Sure.

"Stop starin'," I'm Not Sure. You look like a glazed doughnut," alleged Whatever.

"What's the idea! What do you want sir?" asked the young woman.

"You're a beautiful young girl and I'm lonely and I wanted to ask you for a date," alleged I'm Not Sure.

"I don't even know you sir," exclaimed the young woman. "I'm an employee here and it's my job to sell TVs."

"Of course you do and we're buyers, stupid buyers who are here to buy two TVs," smiled I'm Not Sure.

Hearing I'm Not Sure, Whatever turned his head to see who I'm Not Sure was talking to.

"Aha. Now I can see how you could lose your focus about buying a TV here," admitted Whatever. "This girl is fantastically beautiful."

I'm Not Sure didn't hear much of what Whatever was saying as he began to talk to the young woman.

Seeing no rings on her left hand, I'm Not Sure in a bumbling manner said to the young woman, "Hi, I'm Not Sure and this is my friend, Whatever and believe it or not."

"What do you mean, believe it or not?" asked the young woman.

"Believe it or not, I have an idea," insisted I'm Not Sure.

"What is your idea. It better be a good one," demanded the young woman.

"You are a beautiful young woman and I would like to get to know you better. After I buy all the TVs you have, would you go on a date with me?" asked I'm Not Sure.

"What did you say you were going to do?" beamed the young woman. "Buy all the TVs I have. If you're going to buy the TVs, would you pay up and get out."

"What did you say your name was?" asked the young woman. "I'll take care of you in a large manner. After I add up your bill, would you pay up and get out? Just who are you?"

"Like I'm Not Sure said before, we're buyers, stupid buyers," laughed Whatever. "Come on, answer the girl, "I'm Not Sure. Where are your manners?"

I'm Not Sure is my name and my friend is Whatever," answered I'm Not Sure.

"I'm sure I know my name," laughed the beautiful girl. "Whatever you think, I'm sure my name is Ann."

"Don't get me wrong and I'm not crazy, except over you," exclaimed I'm Not Sure. "Sweetheart, you're wonderful. It's a good thing I found you here.

Me and my friend are members of the West Side Kids' Detective Agency and we've been around. We have all been friends since the second grade and played on a baseball team together. That is when we were all given nicknames. That's how I got the nickname, I'm Not Sure. What do you do to keep you busy? My heart is all ears."

"Oh, shopping for a new computer, so I can use it to become an author of short stories. Why do you need two TVs?"

I'm a private detective in Davenport and am looking to upgrade our detective agency," answered I'm Not Sure.

"How many people work in your detective agency business?" inquired Ann. "Are these people more like you?"

"Yes, there are eight more of us that are like us. Hannibal was our leader. Now Scooter is our leader," clarified I'm Not Sure. "Wait until you meet him. With Scooter, laughter is an instant vacation. The more you get to like him, the less you want to get to know him better. When he stops talking, he starts thinking and everything he does is stupid. He's been up the river so many times that he has been called Showboat."

"Oh really. Why would you say that about your friend?" reasoned Ann.

"Scooter is a good friend, but you have to experience his behavior to understand," jested I'm Not Sure. "All of Scooter's people skills come in a cup of coffee. An example of how stupid he is, is the time he went to get Hannibal a cup of coffee and brought him back a cup of paint."

"You're putting me on. Nobody could be that stupid," declared Ann.

"Well, if you come to our detective agency, don't let Scooter bring you any coffee," exclaimed I'm Not Sure. "All of us go by our nicknames from our baseball team. Scooter was our catcher and he did it really well. We played baseball together from second grade through high school. When we were in high school, we won the state title every year we were there."

"Oh, I really like baseball," declared Ann. "I played baseball when I was in junior high school. My favorite team is the Chicago Cubs."

Timidly, I'm Not Sure asked, "I will give you my real name, if you will accept my invitation for a date sometime. Give me your phone number and I will put it on speed dial and call you."

"I guess it's OK. You seem to be a nice guy and we like the same sport, baseball," reckoned Ann. "Here is my phone number. I see your friend is frantically motioning you over to him."

"Thanks for trusting me. You won't regret it," reassured I'm Not Sure as he left to see what Whatever wanted.

"Cut it out, will ya, I'm Not Sure. It ain't what we came here to do. I know she is beautiful, but we have business to do here," complained Whatever. I told an employee to take the TVs and accessories to the pick up department while you were wasting time talking to that girl. I processed the purchases for three TVs and the accessories for $4,219.00 and now we can load the SUV from there."

After the SUV was loaded up and the boys drove away, I'm Not Sure said to Whatever, "Wow! Ann is so gorgeous and nice. Well, I, uh, ah. I'm sure going to try my best to have her accept my marriage proposal in the near future."

"You're talking away ahead of yourself," laughed Whatever. "You are a mad impetuous fool. You lost your buttons when you started to talk to her. You need a dame like you need a new head. You haven't even had your first date and you can't be sure what's going to happen. I can see it now, Mr. and Mrs. I'm Not Sure. For now, let's go home and unload the TVs and accessories.

After Whatever and I'm Not Sure arrived back at the agency, seeing the two detectives, Stella's ears bolted straight up, noticing that somebody was entering his space. By now Stella has lifted his back leg up to many areas outside, so people beware.

"I have Stella on a leash," warned Scooter, before opening the front door to the agency. "But beware of him anyway. What kept you guys so long? Hannibal and myself need the SUV to get the surveillance equipment before dinner time.

"While we were in the store buying TVs, a girl caught my eye," explained I'm Not Sure. "You should see her. She is beautiful."

"This girl is going to take up a lot more of I'm Not Sure's time," laughed Whatever. "He plans to marry her and he hasn't even dated her yet."

"You didn't forget about buying some TVs?" asked Scooter.

"As a detective, I thought it was my job to get on I'm Not Sure's case to pry him away from Mrs. I'm Not Sure, so we could get back here with the TVs," jested Whatever. Watching TV is America's number one sport. You can learn a lot about watching TV and I knew you needed to learn a lot as soon as possible."

"What else? Well, bring them in and get them hooked up as soon as possible," exclaimed Scooter.

"Come on, I'm Not Sure," requested Whatever. "Let's get them installed before dinner time. After dinner, I'll be able to watch the Chicago Cubs game."

"We'll have to eat in the kitchen," added Hannibal. "Two of the other agents are working on a case. The evidence they are examining is laid out on the dining room table."

Whatever and I'm Not Sure then unloaded the TVs, putting one in the living room, the second in the dining room and the smaller TV went into the game room in the basement.

As the boys were sitting, eating in silence, Hannibal looked up at Smiley and said, "Would you take Stella for a walk around the neighborhood after you're done eating?"

"I wanted to help with the new case given to us by the police department," acknowledged Smiley. "I can do that after I take Stella for a walk."

"After Scooter is done eating, making a pig out of his own self, we're leaving in the SUV," reckoned Hannibal.

Chapter Twenty-Seven

THE INVESTIGATING SURVEILLANCE EQUIPMENT INCIDENT

After Scooter and Hannibal were done eating, they walked out to the SUV and paused in the driveway. "The winner of rock, paper, scissors gets to drive," suggested Scooter. "What about it?"

"Nothing about it," exclaimed Hannibal. "This time, be careful so we don't both end up in the lamp, like we did last time."

"OK, Let's go! One! two! three!"challenged Hannibal.

"My rock beats your scissors," bragged Scooter. "I'm driving to The Establishment, so we can get the surveillance equipment we need. You're shotgun."

"Eh yep. Uncle Columbo said he would put in a good word for us at The Establishment. They are expecting us to be there soon. Well, let's go, while the gittin' is good!" declared Hannibal.

"What else?" replied Scooter. "I'll stay off the strange roads and we can get there in a hurry."

"It's just strange that you would say that," alleged Hannibal. "Just pay attention to where you're going, so we don't end up at Friendly Freddy's. Hey, what's the matter with you?"

"There's a fly pestering me," alleged Scooter.

"Point him out to me and I will murder him," promised Hannibal.

"Say, you shouldn't have hit him so hard," screamed Scooter.

"I was just getting the kinks out of my arm in case I have to hit you in the head with my broken down teapot," exclaimed Hannibal. "Your head will be shiny, if you don't shut up."

"Temper, temper, Chief. If you do that, I'm going to put you back into your teapot," challenged Scooter. "I think that can be arranged very nicely. Let me be the judge of that."

"I don't like the way you said that. If you do that to me, I don't want you to be a stranger," growled Hannibal. "If you put me in the teapot, you're coming with me."

"Wuz you sure you were given a driver's license?" challenged Hannibal. "I think we're lucky we got here in one piece."

"Is that so? Is that so? Where do you think I got my driver's license, out of a Cracker Jack box, Mr. Know It All? Just because you road shotgun, that doesn't mean you can shoot off your mouth," exclaimed Scooter. "Just wait. I'll show you. Next time we play rock, scissors, paper to see who gets to drive, I'm going to use one of my bricks to play that game, instead of a rock. Your scissors won't have a chance to win against my brick."

"Scooter, will you take the clams out of your ears? Next time, make a wish when you are behind the wheel, then you won't have to worry about having a driver's license and we won't have to deal with the traffic," proposed Hannibal. "You remind me of a traffic signal. You need to use your brain, so you are mentally aware and don't get lost in the traffic. Yet every time you try to use your brain you get into trouble. You look as sharp as a dead anchovie. You can never go anywhere by yourself. What are you trying to do, give me battle fatigue?

"What are you talking about? I'm always aware that I'm mentally lost. Who needs a driver's license. Was this trip really necessary? Next time, I'll just wish us here at The Establishment and nobody will have to drive," reassured Scooter.

"Now that we're here, let's go git our surveillance equipment," requested Hannibal.

After Hannibal and Scooter went into The Establishment, they approached the lady at the front desk. Seeing the two friends, she looked up at Scooter and Hannibal with a polite smile.

Smiling back, Scooter and Hannibal introduced themselves.

"It's nice to meet you. My name is Carol. Detective Columbo said you were coming, so I was expecting you.

"Likewise, Carol. It's nice to meet you," responded Hannibal. "This is really a nice spot. A beautiful layout, I calls it. This sure is a lot of store to be in one place, ain't it.

We would have been here sooner, but we had to fight the traffic all the way here. If I was given a wish, we would have been here sooner. Now that we're here, we need to look at some surveillance equipment to cover the inside rooms and the outside property for our detective agency."

"Don't forget, we need two drones and compatible laptops for the aerial viewing," clarified Scooter. "We have a little business to do here and want to get a good price on the equipment we need. Don't get into our pockets. We don't want to take a beatin' like that."

"Come on Scooter. Women and fighting don't mix," declared Hannibal. "Who says anything about fighting with her. Carol, Scooter won't bite you. He was born with that face. I think this store is going to be the means to finding ourselves."

"That's a great idea. Whoever came up with that idea has to be pretty smart," reasoned Carol. "Men are doing great things with our security equipment."

"Awe shucks. It weren't nothing at all," replied a bashful Hannibal. "Once in a while, I do come up with some good ideas."

"That's wonderful that you came up with this idea," exclaimed Carol. "Because we have many different kinds of surveillance equipment in stock. We service all of Scott County. I will have Harry show you our inventory. Harry, these boys tell me they are here to buy security equipment to give them the means to finding themselves."

"Go on Carol, we ain't lost," insisted Scooter. "Hannibal, let's step up to this old man with this young face."

Harry looked to be in his late 40s, with dark short parted hair and no facial hair. He was wearing a long sleeved white dress shirt, with a cartoon necktie, black dress pants and black walking shoes. Harry was friendly and thanked the detectives for coming.

"Hello. My name is Harry. Thanks for coming. I understand you are looking to buy surveillance equipment."

"I'm Hannibal and this is my friend Scooter. You may have heard of us. We own the West Side Kids' Detective Agency here in Davenport. We always get our man, even if it's a woman. We thought we could upgrade our detective agency with some surveillance equipment."

"Ya, I'm the leader of the agency and this was all my idea," boasted Scooter.

"Was not," maintained Hannibal.

"Were so," challenged Scooter.

"Boys! Boys! Wait a minute. I don't really care whose idea it was," growled Harry. "Just follow me, so I can take you on a tour and show you our equipment."

"After looking at all the equipment the store had to offer them, Hannibal and Scooter agreed on the drones, laptops and the other equipment they needed.

"Harry, could our equipment be delivered and installed tomorrow morning at our detective agency?" asked Hannibal.

"I will be happy to make sure your equipment is delivered and installed, ASAP. (as soon as possible.) Anything to help the local detectives and the Davenport Police Department. I will take you to the finance department for you to pay for the equipment, drones, laptops, shipping and installation."

After they entered the finance office, Harry introduced the pair of detectives to Bill, who was an African American. Bill explained the cost of everything and the total, which came to $10,210. As Scooter handed Bill the debit card, he asked Hannibal if there was enough money to cover the cost of the equipment.

Hannibal replied, "If there isn't, we will come back and pay them on Tuesday."

After returning to the SUV, Hannibal and Scooter began counting to three to play scissors, paper, rock. Hannibal presented Scissors, as Scooter presented paper.

"Why is it you win so often?" complained Scooter. "I never saw so many people in one man."

"That's because I am the genie out of the teapot. I have the power and a driver's license," laughed Hannibal. "Let's see you pull a hat out of a rabbit."

"I have a better idea," reassured Scooter. "Since Harry interfered with our deception as to whose idea it was to buy the equipment, drones and computers, I am going to make a wish, Mr. Genie of the lamp."

"How may I serve you, Mr. No Brains," laughed. Hannibal.

"Well let me see," replied Scooter.

"What do you want to wish for, glasses?" laughed Hannibal.

"No! That's not it," answered Scooter.

"Maybe a brain that works when you wind it up," replied Hannibal as he continued to laugh.

"Well, maybe I should wish you a brain that works whenever you need one," reasoned Scooter. "But what I'm going to wish for is that you put Harry's cartoon necktie over his mouth for an hour, so he can see what he has to say to his customers."

"What are you talkin' about? That doesn't make no sense, none what so ever," declared Hannibal.

"Just do it or you will be bottle bound," challenged Scooter.

"That's a lamp, a lamp. Not a bottle or broken down tea pot, ole buddy of mine," insisted Hannibal.

Hannibal then slid into the driver's seat, started the engine and pulled out of the parking lot. Scooter sat there as shotgun with his mouth wide open, in a silent scream. After driving back to the agency in silence, they arrived with empty stomachs.

"I wonder whose turn it is to make dinner?' reckoned Scooter. "I must have a double appetite, because I'm so hungry, I could eat for both of us."

"I believe that it's your turn to make dinner tonight. I hope the dining room table is clear of evidence, so we can eat in the dining room," declared Hannibal.

"All work and no play makes a man stupid," proclaimed Scooter. "You don't want me to be stupid, do you?"

"You've been on a merry-go-round since I've known you," alleged Hannibal. "There ain't nothin' wrong that a new head couldn't fix. It could be worse, but I don't think so."

"It's my head and I'll do anything I want with it," challenged Scooter.

Chapter Twenty-Eight

THE DINNER WITH THE
DETECTIVES INCIDENT

After the two detectives walked into their detective agency, You Don't Say approached them and said, "You won't believe what our case is all about. Wait until you see the evidence we have."

"I will be anxious to hear about it after dinner," replied Scooter.

Scooter then went into the kitchen to start making dinner. As he was making dinner, Hannibal came into the kitchen and asked what he was doing.

"I'm cookin' a hot dog dinner. What does it look like I'm doin', reading a book?" asked Scooter.

"Well, I'm going to rest, cuz, I'm tired of watching you work and I don't want to watch the work that makes you stupid," admitted Hannibal.

Forty-five minutes later, Scooter had just finished his hot dog dinner. It consisted of hot dogs, french fries, green bean casserole, dinner buns and peanut butter under grape jelly for those who don't like hot dogs.

"OK gang, it's time to eat," stated Scooter. "Sit down and make yourselves homely."

As the gang sat down to eat together, a round of jokes were merrily given, because they all knew that it was hard to be sad, when you're laughing.

"Let's have a round of beer. Ya know, root beer?" Scooter joyfully stated. "Don't yell fire. The sandwiches will beat you to the door."

"Pardon me, while I depress the idiot," exclaimed Hannibal.

I hope somebody remembered to feed Stella, his favorite food, Puppy Crunch Chow, Chow. Maybe then, he won't be looking at us thinking we could be his next meal."

"I fed Stella a half hour ago," acknowledged What. "Why didn't the dog want to play football?"

"I feel like a genius and I haven't got a thing to say, proclaimed Scooter. "Oops, there goes my private eyes. Where's my dog?"

"Scooter, who let you out without your muzzle?" proposed Hannibal.

"The dog didn't want to play football, because he was a boxer," laughed What.

I've got one. I've got one," laughed Who. "What kind of dog chases anything red? A bull dog."

"I've got one better than that," insisted Scooter. "Why are chimneys so expensive? Because the price of chimneys have gone through the roof."

Looking at Scooter, Hannibal says to everyone, "Drop dead, Scooter, you imbecile. That joke wasn't better than Who's joke. What are you trying to do, unfool everybody?

"I hope Stella sleeps well in the kennel we put in the basement," grinned Smiley.

"OK, You Don't Say. Now that we're all done eating, tell us about the case and show us the evidence you was so excited to tell us about?" asked Hannibal.

"Remember when Dr. Fine and Charlie, The Chill was waiting outside, the Burlington By The Book store?" I Don't Know began to say. "They were seen traveling north on Highway 61, after they saw the police enter the store. And they haven't been seen since.

The Burlington Police Chief, Tony Hands, told Davenport Police Detective, Rex Tarillo that they assumed Dr. Fine and Charlie, The Chill were headed home to Davenport. Detectives, Sgt. Tarillo and

Capt. Columbo went to their residence, but was not able to contact them. So the Davenport Police Department assigned the case to us. We have been reading the Scott County Sheriff's report of Dr. Fine's car found empty at the Round Lake Park. The investigators found their cell phones that were left in the car.

"I'm Not Sure then added, "Dr. Fine's car has then been towed away, but I think we should search it ourselves for any clues. Neighbors at the campground saw the car pull up to the edge of the woods late at night, while trying to sleep. Some campers were awaken by a brilliant light and a humming sound."

"We should also look into the wooded area," I Don't Know suggested. "There may be clues of what might had been the fate of Dr. Fine and Charlie, The Chill. The police investigators may have missed some evidence."

"First of all, let's get our purchases installed, connected, situated in the proper places to be effective and running well tomorrow," commanded Scooter. "Then later we can divide up and start our team detecting skills. It's been a long day and I think we should all get a good night's sleep."

After a restless night for Stella, he barked and barked, until What came to unlock the kennel he was in. What filled the food dish and water bowl for him. It was a new environment for Stella, but What thought Stella would adjust quickly if the team played with him.

As the rest of the team were waking up, a pot of coffee was made by Scooter. As long as there wasn't anything white in the coffee, everyone was happy to drink it for energizing the start of the day. Each of the boys could choose what to add to the coffee. They usually choose pop tarts or bacon and eggs to eat with their coffee. Milk was available for a white mustache.

The early morning was scheduled for the installation of the supplies bought yesterday. As Scooter and Hannibal waited for the delivery of the security cameras, Who opened up the back door, to let Stella out to romp in the back yard. His nose was busy sniffing every square foot of the yard.

Chapter Twenty-Nine

THE INCIDENT OF INVESTIGATING DR. FINE'S CAR

"Scooter, now that it is our turn to go shopping, we need to leave now in the Ford Taurus to buy two more vehicles," stated Hannibal. "Those vehicles will pay off in the long run, because we can investigate more than one case at a time."

"I knew that," reassured Scooter. "I think we should go to the Ford dealership to purchase two Ford Explorers. They don't make them like they used to. Before we do that, let's go to the Rock Island Arsenal to shop for several night goggles with infrared capability and temperature detecting devices in case we are searching in dark places."

"I didn't think of that," acknowledged Hannibal. "I asked you how you could read a book in the dark, when we stayed overnight at the Goldfish Palace Casino and you told me that was because you went to night school. So why would you need night goggles?"

"I know I said that. I said what I said," answered Scooter. "I lied. I never went to night school, because it was past my bedtime. I am recommending the night goggles for our agency."

"I didn't think you knew nut-in', n-u-t-i-n. I should have stopped at nut," reasoned Hannibal.

While Hannibal and Scooter were on the way to the Rock Island

Arsenal, Smiley and I'm Not Sure drove the SUV to the police compound, to check out Dr. Fine's car. While on the way, Smiley asked I'm Not Sure where Scooter and Hannibal went.

Answering Smiley, I'm Not Sure replied, "I reckon that Hannibal and Scooter went shopping for Ford Explorers and night goggles for dark investigations. We certainly can use two more vehicles.

When Scooter took his Ford Taurus to Friendly Freddy's, a man by the name of Doctor Auto, handled Scooter's car personally and said it only had a few months to live. He could hear funny noises and parts falling out of the car. Everything was falling apart and there was no hope. When he started the car, Doctor Auto knew the car was in trouble when he saw a puff of black smoke coming out of the tailpipe."

When Smiley and I'm Not Sure pulled up to the police compound, Harry, the owner of the towing company was standing next to Dr. Fine's car.

The boys introduced themselves to Harry, who was a tall man, with a slender body frame, red hair and was wearing a surprisingly clean overall, with a blue and orange flannel shirt.

"I was told that you hauled Dr. Fine's car here. Where can we find it?" asked Smiley. "It's a four door Chevy Impala. It was brought here recently."

"You can find it in the second row over there, pointing to the east section of the parking lot," instructed Harry. "It's the only Chevy over there."

After Smiley and I'm Not Sure found the car, they looked into the glove compartment. Dr. Fine placed everything in there, even the sink if he could have made it fit.

I'm Not Sure thumbed through all the papers and saw a receipt for a gas bill from Blue Grass, dated the day he pulled into the Round Lake Campground. The windows were up, but the front passenger side window was covered with a tarp, because the window was broken.

The trunk had blankets, a spare tire, empty pop cans and a small case with a handgun. The car had some blemished paint on the hood, like it was under extreme heat and the undercarriage looked to be off center, possibly caused by driving over rough roads and a lot of vibrations. Under the hood, there were no liquids of any kind...no antifreeze, brake fluid, windshield solvent and oil. Even the battery was dry.

All these observations were written down by I'm Not Sure.

"Thank you Harry. For right now the Chevy will have to stay here at the police station," reckoned Smiley.

"That works for me," reasoned Harry. "The longer the car sits here, the more I will be paid."

Smiley and I'm Not Sure then went inside the police station to tell Detective Columbo and Detective Tarillo about their observations.

"What do you think about your observations?" asked Detective Columbo. "Do you think something fishy is going on?"

"There is an unknown terror about what Smiley and myself seen," exclaimed I'm Not Sure. "The car was really roughed up and all the fluids drained."

"Is it possible that Dr. Fine and Charlie, The Chill was murdered?" asked Detective Columbo.

"I don't think so," reckoned Smiley. "No blood was found in the car, but it could have been a violent kidnapping, since Dr. Fine and Charlie, The Chill are still missing. Right now, it's just a mystery to be solved. Maybe our other team members can find clues where the car was found at the campgrounds."

While Smiley and I'm Not Sure were at the police compound, Because and You Don't Say drove to the Round Lake Campground in the SUV to investigate the wooded area.

"What a beautiful place to camp," stated Because to Howie Brosky, the park manager. "I'm Because and this is my friend, You Don't Say. Here is our card. We are with The West Side Kids' Detective Agency. We were hired to investigate the disappearance of Dr. Fine and Charlie, The Chill. Would you show us where the car was found?"

"The car was parked over by the wooded area. I'll drive over with you to show you where the car was parked," acknowledged Howie. "It is now roped off with a yellow crime scene ribbon."

Five minutes later, the trio pulled up to the crime scene.

After getting out of the car and looking around, You Don't Say proclaimed, "Here's the tire tracks from Dr. Fine's car. Looks like the tires were bouncing on the ground. Nothing else is unusual on the ground."

"Let's go into woods to see what we can find out," suggested Because. "We might find just what we're looking for."

The two detectives then dodged through the wooded area and into a small opening, cleared of grass and twigs. The circular space seemed to be out of normal in the area. There were a few cigarette butts on the perimeter.

"There had to be something going on here," reasoned Because. "What happened here, I don't know."

"Hello, anybody out here?" shouted You Don't Say. "Listen, Because. It's time we shake some trees and see what falls out. Just a warning, anyone or anything sleeping in the trees will be shot!"

After doing that, Because cries out, "I see a piece of cloth falling to the ground, near the circle. Do you suppose Dr. Fine and Charlie, The Chill went upward?"

"Nah, that's not possible. They can't fly," laughed You Don't Say. "Let's get outta here. It's giving me the creeps."

"I know. I feel the same way," agreed Because. "Let's drive around the lake. I wish Stella was here, because I feel so uncomfortable here. Let's run."

A couple minutes later, the two detectives were sitting in the SUV, with Because behind the wheel. Because started the SUV and accelerated to fifteen miles an hour.

"I don't see the lake. Do you, You Don't Say?" asked Because.

"No, I don't see the lake," answered Because. "Are we hallucinating or is the sun shining just right that the reflection of light creates the absence of water."

"I think your explanation is weird," frowned Because. "A lake by definition needs water. Come to think of it, I need a drink."

"Listen, it is the sounds of nature," reckoned You Don't Say. "It smells the scent of nature. As you watch it, it is the vision of nature. It feels like the sense of nature. If you taste it, it is the flavor of nature, but don't put anything in your mouth."

"Why naturely. That all makes sense, but I still need a drink of water," replied Because. "What doesn't make any sense is why the lake has no water. I feel the vibe to leave here as soon as possible and go back to the agency. I'm beginning to feel a little nauseated. Let's get out of here and now."

When You Don't Say and Because arrived back at the detective agency, the gang was watching the news on the newly connected 64 inch TV. The two detectives couldn't believe their ears. The news was about the water in the Round Lake. It was not known how the lake was drained.

"Hey you guys. You Don't Say and myself have something to tell all of you," proclaimed Because. "We just came from Round Lake and can verify the news that you are listening to. The whole area felt weird. Where are Scooter and Hannibal?"

Answering Because, What replied, "They are playing with Stella and then they are going to take the Ford Taurus and go to the Rock Island Arsenal to shop for the night goggles we need for dark investigations and then go shop for two Ford Explorers.

The first choice that Detective Columbo recommend to our buddies was the goggles used by SWAT teams and FBI agents. He told them to start looking at the Rock Island Arsenal. Detective Columbo had called the Rock Island Arsenal and told them that he recommended these two private detectives purchase these items from them. Detective Rex Tarillo told me that Scooter and Hannibal has to stop at the visitor's station to get a pass in order to be on Rock Island Arsenal premises. Their profiles will need to be checked."

Chapter Thirty

THE INCIDENT OF THE WAR WITH 1ST SGT. DAVE HOGAN

After Hannibal and Scooter arrived at the Rock Island Arsenal entrance, they stopped to talk to the security officer. The security officer behind the glass cubicle shook his head for a while, before making a pass card for Scooter.

"Go in peace and leave the Rock Island Arsenal as it is now," demanded the security officer.

"Yah, right.," murmured Scooter.

"Hannibal then fired up the Ford Taurus, which sounded like a puppy that ate too much. They drove to the security gate and stopped to show their driver's licenses and passes, before they were allowed to enter. After that, they drove to building 14, that had the night goggles.

1st Sgt. Dave Hogan greeted them with a grin, because Rex Tarillo told him what they wanted and who they were.

Scooter saluted 1st Sgt. Dave Hogan and asked, "Sir, is this the place and nowhere but the place where we can get goggles that can allow us to see people in the dark and to show thermal images of human bodies?"

"Yes, you found it. This is definitely the place," answered 1st Sgt. Dave Hogan. "Why do you salute me and call me sir? You're not in the army and that's a good thing for our country. I suppose even detectives may even hunt people in the dark, like the military. But remember, the person has to be alive. If they're dead, the body temperature decreases over time."

"Do we need an image receiver with the goggles in order for someone far away to see the same vision?" asked Hannibal.

"Yes, with proper compatibility to the units," explained 1st Sgt. Dave Hogan. "If you have computers, perhaps that's all you need."

"Since we already have computers, then we will need four night vision binoculars for our West Side Kids' Private Detective business to get us the information we need to know," replied Scooter to 1st Sgt. Dave Hogan, as a corporal pulled up to building 14 to give 1st Sgt Dave Hogan a letter.

"Well, I'll be," smiled 1st Sgt. Dave Hogan.

"Is that good news Dave?" asked Scooter.

"It sure is. I just got promoted to 2nd Lieutenant, confirmed Dave Hogan.

"Hey, that's great news, Dave. That's really great," reassured Scooter.

"Dave what?" challenged Dave. "Now, I'm a 2nd Lieutenant, an officer in The Unites States Army and from now on, you will call me, sir."

"Yes sir!" answered a nervous Scooter. "While we are here, can you supply us with ten handguns?"

Answering Scooter, 2nd Lieutenant Dave Hogan replied, "You learn fast. You're going to live up to my standards. You're probably going to hate my guts for what I'm telling you to do. I can sell you the guns, but you must get permits and licenses to carry them. You can take them with you to your detective agency today, but thereafter, you must follow the laws, because I'm going to check to see if you did that. Is that understood?"

"I got it," answered Scooter. "Will I need a GPS to follow the laws?"

"You're not very cooperative, because you're screwing up. I insist that you call me sir," demanded 2nd Lieutenant Dave Hogan. "It's a good thing you're not in the army, because if you were, you were going to get it and I would have to get rough with you."

"Sir, Scooter was talkin' to me," exclaimed Hannibal. "We're not at war and in your Army, Sir! Although you are now an officer, you don't know who you're talkin' to. We are civilians and don't have to salute you and call you sir. I wasn't going to say anythin' to you at all, but you are talkin' to the one and only, Scooter, The Brick. Scooter, The Brick, if you'll agree on these immediate purchases of war, I will give our beloved 2nd Lieutenant Sir, our beloved credit card to conclude our operation in this war. How much is everything, Sir?"

"Scooter, The Brick means nothing to me," replied an angry newly promoted 2nd Lieutenant David Hogan. If it wasn't for Detective Rex Tarillo, I wouldn't be selling you the supplies you need. I would have you very quietly escorted off the Rock Island Arsenal and thrown in the river, by security. The total comes to $28,000. The corporal will help you load your car. It's nice to see you, but it's better to see you leave."

As Scooter and Hannibal were leaving the Rock Island Arsenal, Hannibal reckoned, "If it wasn't for 2nd Lieutenant Sir, it would have bin a piece of cake to buy the equipment we needed. Evidently, a person will not be a risk to society out of the Rock Island Arsenal."

"If I had thought of it, I would have wished a cream pie thrown in his face. Now 2nd Lieutenant Sir is going to live up to my standards," laughed Scooter. "I know I always screw up and do stupid things. When I screw up, since it's a double good idea that you are a genie, it will payoff in the long run.

Now, I am going to wish that 2nd Lieutenant Sir will forget about getting the letter of promotion, because he never got the letter of promotion. Since we left, the corporal will get the letter of promotion to 2nd Lieutenant. Now, 2nd Lieutenant Sir won't be the head idiot in this man's army. The 2nd Lieutenant will get a letter saying he was demoted to a corporal nobody."

"That's funny," laughed Hannibal. "This time when you screwed up and did something stupid, your brains was falling out of your ears and you did the right thing."

While crossing over the bridge of the Mississippi River to Davenport, Scooter and Hannibal then sat in companionable silence.

"Isn't the Mississippi River a wonderful sight to be hold?"

questioned Scooter. "Did you know that the Mississippi River was married?"

"Nah, you can bet your work boots that I don't know that," declared Hannibal.

"Well, according to my work boots, they was known as Mr. and Mississippi, laughed Scooter.

"I can remember when my dad took me fishing along the river, not too far from the Centennial Bridge," assessed Hannibal. "The river was low and I got stuck in the mud."

"Why were you in the mud?" asked Scooter. "So you could track up your mother's house when you got home?"

"No, I just wanted to touch the water," proclaimed Hannibal. "Ironically, I didn't get that far."

"Now I get it, replied Scooter. "Now I see. It was because your feet was stuck in the mud, before you could reach the water."

"My dad had to pull me out of the mud and I lost one shoe to the Mississippi Mud," explained Hannibal.

"That wasn't good at all. It sounds like you was just a dumb kid," reckoned Scooter. "And you say I do stupid things."

"That still didn't stop me from having fun, because I just took my other shoe off and explored the shore for treasures," Hannibal went on to say.

"You must have been quite a sight with all that mud on you. Did you find any treasures like the shoe you lost in the mud?" laughed Scooter. "Was that your impression of Shoeless Joe?"

"I did find one Indian arrowhead that I still keep with me in my pocket," answered Hannibal.

"Wow! You've had it all this time and I never seen it," exclaimed Scooter. "Now you will have to show your Indian arrowhead to me. Other than your shoe that got away, did you catch any fish, that day?"

"I caught a small catfish and my dad caught a large catfish this long," alleged Hannibal as he smacked Scooter in the chin.

"Ouch!," yelled Scooter. "We need a bigger vehicle if you're goin' to tell stories like that. Now pay attention to your driving before you have another story to tell da police."

"I'm glad you brought that up about a bigger vehicle," reckoned

Hannibal. "We need to buy two Ford Explorers, yet today that is on our list of things to do."

TO THE READER

"Before I continue on with the story to chapter thirty one, I want to take a break and explain where we're at in the book," promised Scooter. "I know you want to know when the Space Aliens are coming. Like any story, it will be building up to the end of the story. I hope you enjoyed what you read and had fun with lots of laughs while you are reading this very exciting book.

I know I am always doing something stupid in this book. But my head is crawling with brains and I am really a smart person. Just to prove that, didn't I wish Hannibal to be my genie in a lamp? Now my wishes all come true, because I'm Scooter, The Brick with a magical genie. So what do you think?

I'm not asking you, Chris Seven, What Do You Think, Murphy. You and your twin brother, Michael Eight Murphy, alias Dr. Zodiac will be returning to the story later.

So read on my dear friend. I know you will have more laughs and fun coming your way. If you like this book, check out the other books that I'm in. What I mean is there are a series of six books with this one. Try reading "Wrestling With Death" or "The West Side Kids in A Pocket Full of Wishes."

I guarantee you that I'm just as stupid in those books as I am in this one. So carry on reader. The laughs are ahead.

Chapter Thirty-One

The Incident of Dealing With Unfriendly Freddy

Later on, Hannibal and Scooter pulled into Friendly Freddy's Ford Dealership.

As they climbed out of the Ford Taurus, Friendly Freddy walked over to greet them by saying, "Hello Neighbor. Oh no! It's not you two again!" growled Friendly Freddy. "What can I do for you this time, if I may ask?"

"We are lookin' to buy two new Ford Explorers, you ole bandit," declared Hannibal. "Although Scooter is with me, this time you will have to deal with me. We're lookin' to trade this pile of junk we bought from you for two Explorers."

""What do you mean I sold you a pile of junk?" asked Friendly Freddy. "Before I place any car on my lot, they are like new. I have Doctor Auto check them over from the tires to the roof and you can't buy better used cars anywhere."

"That car was used, OK?" reassured Hannibal. "The only reason I bought it from you was that I needed some transportation in a hurry. You told me when I bought it from you that it was worth a $1,000.00. I know I only gave you $500.00 for it and I want that much for it on a trade in."

"It was well worth $1,000.00 when I sold it to you," exclaimed

Friendly Freddy. "I don't know what you did to that great running cream puff of a car. When Scooter brought that car here a few days ago to have Doctor Auto check it out, parts were falling off of it and Doctor Auto said it only had a short time to live. If you want to get rid of that car, I would have to charge you to dispose of it or give it to the junk yard for parts, that is if you can find the parts that fell off the car."

"No deal! You're not dealing with Scooter this time," exclaimed Hannibal. "I'm on to your schemes. You need to give me a better deal than that, if you want to sell me two brand new Ford Explorers, with all the parts that come with it. If Scooter wishes me to get the kind of deal from you that I want, you better do it."

"I can't do that. What are you talking about," challenged Friendly Freddy.

"In that case, I think Scooter and my own self should have a meeting of the minds away from your prying ears," declared Hannibal. "I hope your ears don't mind the secrecy of our meeting."

Hannibal and Scooter then walked away from Friendly Freddy to talk about their plan of action.

"Scooter, I gota' idea," revealed Hannibal to Scooter. "What do ya say if you wish me up several rolls of $1,000.00 bills and that I hide them inside the front hub caps of our car? Let's insist the Doctor Auto with the assistance of Friendly Freddy, that they check out our car real good like, so they can find the money.

After that, I'm sure that Mr. Friendly will want to give us more than what we paid him for that broken down Ford Taurus. After we trade and leave, you can wish me to have those $1,000.00 bills turned into shreds of paper. Freddy will never figure that one out."

"Ya, ya. Let's do it," smiled Scooter. "I never thought having a genie could be so much fun. Especially if that genie is my best buddy."

"OK Mr. Freddy, Scooter and yours truly has come to an incision," reassured Hannibal. "First I want you and Doctor Auto, exclusively to check out the condition of our cream puff, to see if you can derive at a better price for us. Next, I want you to show me the invoice of what you paid for these here Explorers of my choice and then we can deal from there."

"Well, Doctor Auto and I will take another look at your cream puff, but I think your cream puff is still going to end up in the junk yard," exclaimed Friendly Freddy.

"So take your time. Take your time," reassured Hannibal. "Scooter and myself will be taking a load off our feet and be viewing the Explorers that you have on the lot, while you check out our beauty. Where are your beautys' at?"

"Oh, you mean the Ford Explorers. There are four of them sitting over at the corner of the lot," explained Friendly Freddy

"Come on Scooter. Let's go look at what we came to see while Mr Freddy and Doctor Auto see what we want them to see," instructed Hannibal.

"I'm with you, ole buddy of the best. Just do your magic and away we shall go," exclaimed Scooter.

"Don't go too far. We have to explore the Explorers," laughed Hannibal.

Walking over to the Ford Explorers, the first one they saw was a blue Explorer St-Line, with a sticker price of $45,510. Next to that one was a black Timberline Explorer for $47,570. After that, they viewed a blue ST Explorer for $48,510. And the last Explorer was a gray Explorer Limited, priced at $46,820.

"Which one do you like?" asked Hannibal. "They all have the equipment we want."

"I was hoping to get a black and white one. You know, like the police cars," admitted Scooter. "But, sigh, I guess I will settle for the two blue ones. Maybe we could have them painted black and white with the West Side Kids' Detective Agency painted on the sides of the Explorers."

"I'm sure we can get them painted like the black and white police cars," proclaimed Hannibal. "But there is no sense for what so ever to spend the money to repaint the Explorers.

"Maybe I could explore the idea and wish them the color I want after we buy them," justified Scooter.

"I don't think so Scooter. I tell ya, black and white Explorers painted like police cars. I don't know what you're thinkin'," answered Hannibal. "I don't think Uncle Columbo would advise that. We're detectives, not policemen. Let's just take the blue ones and check out any incentives to buy them. Maybe after Friendly Freddy finds all those $1,000 bills in the hub caps, that could be the big discount they are lookin' for us. Let's go see if Friendly Freddy has found our discounts."

A few minutes later, Hannibal was talking to Friendly Freddy about the Explorers.

"Well neighbor, that Ford Taurus was in better shape than what we thought," alleged Friendly Freddy. "You know as Friendly Freddy, I always give the best price on all of my cream puffs. Since you want to buy two Ford Explorers, I can give you a $2,000.00 rebate on each Explorer and $1,500 for your Ford Taurus.

"You, Sir, I will accept your price. You have a deal," exclaimed Hannibal.

"How are you going to pay for these two cream puffs?" asked Friendly Freddy.

"Would you accept a check from our detective agency account?" asked Hannibal.

"No, I don't think so," confessed Friendly Freddy. "I need a cashier's check to pay for these Explorers."

"I didn't know that," reckoned Scooter.

"You don't know nothin' anyhow," reassured Hannibal. "OK Freddy. You tell me the entire amount and I will have one of the boys from our detection agency bring you a cashier's check for that amount," declared Hannibal.

"Then after you call one of your boys, Doctor Auto will get your Explorers ready to go while we're waiting," acknowledged Friendly Freddy. "You come in and sign the paperwork."

"After the paper work was signed, Hannibal asked Scooter, "Which Explorer do you want to drive back to the agency?"

"I want to drive the blue Explorer to our agency," declared Scooter. "Which one did you think I wanted to drive or did you think I was just going to stand here and wait for a bus?"

"Oh, I thought you wanted to drive the black one back," challenged Hannibal.

"I didn't know that," maintained Scooter. "I thought we bought the two blue Explorers."

"Of course we bought the two blue explorers," boomed Hannibal. "You mean you signed the paper work with me and you don't know which ones we bought."

"I knew we bought the blue Explorers, but I thought you was trying to confuse me," confessed Scooter.

"Oh yea," replied Hannibal. "You was confused the moment you got out of bed twenty years ago."

"OK, Mister Genie of the bottle," screamed Scooter. I would get rough with you only there is only me stopping me."

"What's stopping you ole master of the no brains?" roared Hannibal.

"Me! Chief-ole-boy. Don't let me do something I'll be sorry for," cried Scooter. "Why don't you stop me when I'm talkin' like this?"

"Then you tell me which Explorer you want to drive or I'm going to break the rest of your nose and then wish you wasn't here," bellowed Hannibal.

"Really? You would do that to your best buddy?" babbled Scooter.

"In your case, yes," insisted Hannibal. "Now make up your mind what you want to drive, before you drive me nuttier than you."

"Oh, is that all you wanted to know. Why didn't you just ask me?" exclaimed Scooter. "I want the Explorer with the equipment and the handguns covered up in the back. While you're driving the other Explorer, don't drive toward the oncoming traffic and make sure you stop at the stoplights."

"Yes mom," replied Hannibal sarcastically. "Sometimes I don't know if I'm cummin or goin' with youse."

An hour later, Scooter and Hannibal drove the new Explorers back to the detective agency.

After they walked back into their detective agency, Scooter reminded Hannibal of the wish they had planned at Friendly Freddy's Ford Dealership.

"Oh, ya," replied Hannibal. "Your wish is my command. Wish away ole buddy."

"Are you ready, ole genie of mine?" asked Scooter. "I wish that the rolls of thousand dollar bills we left in the hub caps of my old, but not forgotten Taurus, be turned into shreds of paper that is worth nothing, but pieces of paper."

As Scooter was making his wish, Friendly Freddy and Doctor Auto were sitting at Freddy's desk, dividing up the money when it turned into shreds of paper.

"What just happened to all of our money," screamed Friendly Freddy. "Let's put this money in a case and take our case to the Supreme Court."

Chapter Thirty-Two
THE INCIDENT OF THE NDA INSTRUCTOR

The next morning, Scooter called for a general meeting with the secret agents.

"Everyone did well in updating this here Detective Agency," assessed Scooter. "You could say we are modernized. I want to thank everyone for your time, effort and expertise in getting this agency, to be the best in Scott County. With all this equipment, we need to learn how to use them efficiently, including the handguns."

"You don't say. You mean we get to shoot the handguns?" asked You Don't Say.

"Shoot a handgun, laughed Whatever. "Why would you want to shoot the handguns, you Knuckle Head? What did they ever do to you?

I wouldn't be surprised if it was Scooter asking that question, by shooting off his mouth. But I would think you would know better. You don't shoot a handgun. You put ammo in it and use it to shoot at a target."

"It sounds like we all need shooting lessons," added Scooter. First everyone needs to take a class in gun safety to get a permit to carry a gun. After that, we need to practice, practice and practice some more shooting our handguns.

I will arrange a safety gun instructor to teach us and help us get a permit to carry. As a FYI, we are detectives, who are required to attend a seminar on the activities of a detective for licensing. Is everyone clear on that?"

Scooter, if you are clear on this, I'm sure everybody else is too," chuckled I'm Not Sure. "I will comply as long as I don't have to stand next to Smiley when we are practicing shooting."

"Why is that? What are you talking about?" asked Smiley.

"I was almost a victim of your carelessness, swinging a baseball bat at a practice," stated I'm Not Sure. "You are dangerous to be around with a weapon in your hands."

"Thanks for the information, I'm Not Sure. I didn't know that," laughed Hannibal.

"Well, I knew that,"insisted I'm Not Sure.

"OK, OK, you made your point," acknowledged Hannibal. "Now that we know, all of us will watch out for Smiley and be sure he is aware of the position of the handgun."

"Gang, listen up," boomed Scooter. "Another thing we need to pass as detectives is to be physically and mentally fit. I will arrange for an instructor to handle this. The one I'm going to hire is recommended by the National Detective Association, that is best known as the NDA."

"Scooter, he better be good if he has to get us to be physically and mentally fit to use a hand gun," laughed I'm Not Sure. "He doesn't know what he's in for, if he has to deal with you. After working with you, he may want to volunteer to be one of our targets."

"You don't say. Ain't you the funny one, I'm Not Sure. "Maybe I should make you Smiley's partner in this class," acknowledged Scooter. "Before I dismiss you all, I will want everyone to have your eyes and ears tuned to the Dr. Fine and Charlie, The Chill case."

The next day, the NDA sent an instructor to give the West Side Kids' Detective Agency a seminar for their annual detective renewal license. The seminar stresses physical and mental heath to cope with the life's ups and downs.

Instructor Chan Woetrom, from the NDA introduced himself to the detectives. He also introduced his assistant, Betsy Bones.

"This may be a shock to a selected few people," began Instructor Chan. "But life is basically unfair."

"Are you talking to all of us or just Scooter?" laughed I'm Not Sure.

"I don't understand. Why do you ask that about your leader?" asked Instructor Chan.

"You'll see," chuckled I'm Not Sure as everyone else began to laugh. "Just remember how unfair life is once you start working with Scooter."

"Why do all of you boys follow Scooter, if you feel that way about him?" asked Instructor Chan. "When we work together as a team, the odds become even and we are as strong as the weakest of one of the team. The mind is a very powerful asset."

"Because we're all friends and they knows what will happen if they doesn't," reassured Hannibal. "Besides, we're all Scooter's friends and we all know he has a powerful weak mind. You never know when he's gonna shoot off his mouth and say and do things next. That's when I have to straighten out his head from his ears."

"Oh, I see. I understand. No, I don't see or understand," replied Instructor Chan.

"Let's put it this way," explained Hannibal. "You may have a powerful mind to start with and I hope you do. You'll need it if you're going to work with Scooter, The Brick."

"That's right Mr. Chan," exclaimed Scooter. "At one time, I was a professional wrestler, known as Scooter, The Brick. I had a wrestling match with three mean professional wrestlers and won all three matches without laying a hand on them."

"Sure you did," replied Betsy Bones. "I'm glad you told me. Well, let's move on. Everyone here should know some form of mixed martial arts.

I believe in "The way of the intercepting fist". With this technique, you can thrust your fist, from just inches away, into a person's body and render that person help-less. If you have so much confidence in your mind, into the thrust, then you can control your opponent.

Everything that goes up, must come down. But there comes a time when everything that's down, can come up. Simply of thought and simply of power will get the results you want. Your mind will not let you be defeated. The key to success is sincerity. If you can fake that, you've got it made. It will give you greater effort to achieve your goal.

No limit is a state of mind. It is better to have a mind that has no dwelling place. Simplicity is daily decrease.

"Let me show you," requested Chan.

Betsy then picked up a board and held it with two hands in a bracing stance, while Chan held his fists just inches from the board. After what looked like a few seconds of meditation, Chan thrust his fists through the board, which sounded like a popgun.

"In order to get to this level of power," explained Chan. "A person has to practice with a conditioned mind set. Be quick to learn and wise to know. Define your goals clearly, so that the others can see them as you do.

Of course, you must be in physical shape. The regular running, stretching and strength building are necessary. If you ask me what is the single most important key to be ready to face your opponent, I would have to say it is avoiding stress and tension. And if you didn't ask me, I still would have to say it."

"Life is better, when you can dance," reassured Betsy. "Imagine yourself floating and discover a world of joy, confidence, health, energy and fun. Dress simply. If you wear blue jeans and your favorite shirt, don't wear anything else on it...like lunch or dinner."

"Empty your mind. Sincerely, if you can fake that, you've got it made," emphasize Chan as everybody began to laugh. "Be formless, shapeless, like water," Chan continued to say. "Now shape yourself into the person you want. Let's begin our training. What did I say that was so funny?" asked Chan. "Well, what about it?"

"Nothin' about it," replied Hannibal. "If you want to start our training, I suggest that you start with Scooter first, because you won't have to wait for him to empty his mind, because he doesn't use his head for a dwelling place to keep his mind."

"Does that mean I git to go first, Chief?" asked an anxious Scooter. "I'm ready to go. I have my brick here and some chemicals I made up to drink that will make me strong as an ox."

"I don't think Chan can train a knucklehead that already has an empty mind," assessed Hannibal. "I don't want you to be giving Chan the creeps and having him depart from our agency before he can show the rest of us up on how to be trained."

"I can train Scooter. I'm sure of it," replied Chan. "The function and duty of a quality human being to anything, is the sincere and honest development of each potential."

"OK, you can start with Scooter first, but if you want to avoid the stress and tension, I'm agona suggest that you start with someone else. Are you going to start with Scooter? Don't say I didn't warn you," proclaimed Hannibal.

"OK Mr. Chan. Have Betsy hold a board up like she did for you and watch me tear it in half," requested Scooter. "I'll bust it to pieces. It will all be splinters when I'm done with it. Then I'm agona ask Betsy if she would like to be my partner and dance with me."

"No Scooter, you're not ready for this," replied Chan. Let's start out getting you physically fit. You need to start with the running, stretching and strength building.

"No, I don't have to do anything like that. That can take a lot out of a man. My doctor told me that exercising could add ten years to my life. Now, I feel ten years older.

I would rather be a failure at something I enjoy, than a success at something I hate," reckoned Scooter. "There ain't nothing a man can do, if he believes in himself. I'm Scooter, The Brick. I would say I'm kinda strong. I may think I'm kinda strong. I let my drinking do the talking. After I drink my chemicals, I will be physically strong, strong as an ox and calloused inside."

"But sir, how can I help you if you don't want to follow the procedures?" asked Chan.

"Let him bust that board to splinters," declared Because. "We all want to see him do it."

"Go ahead Chan," reckoned Hannibal. "Everybody has something to conceal. With Scooter, things are never so bad that they can't be made worse. I don't think he tries to be a character. I think he is one.

Let him get it out of his system so the rest of us can start our training. After that, we better call the ambulance for Scooter and while we're waiting for it to come, we can all have some coffee to get our brains working."

Everyone laughed at that comment.

Scooter then said, "Here's to my chemicals. Everybody believes in something. Now I believe I'm going to drink some of my chemicals so I can forget the running, stretching and strength building."

Scooter then took a drink of his chemicals and said to Betsy, "Give me a few minutes and then I will be ready for you to hold that board up that is soon to become splinters."

A few minutes later Scooter said to Betsy, "Grab the board, I'm ready. Look out board, I just drank my chemicals, my mind is empty and I'm comin' after you."

Betsy then held a board up, like she did before. Scooter picked up a brick in his right hand and hit the board, breaking it in half.

"You're not as dumb as you look," exclaimed Betsy.

"I couldn't be and live," replied Scooter.

After an hour of practice, the NDA stopped the exercise and offered to sign papers of participation proving that each detective completed his requirements for license renewal.

"Thank you Woetrom and Bones for the seminar and demonstrations," declared Scooter. "I wish you a safe return to your headquarters."

"You are welcome, Scooter, The Brick," replied the instructors. "You gave us a demonstration of your own that we didn't expect."

"After that demonstration of Scooter's, I hope you will be prepared for Scooter and still come back next year," requested Hannibal.

"You write us a check and we'll gladly be here next year," assessed Chan.

Chapter Thirty-Three
THE INCIDENT OF A
SPECIAL NEWS REPORT

Before lunch, Because took Stella out of his cage, for a walk around the block and into the back yard to play fetch.

Now that it was lunch time, the detectives sat together eating peanut butter sandwiches and their choice of beverage. As everyone was sitting at the large dining room table, Scooter reminded the gang about having a gun safety class, where they will shoot their weapons that afternoon, starting at 2 p. m. at the Davenport Police Weapon Range.

"All right! Oh boy! I finally get to shoot my handgun," Smiley gleefully responded.

"There will be a target down the field we will shoot at," acknowledged Scooter. "Remember that safety is the number one priority."

Later on that day, it was five 'o clock and the gun safety classes and practice at the firing range was over. It was a long day and everyone was ready to go back to the West Side Kids' Detective Agency, in the new blue battleship Ford Explorers. Luckily, no one argued about which Explorer to get into and who was to drive. No one got shot!

Upon opening the front door, to enter the agency, the detectives arranged to have a rock, paper, scissors game, to determine who gets to shower first. Somehow, they established an order of who takes their shower next. If it wasn't your shower time, you helped with dinner set up and fed Stella.

While waiting for his turn to shower, Scooter took Stella to the back yard to play fetch. Stella was getting really good at fetching and bringing the ball back, dropping it at your feet. Stella was doing this without the reward of a treat.

Scooter thought that Stella could be taught other commands, like shaking paws (hands) and bringing other items to you.

As the West Side Kids sat around the table, eating their dinner of hamburgers and french fries, I Don't Know brought up the idea of hiring some people to clean the house and to cook the meals.

"We have plenty of money to do that, don't we?" asked I Don't Know. "Then we could simplify our lives and concentrate on our detective work."

"We could hire two ladies to clean and cook for us three times a week," added What.

"I hope that would include our laundry needs as well," declared Who.

"As your new leader," replied Scooter. "I'm sure it's possible, because I don't want to have to do everybody's laundry anymore. Who, What, and I Don't Know will be the three volunteers I need to do the applicants. You will be the ones to question the ladies. "I will have an advertisement put in the Davenport Quest newspaper."

After everyone was finished eating, some of the detectives were watching TV.

"There's a special report on the TV that is interrupting our favorite show," exclaimed I Don't Know. "Everyone better come over and watch it. It's about some unusual happenings going on around the Quad Cities."

The local TV channel was showing videos of damaged and disturbed properties. There were reports of heavy fog blinding residence and travelers on I-280 by Round Lake.

The report continued interviewing an East Moline resident who said he saw something huge, far west over Round Lake in Davenport two nights ago. It was dark and kind of blended into the night sky. The foggy lights he saw, thought to be coming from businesses. Because of this, he thought it was nothing to report to authorities. He said it was just the usual weather effects common around the Quad Cities.

Another witness of this like event said, he saw a huge saucer-like object, hanging over Buffalo, Iowa. It looked like it was sucking up material from the quarry and the Mississippi River. It stayed for like one hour and then it disappeared.

Many of the people, who reported having seen them, are very reasonable, rational, trustworthy people. The kind of people who are very down to earth and matter of fact. They aren't claiming they know what they saw or that it is definitely aliens. They have no idea what it was.

These reports were just a couple of many more witnesses of these events. The Police Departments all over the Quad Cities were being flooded with calls, saying that they had seen something similar.

One woman reported seeing a huge disc-shaped flying object over the landfill in Buffalo.

A camper at Round Lake Park mentioned, "It was so thick with fog, that he couldn't see six feet in front of him. He did think he saw beams of light shining towards the woods."

The local TV channel turned their news over to the National Special Report. Their news supported the local scary happenings around the Quad Cities. The National News stated that enormous saucer looking objects were seen by different reputable people from the West to the East coast and especially in the Alaskan Mountains. Each report originated from places with bodies of water and nuclear plants. The news ended with a statement advising people to be on alert for abnormal incidents.

"What is going on?" questioned I Don't Know. Strange things are not only happening here, but around the country."

"Could it be weather related?" asked Whatever. "It could be a huge dark tornado clouds and the fog could be different moisture temperatures. But what's causing the vacuum like action?"

"Whoever watched the news will be aware of strange things that are happening," declared Scooter. "As detectives, we better be on alert too."

Stella was laying on the floor in the living room, while the guys watched the special news report. Stella's ears were seen moving up and down throughout the report.

After everyone went to bed, they all had a restless sleeping night. During the night, Scooter could hear Stella making a worried growl sound, for several hours until he settled down to sleep in his bed cage.

Since Scooter couldn't sleep to Stella's noises, he spent some time in the basement chemistry lab to create a formula, for a better brick. He put the chemicals in the brick form mold and waited for it to solidify.

At 5 a. m., Hannibal was awaken by a ringing sound. It was the cell phone on the night stand. Hannibal reached over and touched the green button circle and heard, a voice that sounded like Uncle Columbo's, "I hope I didn't wake you up."

Hannibal replied, "Nah, I had to get up to answer the phone anyway."

"Yes, this is your Uncle. I assume you heard the special report on the TV last night. We need to meet at Round Lake to investigate and find some answers."

"OK, Uncle," replied a sleepy Hannibal. "I will bring Scooter with me. We will be there by 9 a. m."

"Copy that," replied Uncle Columbo and then he touched the red button on his cell phone to hang up.

Around 6:30 a. m. everyone was starting to wake up and got up to get dressed, to be ready for breakfast.

At the dining table, Scooter sat drinking his coffee and stated, "This reminds me to tell Who, What and I Don't Know to get an advertisement in the newspaper for a cook and a housekeeper. The sooner, the better. Just say in the paper what we want. Put in our address and phone number for the people interested in working for us. The rest of you can maintain the business while Hannibal and myself meet Uncle Columbo, at the Round Lake.

Chapter Thirty-Four
THE INVESTIGATING ROUND LAKE INCIDENT

When Hannibal and Scooter arrived at Round Lake, Uncle Columbo and Detective Tarillo were already looking into the dry lake.

Scooter yelled, "Have you found anythin' yet?"

Detective Tarillo shouted back, "No, not yet. I have noticed some charred grass and logs. However this happened, the event not only took the water, but it was also hot enough to burn foliage on the floor of the lake."

Now standing together with the Davenport Police Detectives, Hannibal offers, "We know that the fluids in Dr. Fine's car were also gone. Do you suppose it is related to the same event?"

"And the heavy fog was from the steam coming from the lake's vapor," added Scooter.

"I agree to everything we found so far," declared Uncle Columbo. "But we still don't know what happened and there are still two people missing."

"The frustration is beginning to jam my brain circuits. If I only knew what I didn't know," declared a frustrated Detective Tarillo. "I think I better investigate the surrounding woods and I need everybody to come with me."

Detective Tarillo began to lead the way as Uncle Columbo,

Hannibal and Scooter followed him along the dry shoreline and into the woods. After looking high and low, the four fearless detectives noticed more birds were found dead, in a matter not normal.

Scooter, in an apologizing voice complained, "I woke up this morning feeling fine and now I feel a little sick. I wonder if my sick feeling is related to what has happened here?"

"Maybe it was because you made a pig out of yourself with all that food you ate for breakfast," laughed Hannibal."I don't think so," replied Scooter. "Just because I eat that much, doesn't mean I make a pig out of my own self. A healthy breakfast is the most important meal of the day."

"Look!" demanded Sgt. Tarillo. "There's an open circular area that is unusual for this terrain. Within the circle, there are cigarette butts and would you believe a shoe?"

"What size is the shoe?" asked Uncle Columbo.

"It's a men's size 10," answered Sgt. Tarillo.

"Ugh, I'm not feeling so healthy either," declared Uncle Columbo. "I think we are not feeling so well, because of the food we ate. I think we should compare notes with the Scott County's Sheriff's Department's investigation. I forecast that the Iowa Department of Public Health will be coming here to investigate. They will probably close the park and campground until the cause is solved and safe for people."

"Let's get back into our cars and dash back to the Davenport Police Headquarters," suggested Scooter.

As they drove back to the Davenport Police Station, both Hannibal and Scooter acknowledged that they were feeling much better. There was a companionable silence as both detectives began to think that this case will need more specialists to solve the mystery, behind the Round Lake Park event.

Back at the Davenport Police Station, Uncle Columbo and Sgt. Tarillo were sitting at their desks in an open bay room, making calls.

Detective Columbo informed Deputy Juan Gomez, of the Scott County Sheriffs Department of their findings at Round Lake Park. Because the report included everybody feeling sick, it was agreed to call the Iowa Department of Public Health, which deals with radiation.

Detective Tarillo then called the Round Lake Park manager, Howie Brosky, to inform him of their investigation and told him that he could expect the Iowa Department of Public Health to close the park and campground, until it is safe for people to visit the park.

"What do you do for a dry lake?" asked Detective Tarillo.

"I suppose after we get the OK, we will open the underground spring again, to refill the lake," acknowledged Howie. "Right now, the spring water is closed off. The rain and melting snow will also help fill the lake."

"Uncle Columbo, did you and Sgt. Tarillo feel better after driving a short distance away from The Round Lake Park?"

"Yes we did, nephew," reassure Uncle Columbo.

Chapter Thirty-Five

THE INCIDENT OF THE CALL FROM BETTY AND KELLY

On the way back to the West Side Kids' Detective Agency, Scooter suggested to Hannibal, " You and my own self could use some R&R tonight. Do you agree good buddy, Hannibal?"

"Ya, I know what you mean. I'm up for it," replied Hannibal. "Let's call Betty and Kelly for a double date. We could take them out to eat and show them where we won the district baseball tournament."

"I hope they are available and not busy on this short notice," gushed Scooter.

Scooter then called Burlington By The Book, bookstore to talk to Kelly and Tim answered the phone, "Hello, this is Tim at Burlington By The Book. How may I help you?"

"Hello, this is Scooter at the West Side Kids' Detective Agency. May I talk to Kelly?"

"Kelly's not here today," emphasized Tim."She is home. She told me you might be calling her sometime. I can let her know that you called to talk with her."

"Thanks," replied Scooter. "I hope your bookstore is back to normal after the ruckus the other day."

Back at the West Side Kids' Detective Agency, the phone rings and Because answers, "Good morning, this is Because speaking at the West Side Kids' Detective Agency. We aim to detect anything you need."

"Good morning, Because," This is Kelly. I would like to talk to Scooter."

"Who, tell Scooter that Kelly is on the phone," yelled Because.

After thirty seconds, Scooter picked up the phone and said, "Hello, this is Detective Scooter.

"Hi Scooter. I'm glad you called me."

The feeling eventually passed like a storm that gives way to clear skies.

"Hi Kelly. How are you doin' today?"

"Fine. I'm happy you got back to the agency," acknowledged Kelly.

"I will have to tell you the story, after leaving the bookstore," promised Scooter. "Can you and Betty come to Davenport, for a double date? Hannibal and myself will take you and Betty out for a meal and show you more of Davenport."

OK, that sounds fine and I'm sure Betty can come too. What time do you want us there?"

"6 p. m. would work for Hannibal and myself," gulped Scooter. "Or if you want to put the pedal to the metal in your new cars, I will see you sooner."

"OK, I will plan on coming. I will call you back if Betty can't make it," reassured Kelly."

"That sounds really great, really great," exclaimed Scooter. "I will see you later alligator."

Scooter then hung up the phone and asked Because where Hannibal was.

"He's upstairs cleaning the bathrooms," answered Because.

"Alright!" laughed Scooter. "That's a good job for him. It was my turn last week."

Scooter then climbed the staircase to find Hannibal kneeling in one of the two bathrooms upstairs.

"Gosh, Scooter, you scared me. I was focused on cleaning the bathroom floor." explained Hannibal.

"Do you do windows too?" asked Scooter.

No, I'm just cleaning the bathroom floor, so you will have a place to sleep tonight," smiled Hannibal. "Now why did you climb all of those steps just to tell me what's up?"

"I called Kelly and she said if Betty can come on the date tonight, they will be here at 6 p. m.. If they can't, Kelly will call back to inform us," Scooter said to Hannibal. "I wonder who will be driving to Davenport."

"Remember, at 2:30 p. m. we have the firing range practice for one hour," reminded Scooter.

"We will have to keep Smiley in line," declared Hannibal. His safety technique is getting a lot better."

Chapter Thirty-Six

THE INCIDENT OF THE TARGET PRACTICE

"Is everyone back from their assignments, for the firing range practice? Did anybody get shot?" asked Scooter.

"Yes, master, everyone is back. No master. Nobody got shot and everyone is alive and well," responded Hannibal.

"OK then, let's all git into the two Explorers and go to the police firing range, that is near Buffalo, Iowa," instructed Scooter.

A little while later Sgt. Tarillo, met the West Side Kids at the firing range, where they were all standing in line facing their targets.

"Does everyone have their guns loaded and on safety?" asked Sgt. Tarillo. "The gun is no protection if you can't control what it does."

"Why does the target have to be so far away?" asked Smiley.

"In your case, so you would have to shoot it, instead of hitting it with your gun," laughed Hannibal.

"It's not that far away. You don't want the assailant to be so close to disarm you," explained Sgt. Tarillo. "First you say, stop."

"You don't say?" laughed Scooter. "I always thought that you shoot first and ask questions later if the assailant is still alive."

"Scooter, turn on your ears and listen to Sgt. Tarillo," demanded Hannibal. "He can't learn you nothin' if you keep flappin' your jaw.

Sarge, I'm sorry I interrupted the meetin' of the minds. You may uncontinue with my compliments."

"OK you guys. Just keep shut and I will continue with the class," commanded Sgt. Tarillo. "Now, I'm going to start over again. First you say stop and Scooter, yes, I do say.

Next, you tell the assailant to identify themselves and then you tell them your authority. Next you demand that they drop any weapons, put their hands up, turn around and walk backwards towards you."

"What if they don't put their hands up empty?" asked What.

"Then you offer them a candy bar, in exchange for their gun," alleged Sgt. Tarillo. "No, of course you don't. You explain to them that you will shoot them, if they don't obey. You need to keep yourselves safe. OK everyone, get into a baseball batting stance and extend both arms outward with both hands on the handgun.

Smiley, don't place your fingers on the trigger yet. Point towards the target, release the safety and calmly squeeze the trigger. OK, go!"

All the guns fired, but too many rounds hit the dirt, spraying dust all around. Four of the ten targets were hit. Everyone stopped after one round was fired.

"Not bad for a bunch of grasshoppers learning to shoot," exclaimed Sgt. Tarillo. "Don't actually aim the handgun, point and ease your breathing, to squeeze, not pull or jerk the trigger. Let's do it again, until we get it right."

Everybody then pointed their handguns at the targets and fired. This time, seven of the ten targets were hit.

"OK detectives, that's better," reassured Sgt. Tarillo. "Continue to fire eight more times, then the practice will be over today. I will inspect each named labeled target."

"That was fun," boomed Smiley. "I didn't put anyone at risk."

"Right now, point that gun to the ground!" yelled Sgt. Tarillo. "Put them in your cases and take them back with you to the West Side Kids' Detective Agency. Hannibal, make sure that everyone has taken the safety course, so they can get a permit to carry."

"I could feel it in my bones when I hit the target and it was very satisfying," boasted Scooter. "Sgt. Tarillo, when are we going to get holsters, so we can learn to fast draw?"

"Scooter, you're not going to get any holsters," laughed Sgt. Tarillo. "Who are you trying to be, Wild Bill Hickok? "If you tried to fast draw, you would probably shoot your foot off."

"What are you being so nasty to me for?" asked Scooter. "I was just having a good time and because of that, you're picking on me again, like you think I'm a fool."

"Scooter is right," claimed Because. "I was being picked on before we started this class. "I want to learn how to fast draw, like Scooter."

"This isn't the wild west and I'm not Wyatt Earp," replied Sgt. Tarillo. "This is a class to teach you the tools of your trade."

"Oh, gee. I wanted to learn how to fast draw," exclaimed Because.

Chapter Thirty-Seven
THE TAKE US OUT TO THE BALL DIAMOND INCIDENT

Later on, back at the agency, everyone was hungry and ready to clean up.

"It sure will be nice when we have a cook and a housekeeper," reckoned Scooter "I hope we can hire these people soon, because when we all come home after a hard day's work, dinner will be on the table waiting for us."

After eating, feeding Stella and having a quick shower, Hannibal and Scooter were anxiously waiting for Kelly and Betty to arrive.

At 6:45 p. m. the girls finally arrived. Their presence was known before the doorbell rang, thanks to the security system. Both detectives noticed that the girls' hairs were up in a bun.

"Why are you girls so late?" quizzed Hannibal.

Betty then explained," We had our hair done just for you two and it took longer than we expected.

"I see you want to be our little bunnies," alleged Scooter.

"Yah, more like Easter Bunnies," laughed Hannibal. "OK, without joking, you two look very nice, which is better than good."

"Yaaa! Like now we won't be embarrassed to have you ride in the Explorer," teased Scooter.

"What are we going to do tonight?" asked Kelly.

"We don't have a plan. We will let life surprise us a little," explained Scooter. "Maybe we will hunker down in the dark."

"I have an idea," grinned Betty. "Why don't you take us girls to a baseball diamond?"

"As you wish," Hannibal agreed. ""Your wish is my demand."

Before the two boys climbed in to the Explorer, they again began to play rock, paper, scissors as the girls watched. Hannibal won again, without any complaint from Scooter and then climbed into the driver's seat. He started the engine and then began to drive through the bumpy roads of Davenport and arrived at the baseball diamond, just north of Eldridge. Because how rough the streets were, everyone was irritated by the uncomfortable ride.

While everyone was getting out of the Explorer, Scooter gleefully predicted, "Girls, I'm going to use my chemistry lab in the basement, to create a formula to make more superior materials of the stuff we have today for the roads."

"Wow! Look at this baseball diamond," beamed Kelly. "With the lights and all with a large pond, by a bicycle path going further north."

"This is the diamond where we won the game that led us to the state tournament several years ago," beamed Hannibal. "The finals were in Des Moines."

"Let's get on the field and play ball!" requested Scooter, like an umpire.

"What was it like?" questioned Kelly.

"It was full of hard competition and lots of emotions," explained Scooter. "Whenever a batter hit a single, the dugout would get up and bounce on one leg. When a batter hit a double, the dugout would jump up and down on two feet. Whenever a batter hit a triple, the bench players of the dugout would jump on two feet and have one hand in the air."

Hannibal then added, when a batter hit a home run, the rest of the team would waddle, like a penguin, up to the home plate to greet the happy batter. And believe me, we had a lot of action with the feet, arms and the dance to the home plate that game!"

"What if the batter struck out?" asked Betty.

"They had to sit next to Scooter on the school bus, when we went home," smiled Hannibal.

Betty then joyfully challenged Hannibal, "I'll race you around the bases. Give me a head start to first base."

As the race began, Hannibal raced around the bases behind Betty, and caught up with her at third base and he wrestled her to the ground playfully.

"I think you are out of the baseline," joked Hannibal.

Scooter didn't want to be left out of showing the girls what he could do, so he suggested to teach Kelly how to slide into home.

"When it comes to a close call, to be tagged out at home plate, we can extend our hands and slide face first. Now I'm going to show you how this is done," offered Scooter. "Watch this! Ouch! That hurts! There are two many rocks around home plate and I think I landed on all of them at once. Now I have a tear in my favorite shirt and my clothes are dirty. Do you want to try that Kelly?"

"NO, thank you! Do you think that I'm crazy?" Besides, I don't want to get my hair dirty and messed up.

I have a better idea. Why don't we all sit in the bleachers and watch the sunset. I think I have some thread and a needle and I can repair your shirt and you will never see the damage."

"That's a wonderful idea," stated Betty.

The foursome then went over to the bleachers to sit in silence while Hannibal put his arm around Betty and Kelly sat there sewing away, as they watched the sun set.

"Ouch!" yelled Scooter. "You're sticking me with the needle. I think you're sewing the shirt to my skin."

"I told you I would be sticking you, if you didn't take your shirt off," scolded Kelly.

"Scooter, you're at it again," scolded Hannibal. "When did the young and in love turn into having your shirt sewn to your body? Quit being stupid and take your shirt off, before I sew your lips together. Hurry it up, because I want to take the girls down the bicycle path to the pond."

After a few minutes, the two couples were standing by the pond. Hannibal and Scooter immediately picked up some rocks and threw one rock at a time skipping it across the pond. Both of the boys started to be competitive, when Hannibal skipped a flat rock further than Scooter.

"You must have the magic!" boomed Scooter.

"And you control my magic, whenever you wish," beamed Hannibal. "If I had a wish, I would skip you across the pond."

"Listen to the sounds of nature as the sunlight is diminishing," stated Kelly.

"Diminishing? Diminishing? You're learning me a lot of new words. Where did you learn them from? asked Scooter. "I like the way you say things to me. I also liked the way you sewed my favorite shirt back together, after you cut the thread out of my skin. Continue if you will."

"OK Scooter. I guess that's a compliment," admitted Kelly. "Anyway, as I was saying, look at the beautiful colors of the sunset. The flowers are closing their petals."

"What time does the flowers close?" asked Scooter.

"Soon Scooter, soon. Now let me finish what I'm saying," scolded Kelly. "I'm trying to be romantic and well you're behaving like, like Scooter. It's getting darker by the minute and the moon is so bright. Isn't this so romantic? Scooter, look into my eyes and what do you see?"

"One red eye and one green eye. I don't know whether to stop or go ahead. I know. I know, I owe you a kiss, but it's not dark enough for me yet," whispered Scooter. "It's a good thing Hannibal didn't sew my lips together or you would never get one."

"Did you just see the moon wink at us?" murmured Kelly. "Either that or something very large moved in front of our vision of the moon."

"I know what it was," reckoned Scooter. "It was a baseball I hit at our baseball tournament here and it still hasn't landed anyplace."

"Oh go on," smiled Kelly. "The next thing you're going to tell me that it is a flying saucer, with space aliens."

"Listen to the symphony of life!" Betty continued to say. "The gentle wind, without sound, making the tree leaves rustle in the air, the chirping of birds, the croaking of frogs in the pond. Listen to our footsteps as we walk around the pond with the buzzing of insects about our faces. Can you hear my heartbeat for you, Hannibal?"

"Yah, if you can shut up for a minute, so I can hear it," acknowledged Hannibal.

"Hey guys, I see a light beyond the treeline," Scooter, curiously stated. "You stay here and I will be right back. It's probably just a group of fireflies."

"Don't get lost in the dark," jested Hannibal. "Watch your step. Those space aliens might abduct you and never want to come down to this here Earth of ours."

Scooter then got up and jogged to the tree line and then walked to the other side of the trees as the other three saw him fade away in the dark of the night.

As Scooter approached an open field, he saw a silent object hovering just above the ground. His eyes were adjusting to the object which began to focus into a semi-truck size flying object. There was one window showing a flashing light, broken by a figure looking like a peanut shell, with two large round eyes.

Faking a calmness he didn't feel, Scooter approached the window so close he clearly saw the peanut head raise up and show two fingers and what looked like a thumb.

Scooter was trying to register these disjointed facts in his mind, but he could only scream, "The Space Aliens Are Coming! The Space Aliens Are Coming!"

Scooter gave him three fingers back to the alien and fled the open field, through the treeline and passed Hannibal, Betty and Kelly shouting, "The Space Aliens Are Coming. I need to tell everyone that it's real. I'm going to run back home. I'll meet you there."

Off on a journey of goodwill, Scooter sprints into Eldridge shouting, "The Space Aliens Are Coming."

Doors were opening, porch lights were turned on and people were coming out of their homes to hear Scooter's words, "The Space Aliens Are Coming."

People were saying, "Are you crazy?"

Scooter shouted back, "You'll find out! I may do stupid things, but I'm not crazy!"

Scooter continued his run to Davenport. Once, he saw Hannibal and the girls in the Explorer traveling fast toward home.

When Scooter arrived at Davenport, he screamed, "The Space Aliens Are Coming" into all the streets he went through.

Some people were saying, "Thanks for the warning, you nut head. You must be drunk!"

And Scooter would reply with, "But I'm not, you unbeliever!"

While Scooter was running home announcing the coming of the aliens, to the Quad Cities, Hannibal, with the girls driving home, brought up the time when he tackled Betty on third base. Hannibal claimed that he felt a lump on the back of her neck and he wanted to know about how and what he felt.

"I have ignored the lump for many years," explained Betty. "My mom noticed it when I was five years old. She said it would go away when I became an adult."

"How did it get there?" stammered Hannibal.

"I don't know. My mom said there was an incident when I was playing with the cat outside, in the dark. The cat strayed into the nearby woods. I followed it. In the pitch black night, a light beam, shone directly on me. I couldn't see a thing. I must have fallen asleep, because I woke up sometime later wondering where my cat was.

I regained my whereabouts and walked back home a short two hundred yards away. The cat was in the kitchen with mom, while she was washing dishes. I was known to play outside before bedtime. Mom said she called for me twice. Mom wasn't worried because she always knew I took my time listening to nature by a creek.

This time mom said it was about time I got home. Go take a bath. I'll be up in a few minutes to help you, then it is off to bed. While drying me, mom felt the lump on the back of my neck.

I have had it since. As an adult, I don't think it has affected me. I'm touched by your concern, Hannibal."

"You are my sunshine, my only sunshine and I don't want anything or anyone to harm you," reassured Hannibal.

"Oh, how touching," exclaimed Betty.

"Look! There are news reporters at the agency!" shouted Hannibal. "Someone must have told them Scooter was trying to inform people about the aliens and he is running a marathon to do it."

Bright floodlights were shining the front yard, like it was daylight.

One reporter from the Davenport Quest newspaper asked, "Do you know who is the person telling everyone that The Space Aliens Are Coming?"

All the detectives, who were asked, said that they know him and he is a valuable member of their team.

"What did he see?" asked the reporter.

"You will have to ask Scooter what he thinks he saw," answered Hannibal. "We didn't see anything but a light beyond the treeline."

One of the Davenport Quest reporters boomed, "There he is now walking down the street. Can you tell me what you saw?"

"Right now I am very tired," answered Scooter. "I saw a peanut head with three fingers in a flying saucer! Now go away. I will make interviews tomorrow. Go on. Now git."

"I'm so glad you are safe and back home," declared Kelly. "Now, will you kiss me?"

After some memory flashes, Scooter passes out and several detectives carry him into the house.

"We will be talking to youse again at another time," explained Hannibal. "Youse girls should be on your way back to Burlington, because it is getting late."

Chapter Thirty-Eight
THE INCIDENT OF THE REPORTING OF THE SPACE ALIENS

About 11:00 a. m. the next morning, Scooter was awaken by some cheerful noises in the living room. All the West Side Kids decided to let Scooter sleep late, because he had a late night running away from a space alien and letting people know of the invasion.

After getting dressed and his awareness back, Scooter came down the stairs to a sweet smell of cinnamon rolls being made. Scooter walked into the living room to see a familiar face joking with the detectives. Scooter couldn't believe his eyes. It was Amy, his twin sister from Colorado. Scooter then heard everyone laughing about a cow joke.

"If you weren't nice to a cow, you might get spoiled milk." Something like that.

Scooter was too shocked to see his long lost twin. Amy moved from Davenport to get a fresh start from her ex-boyfriend. She went to a culinary school in Colorado Springs to become a chef.

"Hi, Scooter," greeted What. "I thought you would be happy that we gave you some extra time to sleep. We just hired your twin sister to be our cook four times a week. I think we've got a keeper."

"Hi, sis, my head is spinning from this welcome," stated an eye opening Scooter. "So this is my happy hour. You're looking good, because you still have my traits, with your light dyed red hair, blue eyes and a short mustache under your nose. You're wearing a light orange short-sleeved blouse with a belt. Your shoes even match your black skirt with your blue apron."

"We can't help it that we are twins. It's just what nature had in store for us," reasoned Amy.

Look y here. We have a patriotic chef cooking for us. this morning," remarked Scooter. "And the cinnamon rolls, I smell, smells good to eat. Have you been to the gym, too?"

"Awe cut it out Scooter. You're making fun of me. Put it where the sun don't shine" pouted Amy.

"You mean under my armpits," questioned Scooter.

"No, you bumbling idiot!" cried Amy. "I'm moaning because I tasted a cinnamon roll and my tooth screamed in pain. It fell in a hole in my back tooth. I haven't seen a dentist since I left Davenport four years ago."

"I know of a local dentist where 4 out of 5 patients recommend him," emphasized Hannibal.

"What's his name and does he take emergency patients," mumbled Amy.

"His name is Dr. J. B. Sirrod and I will call him to get you treated, straight away," said a sympathetic Scooter.

"Did anybody show Amy around our home, especially the kitchen?" asked Scooter.

"I volunteered and took it upon myself to show Amy around our place while you was still in bed probably dreaming of space aliens," acknowledged Who. "Amy has already made a list of food products to get."

Walking in from the security room, You Don't Say reported to everyone that the news reporters are coming to the door.

"Let's have Stella greet them at the door," demanded Hannibal. "Maybe that will have them turn around and chase a firetruck.!"

"Why are they here?" questioned a tired Scooter.

"Scooter, you look like the walking dead. Don't you remember anything at all? exclaimed Hannibal. "You told the reporters that you would give them an interview."

"Oh yah. I guess I will talk to them outside and answer a few questions," exclaimed Scooter. "Smiley, can you take Stella out for his regular hunt?"

Scooter then walked outside and stood by the flagpole, saluted and then turned to the reporters. Then a half dozen microphones and cameras were pushed into his face, which looks like his twin sister, who came home from Colorado.

With a serious look on his face, Scooter said, "Live today as if you were to die tomorrow. The space aliens have our lifestyles in their hands. We have to work together to stop them."

The Muscatine reporter asked, "What did you see last night? What you're going to tell us, isn't a gag?"

"I've got an inclusive news story for you," answered Scooter. "What do you think? Did you think that somebody told me to run around all night in the streets of Eldridge and Davenport yelling The Space Aliens Are Coming just for a gag when I don't like to be told to run around the streets yelling The Space Aliens Are Coming. The Space Aliens Are Coming. Of course I saw a flying saucer. I saw a huge flying saucer suspended just above the field. There was a creature inside, that didn't look like us."

"I've got an inclusive story for you," laughed the Muscatine reporter. "You're nuts."

Then the Dubuque reporter asked, "What did the creature look like? Do you like talking about creatures and flying saucers?"

"No, I don't like being told to talk about creatures and flying saucers," answered Scooter. "You're going to like what I have to tell you. The creature had a peanut shell shaped head and a light covered body. I saw only one arm, with a hand giving me some three fingered sign."

"I don't like being told what I like," declared the Dubuque reporter.

The Davenport Quest reporter then asked, "What do you think the creature was trying to indicate with his fingers?"

"I think he was saying, he was going to get me peacefully and I also thought that he meant harm to all earthlings."

"Why did you run all the way back home?" asked the Burlington reporter.

"I thought it was the best way to tell everybody what may come of us, by screaming The Space Aliens Are Coming, The Space Aliens Are Coming, like Paul Revere did to warn the people that the British are coming. Both came to control us! But I didn't have a horse to ride. I think the horses were afraid I was hungry!"

"What do you think we ought to do?" asked the Moline reporter.

"I think we should convince the public that there are space aliens watching and controlling and talking, what they need from us," explained Scooter.

"If we can get video sightings, then we can contact the local authorities, who will then believe they exist. Next they will report it to the Federal government. I hope the Federal government will not deny it and give some other excuse for the sightings. Later on, I have to go make some calls to Professor Boblit and the twins, Michael and Chris Murphy."

Chapter Thirty-Nine
THE INCIDENT AT THE DENTIST

"Thank you doctor, for getting me in so soon. I hope to git back to some hungry detectives, yet this morning," said a gracious Amy.

"So you are Scooter's sister. How about that? He's been a rare bird around here!" reckoned Dr. Sirrod. "Let's take a look at your hole in one."

"It hurts to chew on it, when the food has a lot of sugar," explained Amy.

"Aha! I see the hole. Does this hurt when I tap on it?" asked the doctor.

"No," answered Amy.

Dr. Sirrod then stood up and said, "An x-ray will be needed and I will be with you as soon as I figures this out!"

The dental assistant escorted Amy to an x-ray room. For conversation, she said that she sure could use four hands to work with Dr. Sirrod.

Dr. Sirrod looked at the x-ray and claimed that all the tooth needed was a fill in.

"Do you know anything about toothaches?" asked Amy.

"Aha, yes! I've gone to many conferences, to learn all kinds of treatment," answered Dr. Sirrod. "It frequently makes my head ache!"

"Doc, can you get this numb, before you fill it?" asked Amy.

"Absolutely. I have local anesthetic, nitrous oxide and a huge sledgehammer," laughed Dr Sirrod. "While your tongue is numb, don't bite it. When you move your tongue, you will feel a lack of control and you will find your words will slur. Don't do anything to cause a need for the police to stop you. They may think you are drunk."

While working to complete the procedure, Dr. Sirrod stopped and said, "Oops! I've lost my train of thought. I left it at the last procedural step. Assistant, can you help me?"

"What else? Every time you lose your train of thought, you end up in a train wreck," laughed the assistant with smiling eyes and motioned with her jaw, that was covered with a mask.

"Aha," stated Dr. Sirrod. "Amy, would you move your jaw to the right?"

"Which one?" asked Amy.

Dr. Sirrod and his assistant laughed and Dr. Sirrod then answered, "The only one you can move left or right. The lower jaw!"

"What's that?" asked Amy.

"It's a hand mirror to show you the beautiful white fill-in placed in your hole in one."

"Nice," exclaimed Amy. "How long will I be numb?"

"Since you are Scooter's twin sister, I would say always," laughed Dr. Sirrod. "As far as the anesthetic goes, a few hours."

"That's good. If it helps me to feel better, I can be in a better mood at work," reasoned Amy.

"What do you do for a living?" asked Dr. Sirrod.

"I'm a chef who makes cinnamon rolls that cause toothaches," laughed Amy. "I work for the West Side Kids' Detective Agency, where my brother works."

"Tell Scooter that he needs a cleaning, like you need one," declared Dr. Sirrod.

"Scooter doesn't brush his teeth every day!" accused Amy.

"Well, bite my tongue," chuckled Dr. Sirrod. "Pay at the business window on your way out. Make another appointment to get your teeth clean and make sure you brush your teeth everyday. Thank you very much."

Michael Eight Murphy, alias Dr. Zodiac. Chris Murphy's twin brother

Chapter Forty

THE INCIDENT WITH THE MURPHY BROTHERS

That afternoon, Scooter made the call to the Burlington By The Book store to convince Michael and Chris to prepare for the aliens. Scooter's backup was Hannibal, who was listening by way of the speaker mode off of the cellphone.

"Burlington By The Book," stated Chris.

After exchanging greetings, Scooter began telling of his frightful event, last night.

"How dreadful of an experience you must have had," stated Chris. "Have you recovered from this experience? How may I help you?"

"I need you to convince your twin brother Michael Eight Murphy, alias Dr. Zodiac, to spend some money to fight the aliens."

"What?" replied Chris.

"No, What isn't talking to you. Scooter is and Hannibal is here to back me up on this plan to defend Earth."

"I, I, I, mean," declared Chris. "How can I do that? It's Michael's lottery ticket winnings. I already have him spending millions of dollars to expand my business. He's helping me buy the next door business and I will have enough room to create a library of books. I could even have a small museum there."

"That's all fine and dandy, but there is a serious case of space aliens that could ruin all of that for you!" declared Scooter.

"I don't know if it is real about the space alien theory," admitted Chris.

"Let me tell you that it is real stuff," challenged Scooter. "Taking this risk is an essential part of living our dreams."

Hannibal then interrupted the conversation by stating, "He wanted to talk to Michael Eight Murphy, alias Dr. Zodiac.

Chris's twin brother Michael then spoke into the speaker saying, "What can I not do for you?"

"You can stop being selfish, by being a jerk and help the public confront the aliens," commanded Hannibal. "Watch the news! They are saying that there are people missing and others are reporting UFO sightings. Scooter has truthfully seen an alien in a spaceship. By doing what we ask, you can help your family and the world to continue living on our Earth, without alien control."

"OK, now you have my attention," exclaimed Michael Eight Murphy. "What do you want us to do?"

"You better do what I tell you," explained Hannibal. "Or I'll have Uncle Columbo open your closed case. I need you, Chris, Tim and Kelly to have available and to invest in world safety equipment. We, the agency, want you to have a radar system and computers to communicate with orbiting satellites and the International Space Station, ISS. Get those soon, because the buffaloes and chickens are getting very agitated."

"You're getting me nervous too!" answered Michael.

"And another thing," explained Hannibal. "Do not inform any reporters of our findings. Only inform the authorities, like Uncle Columbo and us, including anybody connected with the West Side Kids' Detective Agency."

Scooter then said to Michael Eight Murphy, "I think next, I better call Professor Boblit. If he doesn't answer, I'm going to leave a message to have him call us any time of day or night.

The space aliens don't know who they are messing with. Before I push the red button, we need to give you nicknames. Michael, you can be called Eight and Chris can be called "What Do You Think"! I gave Chris that nickname because Chris is always asking me, "What Do You Think?"

Scooter, protrayed by Ben Hendricks, talking with Professor Boblit.

Chapter Forty-One

The Incident of Scooter Talking To Professor Boblit

Ring a ding a ding.

"Hello, this is Professor Boblit speaking. How may I help you?"

"What's happening Professor Boblit? This is Scooter, your pal, remember? I have a lot to ask you."

Professor Boblit was thinking, "Oh no, not this crazy dude again. OK, shoot, demanded Professor Boblit. "Oh, I don't want you to hurt me. I know, what are your questions that you want answered?"

"That's right. I do want answers to my questions or I wouldn't be asking them," demanded Scooter.

"As you remember, I am the interviewer for the YMBO radio," reminded Professor Boblit. "I receive a lot of information from smart people. That excludes you, but I won't turn you down."

"Why am I seeing space aliens?" whispered Scooter. I do stupid things, and I know I exist, because Hannibal is always bawling me out when I do these things. Hannibal won't stand for nuttin' I do that's stupid. I do so many stupid things that Hannibal never knows when I do somethin' smart."

"Now you're telling me that you think you're seeing space aliens. When did the space aliens you thought you saw, run and hide after they saw you?" questioned Professor Boblit. "There are many people around the world who have seen space aliens. Especially those who have been abducted, but I'm sure you're safe from being abducted.

As I was saying, many people have sighted the UFOs. The abducted have been hypnotized to explained their experience in the spaceship. People like Navy pilots have seen UFOs. Sailors in the Navy ships have seen spacecraft come out of the deep oceans and vanish into outer space."

"What do these aliens want from the Quad Cities?" asked Scooter.

"I don't know, Scooter! Maybe they just want the necessities of life, like we do. You know, we share the universe with other beings. The aliens may be just curious and making a pit stop!"

"Do you think they will try and control Earth and destroy our way of life?" reasoned Scooter.

"It's a possibility," reckoned Professor Boblit. "I have heard and read that the aliens have placed their DNA into the abducted people way back in the ages. These people are hybrids, both alien and human. Some were injected a microchip to keep track of them and to control their mind and behavior."

"Wow, that's not freedom. I feel threatened just thinking about it," exclaimed Scooter. It doesn't seem to be my way of life to have my mind and behavior controlled. What do I need the space aliens to control my mind and behavior for? Hannibal does that for me."

"It sounds like Hannibal has a tough job. Your mind would be hard to change at that," declared Professor Boblit. "Now let me finish answering your question, before I give the space aliens your name and address.

All over the world reports of UFOs and abductions are being addressed to government officials and journalists. The government tries their best to not recognize the problem, because they cannot control it. Civilian programs, like MUFON are pressuring the government to accept the alien theory. I think one day we will all agree to make steps to defend us from alien takeover."

"If the aliens have been visiting us for ages, have we learned anything from them?" asked an excited Scooter. "Like technology and power of all sorts."

"I wish they could spend years on you, Scooter. But then again, you haven't been around for ages, have you?"

Professor Boblit then continued to babble on, "Since the controversial alien spacecraft crashed in the late 1940s, it was thought we learned from their materials and how it travels through space and time. The military may have recovered parts of UFOs and be secretly working to understand them.

The UFOs mysterious phenomenon has possibly moved through dimensions or consciousness affecting people's mind and bodies throughout human history. The MUFON organization analyzes alien spacecraft materials, collect data, listen to witness accounts and focuses on the medical health affects of UFO encounters. Most investigations are largely inconclusive. They simply do not know why they're here and of their propulsion and materials.

The pentagon's new office is called Unidentified Aerial Phenomena or UAP. They are getting reports of blue orbs, white spots and beams of light.

The Defense Intelligent Agency, DIA, is investigating a connection between UFOs and the paranormal. Physics plays an important part in this.

In my opinion, The Pentagon is thinking of a national security threat."

"How can we communicate with the aliens," asked Scooter.

"Music, colored lights and hand signs may be ways to communicate with them," answered Professor Boblit. "Long before recorded history, the mystery of music had its origin. It was once labeled, "The speech of angels." It expresses what we cannot say in words."

"You mean, Hannibal can sing "You are my sunshine" and the aliens will respond," questioned Scooter.

"Yes, probably the response can be of many forms," laughed Professor Boblit.

"Oh, one more thing before I have to hang up. The Space Force Engineers in the International Space Station are monitoring space around Earth to notify us of any strange UFO appearances. The aliens could be intelligent enough to be searching on the opposite side of the Earth, therefore unseen by the International Space Station."

"Are you saying we need to watch our back 40 anyway," gulped Scooter.

"Yes, be on the lookout, " declared Professor Boblit.

"Professor Boblit, thank you for your intel!"

"Anytime Scooter. It's an us team situation, we all need to be aware of."

After Professor Boblit disconnected, Scooter thought of another question. He speed dialed the Professor's phone number.

"Yes Scooter, what is it now?"

"I saw my twin sister from Colorado today. We haven't seen each other for over four years. Do you think she may have been abducted?"

"How do I know, Scooter? Why don't you ask her," answered Professor Boblit. "Now hang up will you?"

"I was just asking and you think it was a stupid question," declared Scooter. "Ain't you a sore one! Good-bye!"

"Did Professor Boblit give you some enlightening information about UFOs and aliens?" asked Hanibal.

"Yes sir, Chief," replied Scooter. "I now know more about the alien creatures and I found out that they are very mysterious. We don't know what they want from us."

"I think I better call Uncle Columbo next to see what he found out about the airport incident, from the Federal Government.

Chapter Forty-Two

THE FINDING OF DR. FINE AND CHARLIE, THE CHILL INCIDENT

Hello Uncle Columbo. Can you tell me what the Federal Government said about the Davenport Airport incident?"

"A representative from the Federal Government told me that it is a secret project that will be used to defend the Midwestern United States against any aggressive unknown enemy. This project was not planned by a terrorist group like you thought. What we saw was the building structure of a rocket to be fired at the enemy.

I was told that we will be getting government agents to help with the UFO sightings, which have cause of alarm for the national security. These two people will be an astrophysicist and a biochemist from the University of Iowa science department. They will help you in the investigation of strange things happening in and around the Quad Cities."

"That's great," boomed Hannibal."When will youse be expectin' them?"

"In a few days," replied Uncle Columbo.

"Have youse heard any news about the Round Lake Park missing people situation?" asked Hannibal.

"The Scott County Sheriff's Department had some reports from motorists on I-280 at the time of Dr. Fine and Charlie, The Chill went missing.

The motorist witnessed a huge dark threatening storm cloud, that caused a very heavy fog preventing him from traveling any further. While stopped on I-280, the cloud presented some fast revolving multi color lights hovering and zipping around, moving in a circle. The incident went on an endless time of one half hour, then the cloud lifted very quickly along with the dense fog.

The motorists said they couldn't believe their eyes of what just happened, because the lake had been drained of it's water. Some of the motorists said they saw a smaller black cloud over the wooded area and a bright beam of light was directed into the ground.

It may have been the abduction of Dr. Fine and Charlie, The Chill," Uncle Columbo continues. "Now that the radiation level is safe again, I think you detectives should try again to look for Dr. Fine and Charlie, The Chill at Round Lake. It's been known that abducted people are returned where they were taken. Take your drone with you and Stella."

"That sounds like an excellent idea," responded Hannibal. "Scooter and myself will do that later this afternoon. Thanks for the information, Uncle."

After Hannibal hung up, Hannibal and Scooter decided to take I'm Not Sure with them to take care of Stella, who was allowed to smell the scent of Dr. Fine's clothes. With Stella, I'm Not Sure took Dr. Fine's clothes with them to Round Lake.

When the threesome and Stella arrived at Round Lake, they noticed the lake was refilling with water from the spring. I'm Not Sure could tell Stella was eager to search for the source of the scent of Dr. Fine's clothes. The detectives were hoping that Dr. Fine would be found with Charlie, The Chill.

I'm Not Sure had Stella on a leash while Hannibal and Scooter were getting the drone ready to fly and the computer system ready to view images from the camera on the drone.

When the drone lifted from the ground, Stella pulled I'm Not Sure away from the lake and with his nose in the air, he ran towards the woods.

"Take the leash off!" yelled Hannibal. "We can find Stella with the drone's camera."

"Look, Stella is leading us towards the woods," exclaimed Scooter. "Guide the drone in the direction of the woods and we should see Stella. I'm Not Sure is trying to keep up with Stella's nose.

"Scooter then laughed and asked, "What do you call a fish out of water?"

"I don't know," answered Hannibal. "What?"

"No, not What or I Don't Know; it's sushi," joked Scooter.

"Oh, you mean it's like, "I know sushi, like you know sushi. Oh what a gal." Not bad Scooter. It's not good either. Now let's quit being comedians and pretend to be detectives so we can search on? Now I can see I'm Not Sure deep in the woods, but I don't see Stella yet."

Next an extremely bright light blinded Hannibal and Scooter for about five seconds.

"What was that?" exclaimed Hannibal.

"Hey, I think it may be a sun spot blinding us," acknowledged Scooter.

"No! You forgot to wear your glasses. For your information, I'm over here. Now look at the screen and quit clowning around!" instructed Hannibal. "The drone's camera survived the intense flash of light and I can see two bodies laying in a clearing in the woods! We can direct the drone higher to see where I'm Not Sure is related to the bodies. Stella is at the clearing now. Look, Stella is sniffing the bodies and licking their faces."

"I've got an idea," proposed Scooter.

"How did you get an idea?" asked Hannibal. "Did you go to a library and read a book?"

"Now you're clowning around. Now listen to my idea," demanded Scooter. "Let's follow the tracking beam to get where I'm Not Sure is."

"Before we both forget you had an idea, I'ma agoin' to call I'm Not Sure to let him know we're comin'," exclaimed Hannibal.

"No, you're not! It was my idea. I'm going to call him," demanded Scooter.

"OK, I guess we have to do the rock, paper, scissors thing," reckoned Hannibal.

"OK, I won," declared Scooter. "Now I'm agoin' to call I'm Not Sure."

"Where are you at, Scooter. Yea, I caught up with Stella where he found the bodies," reported I'm Not Sure. "I have already checked their pulses and their breathing. They are definitely alive."

"Good, we will be there in a couple of minutes!" gulped Scooter. "Call the police and a medical team."

Five minutes later, Hannibal and Scooter arrived at the scene where I'm Not Sure and Stella were at viewing the bodies of Dr. Fine and Charlie, The Chill. Both Hannibal and Scooter then patted and stroked Stella for doing a good job. I'm Not Sure gave Stella a treat of his favorite food and a drink of water.

Everyone looked at the bodies and agreed that they were Dr. Fine and Charlie, The Chill. Both were only wearing pants. Several poking marks were on their bodies.

Hannibal then told I'm Not Sure to go to the campground, to guide the police and ambulance personnel to the clearing in the woods.

Scooter then walked up to each body and started waking them up, by gently slapping them in the face and shouting aliens. Dr. Fine and Charlie, The Chill both woke up in a daze and could not speak well.

"Be calm and relax. The ambulance EMT unit will be here soon," consoled Scooter. "You look like dried fish! We have been looking for you for days!"

After the EMTs arrived, they saw the ghostly faces of Dr. Fine and Charlie, The Chill. The EMTs began to check their vitals, then placed them on an emergency cot and carried them to the ambulance from Davenport. The EMTs told the police that they would take the victims to a Davenport hospital for evaluation and probably some psychological testing. Both men looked very dehydrated.

Later on at a Davenport hospital, Dr. Fine and Charlie, The Chill were hooked up to machines monitoring their vital information and they were resting with blood lines into their arms giving them the needed saline to restore their body liquids. Both the men were bunked in the same hospital room. The doctor said they may be treated this way for a couple of days.

In the meantime, the military officials, suspicious of an alien abduction visited both of the men with questions.

"Question number one. Where have you been?" asked the military official.

"I don't know where," answered both men.

"Question number two. Can you tell us about your experience?"

"No, we can barely know our names."

"Comment number one. We think you were abducted by space aliens into their spaceships."

"No way! I can't believe that!" declared a surprised Dr. Fine. "All I can remember is that me and Charlie, The Chill was having a smoke in our car and we noticed a bright light streak across the darkness above. Then the ball of light grew brighter and brighter. A very bright brilliant light that came closer and closer. Then it was three to four feet off the ground. The light seemed to intercept us and then we heard the glass shatter and suddenly it was in the car with us. The ball of light was extremely brilliant and painful and now we are here!"

"Question number three. Do both of you give the military permission to use a hypnotist to get your memory of your experience?"

"Yep, I guess so. We both would like to know what happened to us," emphasized Charlie, The Chill.

"Comment number two. The antenna of your car appeared to be bent as a result of high velocity blasts of air. It was determined that some sort of electrical thing or force had caused the impact and the damage was inward and outward. It didn't sound like anything you would find on Earth. The area around your car was searched, but nothing was found.

The doctor said you have probing marks in several parts of your body," explained the military official. "I will set up an appointment to have a military hypnotist to hypnotize both of you. Then we will know what happened to you."

Chapter Forty-Three
THE NEW HOUSEKEEPER INCIDENT

While Dr. Fine and Charlie, The Chill were resting comfortably, Hannibal, Scooter, I'm not Sure and Stella were back at the agency, hungry for supper.

I Don't Know and Because came out of the large living room pushing a young college student into the hallway, to meet with Hannibal, Scooter, I'm Not Sure and of course Stella, who was very tired.

I Don't Know then said, "We decided to hire Ann as our housekeeper. She will work here three times a week cleaning this large home."

She is willing to work to supplement her college tuition," added Because. "Her major is short story writing. She plans to write a children's short story book about Space Aliens."

Wow! What do you think the odds were that Ann would be doing that?" reasoned a shocked Scooter. "That fits right in the current business of today. Have you seen the aliens? I have!"

"Oh go on. you're pulling my leg," reasoned Ann. "There is no such thing as real aliens, so how could I have seen any? The only aliens that I've seen are in the movies and on the TV shows. I have also read about them in books.

Since children like dinosaurs, I thought they would like to read and see friendly aliens in a book.

When I saw the advertisement in the newspaper, I thought you may be the detectives I sold some TVs to."

"Now I know who you are," acknowledged I'm Not Sure. "I met you at the TV store. I haven't called you for a date yet, because I have been real busy. Now that you're going to work here, I'm glad I can see you more often."

"I'm Not Sure may not have called you for a date, because he has been busy," recalled Whatever. "After you sold us those TVs, on the way home, I'm Not Sure was already to ask you to marry him. Then you would be Mr. and Mrs. I'm Not Sure."

"I think we need to have our first date, before we can decide to go that far," answered a surprised Ann.

"Have you met our new chef, my twin sister?" asked Scooter.

"So you're Scooter. I wondered what you would be like. Now, I understand why you claim that you have seen aliens. Your twin sister and I had a long talk about you," exclaimed Ann. She definitely looks like you. What I have been told about you, she even seems to act like you."

"Would you like to eat supper with us?" asked I'm Not Sure. "Amy is a chef with over four years experience. This could sort of be like our first date."

"The food really does smell good!" grinned Ann. "I guess this can sort of be our first date."

After supper was served, everybody enjoyed the delicious meal, except for Stella, who was satisfied with his favorite Puppy Crunch Chow and water. He didn't get any splinters from the table scraps.

"Ann, I hope you will be eating with us, when it's your days to work here," offered Amy.

Everyone agreed with Amy, especially, I'm Not Sure.

Ann was to start housekeeping in two days.

I'm Not Sure then walked Ann to the door and out to her car to say goodnight.

"I'll see you in two long days. Good luck at college," wished I'm Not Sure.

Chapter Forty-Four
DON'T MESS WITH SCOOTER, THE BRICK INCIDENT

Two men in blue suits reported to the Davenport Police Station. They said they came from the University of Iowa science department and was sent to help with the strange happenings going on in the Quad Cities. The pentagon hired them to investigate and collect data for the government.

The biochemist introduced himself as Joe Mixer and Frank Stargate as the astrophysicist. Frank couldn't say how long they would be in the area.

Sgt. Tarillo and Capt. Columbo both told these two men that they would be working with Scooter and Hannibal of the West Side Kids' Detective Agency.

"The West Side Kids' Detective Agency has been assigned the investigation in the local area," explained Sgt. Tarillo. "They have sophisticated searching equipment and they plan to work with a group of people from the Burlington By The Book, in Burlington, Iowa. They also have the needed radar and communication systems to be of value in the searching of the unidentified aerial phenomenon. The police department could not get the state funds to purchase the equipment."

"What are the names of the people in Burlington?" asked Joe Mixer.

"Well let's see. There is Chris Seven Murphy, his twin brother, Michael Eight Murphy, his brother Tim and his sister Kelly," answered Capt. Columbo.

"By the way Joe, I have a degree in chemistry if you need me to help!" reassured Sgt. Tarillo.

"Will you give us the phone numbers of these people in Burlington, so we can contact them?" asked Frank Stargate. "Where can we bunk while we are here in Davenport?"

"I believe that By The River Hotel in downtown Davenport is a nice place to stay," answered Sgt. Tarillo. "You can see the Rock Island Arsenal from there."

If you get a room facing the Mississippi River, you can see boats going up and down the river. You can also see the dam," added Capt. Columbo.

"That's good information," replied Frank, the astrophysicist. "I can see why you're a great detective."

A short time later, the two men from Iowa City were unpacking their suitcases into a room at the By The River Hotel. While unpacking their suitcases, they began making plans what to do next.

"I need to eat first, because I'm so hungry, I could eat a horse," suggested Joe Mixer. "There is a diner downstairs in the hotel, where we can eat."

Shortly after eating a large lunch, they decided to call the West Side Kids' Detective Agency. Hannibal answered the phone and Joe Mixer introduced himself. Joe then went on to explain that they are to work with the agency to gain proof of the UFO sightings and the evidence of aliens.

"You must have talked to my Uncle Columbo about us and our assignment," reasoned Hannibal. "In the next encounter with the aliens, we will be prepared to video them for evidence."

"What are your plans to do next?" asked Frank Stargate.

"I believe we need to meet them face to face by willingly putting ourselves in a position to be abducted," explained Scooter, who was listening to the conversation by way of the speaker phone.

"Are you crazy, Scooter? Where is your brain now? Are you in overload?" asked excitedly by Hannibal.

"Wait," said the astrophysicist, Frank. "It's the best way to get to know them as long as we can control our own inquisitive minds."

"I like it when a plan comes together," reasoned Hannibal. "OK, then let's go meet at the Round Lake Park Campgrounds, to start the showdown. We can only hope that the aliens will come back to that location."

In Hannibal's thoughts, he hoped he had the power to get everyone back to Earth.

When everyone met at the boat docking sight, they parked their two vehicles. As they sat there in their vehicles, Hannibal, Scooter and Frank were looking into the moonless dark sky.

As Scooter was looking up into the dark sky, he asked, "What time is it?"

Looking as his watch, Hannibal answered, "It's 8:30 p. m. Why do you want to know?"

"I was just wondering if we are going to be abducted at all," answered Scooter. "I was told that aliens only come out at night, between 8:00 and 10:00 at night. Do clouds ever look down on us and say that one is an idiot?"

"Aliens only come out between 8:00 and 10:00 at night. What a stupid thing to say," laughed Hannibal. "Has the clouds ever told you that youse looked like an idiot? I'm sure they did and then they rained all over youse."

"Hannibal, I was just wondering, since we as humans always try to identify what we think clouds look like," answered Scooter. "I wish you was more influence in silence. Where is Joe?"

"Joe wanted to stay at the hotel and be the one who knows where we are and what we are up to," replied Frank. "He gets kind of lazy and hungry. He prefers to be in the comforts of the hotel wearing his special hat. He's basically like Jughead, but very intelligent in chemistry."

While watching in the pitch dark night, there stood out a small round light that looked like it was getting larger.

"When it gets larger in the night darkness, it must mean it's getting closer," explained Frank. "I've heard there are different alien crafts for specific purposes of exploring, getting samples and abducting people. The mothership is where their control intelligence is. By the way, I almost forgot. They have fighting warships as well."

"Why do they call the flying saucers, spaceships?" asked Scooter. The saucers ain't on bodies of water like our Navy ships."

"That's a good question, Scooter. I guess it's because it is a vehicle carrying something not on solid ground," answered Frank.

"Look at that glow of white light now!" demanded Hannibal. "Do we run for the hills?"

No, Let's see what it does! It may be what we want...an exciting journey into space. OH yeah. It may be our ride to the aliens living room or to a surgery table," gulped Frank.

"It's the size of the campground and it's right above us," stammered Scooter. "I feel the crackling of electricity and my eyes see only white. I wish us to keep our wits about us, Hannibal."

"Copy that, good buddy! See you up there!" replied Hannibal.

The three adventurers then shook their heads and opened their eyes, that was once blinded by the light, to see these peanut shell head shaped creatures looking at them.

"Hannibal, I wish us to understand the communication between us and these creatures," demanded Scooter."

"What ever you demand, I will make it your wish, master of mine," declared Hannibal. "Now that we will understand each other, don't say or do anything stupid."

"Hi, I'm Hannibal, the boss," clarified Hannibal.

"I'm Scooter, the brains," proclaimed Scooter.

"What do you mean, you're the brains?" asked Hannibal. "You couldn't open a safe if you had the combination."

"That's because it's locked," answered Scooter. You're just a schizophrenic freak."

"I don't know what that word means," declared Hannibal. "I'm going to look it up."

"Where are you going to look it up in, the telephone book?" asked Scooter. "I think you're doing it the hard way."

"I think your head is on the hard way," growled Hannibal.

"By the looks of these three humans, it confirms the fact that they are ugly looking creatures, with different sizes and shapes. We have learned that they are determined to live with loyalty and love of others," said one alien. "These traits can interfere with our goal to control them and get what we want to find a better and safer place to live, since our planet became depleted of resources. We don't plan to share other planets with their indigenous inhabitants."

"What you talking about?," shouted Scooter. "We come in peace. Don't go bad mouthing us. Your mouth doesn't even move."

"They must be using telepathy and somehow we can here the words!" exclaimed Frank.

"Scooter, the aliens are coming after us. I think we're going up the river," declared Hannibal.

"What are we doing?" asked Scooter. "Are we going fishing?"

"Do the hit and run play," demanded Hannibal.

"I'm going. I'm going," reassured Scooter.

Five aliens came forth and picked up Hannibal and Frank.

"I'm Scooter, The Brick and you aliens don't know who you're messing with." challenged Scooter. Scooter then dropped a brick on his assailant's foot and escaped into a different compartment of the spaceship. Frank and Hannibal were carried to a table and tied to it. The aliens then scampered into the other compartments of the spaceship looking for Scooter.

Without knowing where the door would lead him, Scooter opened it and he ran to a lab table. He noticed all sorts of liquids and solid materials on the table. He decided to take a vial of blue liquid and a solid pink material. He shoved them into his pockets next to his holster of bricks.

Meanwhile, Frank and Hannibal were helplessly attached to their tables, waiting for their fates and listening closely to any conversations between the aliens. A bright light was placed directly into their faces.

"I pray we get out of this!" exclaimed Frank.

"Don't worry, I just hope Scooter finds his way back to this room," answered a nervous Hannibal. "Just be calm like I am and listen for a while to the pink alien talking to the blue alien."

"Our ancestors have taught us a lot about life on Earth," stated the pink alien.

"To get what we want from the Earthlings, we need to control or terminate them," replied the blue alien. "We need their fresh water and nuclear waste to safely generate the energy to continue traveling through the universe. I am sure the Earthlings will not let us take it without a fight. Our leader has created a bio weapon to wipe out the people. It will take a two week incubation period for the massive infection. It will be an aerosol system settling on the ground and into the lungs of all humankind. The mixing of several viral strains into the aerosol system is called a chimera. It is highly contagious! It will be the plague of all plagues."

"Did you hear that?" Hannibal whispered to Frank.

"Yes, I sure did. It will be the end of the Earth and humankind," answered Frank. "But how will our fresh water be affected? I guess it would be their problem."

"I hear foot steps coming our way," murmured Hannibal. "Oh no! I believe they are going to explore us and implant a tracking chip in our bodies!"

Scooter then rushed over to Frank and Hannibal and announced, "Never fear. Scooter, The Brick is here!"

Scooter then dropped a brick on the foot of each alien and wished to Hannibal that they were back at the campground, near the cars.

Poof, the threesome then found themselves laying in the grass, by the cars. Each one felt the residual static electricity leaving their bodies. They looked up in the star filled, night sky to see a vanishing bright light.

"Well, I'll be," explained Frank. "You guys are fun to be with."

"Guess what?" declared Hannibal. "I activated the video button on my cell phone camera, just before the peanut shell aliens grabbed us. Now, we have real evidence to show Uncle Columbo and the government authorities."

"That's good news. It made it worth our time to get abducted to get that video," replied Frank. "Scooter, what were you doing while Hannibal and I were praying and sweating on the tables?"

"I was searching for the party room," laughed a grateful Scooter. "I slipped past the monsters and went into a compartment that turned out to be a laboratory. I took several samples and placed them in my holster. Here they are! I sure hope that Joe will take the samples to the University of Iowa science lab to analyze them."

"Joe is somewhat lazy," explained Frank. "But give him a chemistry problem and he is enthusiastic about solving it as long as he has plenty to eat and he is wearing his lucky hat."

"Let's go to the hotel where Joe is staying and show him what we have," instructed Hannibal.

"Thanks Hannibal for getting us home," acknowledged Frank and Scooter.

"I'm eager to see what Scooter brought with him from the alien laboratory," declared Frank.

Without saying anything, Hannibal didn't mention the going home incident.

When the three men arrived at the hotel room, Joe was sound asleep. Seeing this, Frank woke up Joe and told him that they had some remarkable, exciting news.

Joe then sat up and wiped the sleep out of his eyes. Scooter then showed Joe the liquid and solid material.

"These samples look very interesting," boomed Joe. "I will need to take them back to Iowa City for analyzing the chemicals that they're made of."

"I would like a small sample of each to work on them in my basement chemistry laboratory," insisted Scooter.

"That's OK," stated Joe, who was getting hungry. "I don't think I can go back to sleep."

"It's fine with me," reassured Frank. "'Why don't you put on your hat and go to Iowa City now?"

"Not until I eat,"demanded Joe. "Right now, food is my first priority. Can you hear me? I gotta eat."

"What's it going to be this time?" questioned Frank. "Fast food restaurants or the world's largest truck stop on I-80.

"I have to get something to eat with probably a lot of coffee," replied Joe. "I'll report back to you in a couple of days."

"While you are driving back to Iowa City, Scooter, Hannibal and I are going to get some rest and then report to Capt. Columbo about our experience tonight," explained Frank.

Chapter Forty-Five
The Space Aliens Do Exist Incident

While Frank Stargate slept at the hotel, Hannibal and Scooter took their samples to the chemistry laboratory, at the detective agency.

"Don't make a bomb like you did at our chemistry class, at the University of Davenport and blow up our house," Hannibal seriously demanded of Scooter.

"After I get some sleep, I'm going to mix some chemicals with the alien samples to create a better brick for my weapon and for those awful roads," declared Scooter.

"Late this morning, we will meet with Frank at the Davenport Police Department to show Uncle Columbo the videos of our experiences with the aliens," replied a sleepy Hannibal.

The next morning Scooter entered the kitchen and seeing his twin sister Amy, Scooter greeted her, "Good morning Amy, Hannibal and myself have an appointment to see Uncle Columbo. Can you make us a quick meal before we go?"

"If you want something fast, how about some Nestle's Quick chocolate protein shake?" offered Amy.

"Is that all you know how to make?" questioned Scooter. "I thought you learned to be a chef and so you can cook vitals that is hot and can stick to our ribs."

"Then how about four hot dogs and a chocolate milk?" suggested Amy.

"Well I guess its alright! It's better than nothin'." replied Scooter.

It was finally one o' clock in the afternoon when Hannibal and Scooter met Frank at the Davenport Police Station. Just making it on time, Capt. Columbo and Sgt. Tarillo were returning back to the station.

"Hannibal called me and told me you three guys have a video to show us," acknowledged Uncle Columbo.

"Just wait until you see this video. It is really wild and should give us the proof we need that there are aliens messing with us," explained Scooter.

"How did you get this video that you are about to show us?" asked Sgt. Tarillo. "After you show us this video, is this something you're going to make us believe? This video isn't from one of your far out hunches?"

"It was just plain magic," laughed Hannibal "Everyone cooperated like actors."

"This video wasn't from something stupid I did. Hannibal was really smart," explained Scooter. "He was the one who had his cell phone camera on after we had been electrified into the spaceship. It was really a hair raising event, because the aliens abducted the three of us.

Those weird peanut shaped characters tried to tie all of us onto a table. Nobody messes around with Scooter, The Brick, because for once I did something smart and used my secret weapon by dropping my bricks on their feet and escaped.

When you look at the video, it doesn't show me racing around the spaceship. I showed up later and dropped bricks on two more aliens, then Hannibal took over from there. They didn't like my bricks, so they sent us back to Earth."

Frank and Hannibal then told Uncle Columbo and Sgt. Tarillo what they heard the aliens talking about.

"The aliens want our fresh water and nuclear material for them to use," Frank began to say. "They will take it any way they can. The aliens can use biochemical weapons and use them by force to get what they want."

"You by all means did your job and have shown us and told us what we feared the most," stated Uncle Columbo. "They are not a peaceful form of aliens. Sgt. Tarillo and I will inform the government and the military authorities of this video and the information that you told us."

Most government agents are assigned to discredit UFO witness sightings. Their explanation of the strange happenings were due to balloons, flares and drone activity."

"Those must be really big balloons. How long does it take for somebody to sit there and blow them up?" asked Scooter.

"That explains your far out hunches," laughed Sgt. Tarillo. "Nobody sits there and blows up these balloons."

"How long does it take for somebody to sit there and blow them up?" laughed Uncle Columbo. "Scooter, you're funny. Now be still and let me finish. As I was saying, sometimes the agents say it was just known military craft being tested. Usually, the government had no interest in the sightings, but after several outstanding reputable people having admitted to seeing UFOs, the pentagon is now curious."

The next day, the Davenport Quest printed an article that said, "A scientist, astrophysicist Frank Stargate and detectives Scooter Hickenbottom and Hannibal Columbo, from the West Side Kids' Detective Agency admitted to being abducted to an alien spacecraft.

While being in the spacecraft, they overheard a conversation (How, it is unknown.) about what the aliens were going to do to Earth's humans.

At one time, a secret program had the mission to silence these people with their alien contact experiences. Now, the pentagon is interested, because Homeland Security is involved.

A psychiatrist interviewed the three abductees to evaluate the authenticity of their stories. The investigative group from the pentagon convinced congress to contribute a sizable amount of funds to the UFO investigation.

It was disclosed that Area 15 existed to help monitor UFO activity in The United States. The Department of Defense has generated plans to organize defense to protect the country, by using force as needed, depending on the purpose of the entities in the UFO spacecrafts.

Many weapon launching sites were made around the mainland of the United States, including Alaska and Hawaii.

When the testimonials were proven authentic, anxiety and concern of danger will focus on humankind for survival."

"That was quite an informative article in the paper!" boomed Whatever.

"We also found that the aliens have a way to change sea water into fresh water, without infectious microorganisms in huge quantities," added Hannibal.

"And those peanut shell aliens also plan to use mind control to change our behavior," gasped Scooter. "If I ever catch a peanut shell alien, I'm going to take him down to my chemistry lab and make peanut butter out of him."

"You don't say? I think that mind control would be useful for you, Scooter," laughed Hannibal. "Just think, you would have alien behavior. Perhaps that would be a big improvement!"

"I need to call Professor Boblit and see what he has to say about our abductions," insisted Scooter. "I'll talk to you guys later."

Professor Boblit talking with Scooter

Chapter Forty-Six

THE INCIDENT OF PROFESSOR BOBLIT

"Hello, Professor Boblit. This is Scooter, The Brick calling you again."

Terrific, I'm glad you called," proclaimed Professor Boblit. "This is one time I seriously want to talk to you. I read about you in the Davenport Quest. That must have been some experience of a lifetime."

"It was very scary," explained Scooter. "It was as scary as watching models walking down the showcase runway, in wild outfits."

"What did the aliens look like?" asked Professor Boblit.

"Well, to tell you the truth," Scooter began to say. "They had a peanut shell, shaped head, two large eyes, a long neck, pointed ears, four arms, with three fingers and two legs with feet in both directions. Their skin color was either pink, blue or gray."

"What did the Earth look like from way out there?" questioned Professor Boblit.

"Before I found some samples that I picked up, I looked through the window," replied Scooter. "Earth looked like a small perfectly round blue object. It was beautiful! What have you read about alien activity?"

"Assuming that there are intelligent beings, guiding these UFOs, they have been exploring and visiting Earth for a long time. Like millions of years. Their technology has also advanced. They have a right to travel throughout the universe!

Each unidentified aerial phenomena has been getting more and more credible. In response to these phenomena, Navy and Air Force fighter jets have been deployed to patrol the country. Our Navy submarines are also searching underwater for spacecraft. There have been reports from top Navy fighter pilots being outmaneuvered by the UFOs.

The aliens have become interested in us since the first atomic bomb explosion. Since then, we have been stockpiling nuclear weapons.

Can their beams of light affect the nuclear material? Our nuclear weapons are more powerful today than what they were in the 1940s and the 1950s."

"Why do they want our water?" asked Scooter.

"Water makes up most of Earth," explained Professor Boblit. "Drinking water is not guaranteed. Water is most important for life on Earth. Could it also be for the aliens from light years away from Earth? Perhaps their water supply resources had depleted and they are searching for water at no cost. They must be desperate beings and we take our water for granted."

"Is that why a bottle of water cost more at a ball park, than at the grocery store? And why would anyone fill a swimming pool full of water? We could conserve the water and not be in the position of the aliens," asked an inquisitive Scooter.

"There is a magnetic force surrounding Earth. To disturb it, Earth may be off its normal angle of tilt and this could cause all kinds of problems for us," instructed Professor Boblit.

"I wonder if the magnetic force field caused me to lose my car keys," reckoned Scooter.

"I don't think you need any external excuses to lose your car keys or anything else," laughed Professor Boblit. "Your mind could be somewhere else like in the empty vacuum of space in the universe."

"That's what Hannibal is always telling me, only he doesn't say it that way," alleged Scooter. "He says that my head is an empty vacuum of space."

"Your head is an empty vacuum space," laughed Professor Boblit. "You're funny."

"That's what Uncle Columbo keeps telling me. Here's another good question for you, Professor Boblit. "Would the aliens give me electricity in exchange for water to cut my electricity bill? OK, maybe even a battery that would last forever?"

"I don't know Scooter. I'm not sure what to tell you," answered Professor Boblit.

"Oh, you know I'm Not Sure, who is one of our detectives?" asked Scooter.

"Just what are you talking about?" asked Professor Boblit. "What's, I'm not sure?"

"You know, What? It sounds like you know the rest of the detectives?" asked Scooter.

"Just who are we talking about?" asked a confused Professor Boblit.

"I thought we were talking about, I'm Not Sure, not, What," replied Scooter.

"I don't know who we're talking about," reckoned Professor Boblit.

"We wasn't talking about I Don't Know and Who," replied Scooter. "Since you know all of us, you should come over for dinner sometime. We just hired my twin sister, Amy as our cook. She makes fabulous hot dog sandwiches."

"I'll have to think about it and let you know as soon as I can figure out what we just talked about," reckoned Professor Boblit. "I have to be on the air in five minutes. I think it was very interesting talking to you. Right now I need to let you go, because my head is like an empty vacuum of space. So after talking to you, I need the time to clear my head."

"I will keep in touch," stated Scooter. "Come over the next time you're hungry for hot dog sandwiches."

Chapter Forty-Seven
THE INCIDENT OF THE HYPNOTIST

Two military colonels, specialized in hypnosis, arrived at the hospital where Dr. Fine and Charlie, The Chill were getting ready for their visit with them. As detectives assigned to the case, Hannibal and Scooter also showed up at the hospital to watch Dr. Fine and Charlie, The Chill being hypnotized.

Colonel Brane chose to work with Dr. Fine and he welcomed him to a sofa. Colonel Dreme said he would work with Charlie, The Chill.

"It says here in my folder, Dr. Fine that you are into hypnotism yourself. So, just be calm and we will find out what your experience was on the alien spaceship," reassured Colonel Brane.

"All aboard," laughed Scooter.

"Scooter, keep your lips glued shut, so Colonel Brane can do his magic by exploring Dr. Fine's brain," scolded Hannibal.

"Wait a minute," interjected Dr. Fine. "I don't remember that I was involved in hypnotism!"

"Aha! I see. It will take time to fully get your memory back," reasoned Colonel Brane. "I have hypnotized many abductees and found out about their experiences in the spaceships. As a hypnotist, you know the routine. Now, let's begin," instructed Colonel Brane as Scooter and Hannibal watched.

"Watch the medallion swing back and forth, back and forth. Your eyes are getting tired, very tired. You are getting sleepy, very sleepy.

You can't stay awake any longer and you must close your eyes and you're going to sleep, sleep, sleep. You are now in a deep sleep.

Now you will see flashes of light behind your eyelids and you will invite them to open up your mind about the incident where you were abducted. Stay calm. Breathe slowly and let your mind select the flashes of light that opens your memory. Now that you are asleep, I will be asking you questions and you answer to anything that comes to mind.

"I was smoking a cigarette with my friend in my car," answered Dr. Fine.

"I was at Round Lake with Hannibal and Frank waiting to be abducted by the space aliens," answered Scooter.

"Well, it looks like you done it to Scooter, Colonel Brane," exclaimed Hannibal. "You re-hypnotized, The Great, Scooter, The Brick, alias no brains. Scooter and myself came to watch you hypnotize Dr. Fine and he got his self re-hypnotized. I always wondered what it would be like to have this bonehead re-hypnotized. Don't let it bother you none because Scooter has no brains, so you have to use your own. Continue if you please."

"Aha, it's a first for me to have hypnotized two people at the same time," proclaimed Colonel Brane. "Let's put Scooter in this chair, while I continue with Dr. Fine. OK, Dr. Fine, let's continue. Did you see or feel anything different?"

"I felt the heat from the cigarette. I saw the red glow of my friend's cigarette. It was very dark and there was no sound," answered Dr. Fine.

"I felt the crackling of electricity and my eyes only saw white," answered Scooter.

"Aha. What came next?" asked Colonel Brane.

"There was this bright light that blinded me and I felt an electrical eruption of my body. I was going blank and then I was flying upward," answered Dr. Fine.

"My eyes that was once blinded by light, saw these peanut shell shaped head creatures looking at me," answered Scooter.

"Aha. Then what?" asked Colonel Brane.

"Time just escaped me and I woke up tied to a table and my

vision was foggy like. It looked like peanut shells were all around me, " explained Dr. Fine. "I heard sounds like there were other people frantically trying to move off of the tables."

"To communicate with these creatures, I wished to Hannibal that we could communicate with each other," answered Scooter.

"Aha. Did you feel safe?" asked Colonel Brane.

"No! I Just wanted to scream and get released so I could go home," answered Dr. Fine.

"When the aliens came after us, Hannibal demanded that we do the hit and run play," explained Scooter. "So I dropped my bricks on these creatures feet and ran for my life, while Hannibal and Frank stayed behind."

"Aha. Now tell me what happened while you were on the table?" questioned Colonel Brane.

"These creatures started to poke and push pins into me. I felt them place something in me," answered Dr. Fine.

"I ran into another compartment. Hannibal and Frank was tied to the table," answered Scooter.

"Aha. What was it they placed into you?" asked Colonel Brane.

"I don't know. Their hands were all over me. It was terrible," answered Dr. Fine.

"They didn't place anything in me, because they couldn't catch me," answered Scooter.

"Can you describe what they look like?" asked Colonel Brane.

"Their heads were peanut shell shaped, with two huge eyes and pointed ears. The necks were long and they had four arms in the upper body position. They had two legs with each leg having two feet. I know that, because they didn't turn around to travel away from the table. Each hand had three fingers and each foot had three toes.

"I told you what they looked like, before you asked that question," boomed Scooter. "Can't you remember nutin'? And Hannibal says I am stupid."

"How did they communicate?" asked Colonel Brane.

"I don't know, because I didn't see their mouths move and I couldn't hear them," answered Dr. Fine.

"What else? Boy! You really don't remember nutin. I already

told you that I wished Hannibal to help us communicate," answered Scooter. "I think Colonel Dreme needs to hypnotize you to help you remember things."

"Hannibal, why does Scooter keep saying that he wished you to help him communicate with these creatures?" asked Colonel Brane. "What do you have in that bag on the floor? It looks like a lamp of some sort."

"Oh, that?" answered Hannibal. "It's just a broken down teapot that Scooter bought at a garage sale. I like to bring the teapot with me, because I like to drink tea.

Scooter always wants me to bring the tea pot with us, just like he does his bricks.

He believes that if he uses it to make wishes, they will come true. Isn't that ridiculous? Besides, with Scooter, you never know what he is going to say and do," answered Hannibal. "You're the one who re-hypnotized the kid. Now is our chance to find out why Scooter is always doing something stupid."

"Aha, now I understand why he keeps talking about wishes. No! with all my education, I don't understand," replied Colonel Brane.

"Why do you keep saying aha?" asked Hannibal.

"It beats me. I just don't know," replied Colonel Brane. "I need to get this over with, so let me finish asking the questions."

"Aha, now I understand," laughed Hannibal. "It seems that you and Scooter think alike."

"OK, Dr. Fine, let's continue, so I can get out of this mad house," exclaimed Colonel Brane. "Did the aliens have a nose?"

"Yes, a very small one," answered Dr. Fine.

"I didn't see any nose," answered Scooter. "All I did was drop my bricks on their feet and ran for the hills."

"Aha," laughed Hannibal.

"What else can you tell me?" asked Colonel Brane.

"They left me alone for some time. I closed my eyes and the next thing I knew, I felt the dog's tongue licking me," explained Dr. Fine. "The ambulance medics came through the trees and took me to the hospital."

"I returned to where Hannibal and Frank was tied to those tables and then dropped my bricks on the aliens feet. Then I wished Hannibal to return us to the campground, near the cars," Scooter went on to say. "We returned to the campground laying in the grass by the cars and looked up in the sky to see a vanishing bright light."

"OK, we're done with the hypnosis and I will guide you out of it," explained Colonel Brane. "You will remember none of this conversation and I want to forget about what Scooter said. Dr. Fine, you will regain your normal thoughts and behavior.

On the other hand, Scooter. If you regain your normal thoughts and behavior, nobody can help you. I think you need to treat your mom to a margarita. You're probably the reason she drinks.

I will count back from ten to zero. You will wake up refreshed and you will ask for a cup of coffee. Ten, nine, eight, seven, six, five, four, three, two, one, zero. That's it. Open your eyes. How do you feel?"

"I want a cup of coffee," demanded Dr. Fine.

"Good. One cup of java coming up!" exclaimed Colonel Brane. "Stay here and enjoy your coffee. I'm leaving, before I'm admitted to the nuthouse."

After Colonel Brane left, he met Colonel Dreme in the hallway after both were done with the hypnotic interviews. They found out that the recordings of both people were similar except Charlie, The Chill saw different colors of aliens, that were pink, blue and gray.

"Well," said Colonel Dreme. "We will put these interviews in our separate folders and give them to Homeland Security. I'll see you back in Washington."

Chapter Forty-Eight

THE LUMP IN THE NECK INCIDENT

Meanwhile, Burlington was having some excitement. The waterworks building was broken into. The police found a hand print with only three fingers. There were reports of UFO sightings. They saw balls of light fly across the sky so fast you didn't want to blink to see it. It probably broke the sound barrier, but no thunder was heard.

Chris Seven Murphy and Michael Eight Murphy informed Scooter and Hannibal that they saw several objects on radar in the Burlington area.

Betty, who was living with Kelly, felt like she was being followed all day. Occasionally, her mind was a blank and in a fog, but she came out of it in seconds.

Betty was called into work the next early morning, to check on the Water Works machinery and quality control gauges, after a security guard reported the break in. Betty reported false information to the CEO of the Water Works.

Before anyone showed up at the Water Works, Betty was confronted by a pink alien. She was controlled by the alien to tell secrets of the Water Works.

The back of her neck was the cause of the pain so she went to see a doctor, who found the lump. The doctor found some movement inside the lump and recommended an x-ray. A metal object in the image, just located under the skin, appeared in the x-ray, so the doctor recommended to remove it.

"What is it doctor?" questioned Betty.

"It appears to be a metal chip!" responded the horrified doctor. "Someone is tracking or controlling you."

"It's been in my neck since I was five years old, when my mom found it," replied Betty.

"In my professional opinion, I believe you have been tracked or controlled by aliens since they have been sighted in spacecrafts around here. Have you had any encounters with them currently?"

I vaguely remember something happening at the Water Works!" exclaimed Betty. "Oh my! I bet I gave the CEO the wrong information. I better call her back and tell her the right story. Doc, since this chip is out of my neck, now I won't be controlled by aliens?"

"Yes, I think we can assume that," answered the doctor.

After getting home from the doctor's office, Betty decided to call Hannibal about her visit to the doctor."

"Hello, is Hannibal there?" asked Betty "Who am I talking to?"

"Hi Betty. This is Scooter, not Who. Hannibal is in the kitchen right now eating his hot dog lunch. Does you want me to git him?"

"Yes, I need to talk to him about my doctor's visit," replied Betty.

"What else? Hannibal, Betty is on the phone," mumbled Scooter. Put down that hot dog and come to the phone.

"I can't hear you! I'm coming!" yelled Hannibal.

As Hannibal walked into the office, he asked Scooter, "Why do you always do that?"

"To get you to come in here," laughed Scooter. "Betty is on the phone."

"Hello Betty, What did you find out from your doc?" asked Hannibal.

"I went to see the doctor about the pain in my neck," explained Betty.

"It wasn't me, was it? Or was it Scooter?" asked Hannibal. "Whatever we did to you, I'm sorry."

"No it wasn't either one of you," proclaimed Betty. "Now listen! I want to finish telling you what the doctor said. The aliens. I have not been acting normal in the last two days, since the aliens have been more active around Burlington."

"Your behavior might be because you like me so much and you can't get me out of your mind," reckoned Hannibal.

"That sure is a fat chance! I do admit that I care about you," reassured Betty. "After the chip was removed, I do feel freedom."

"That's good! Now you can be yourself," insisted Hannibal. "Be careful over in Burlington. These aliens are becoming a world problem. Tell What Do You Think, Michael Eight, Tim and superfox Kelly to be on the alert. Keep informing me what's going on."

"What's my nickname?" asked Betty.

"You know that I know what it is," replied Hannibal. "You have heard me say it before. It's My Main Muffin.!"

"Oh, how sweet!" laughed Betty.

"It is! It looks like I have to go and straighten out the rest of the detectives," laughed Hannibal. "What are you guys watching on TV?"

Chapter Forty-Nine

THE SPECIAL REPORT INCIDENT

"Scooter found a channel that is giving a news break," exclaimed You Don't Say.

"It's all about the activity of those darn aliens," sneered Smiley. "Wait until I get my handgun tuned up."

"Yeah, you might be able to hit the large spaceship," laughed Whatever.

"I think we are going to need a bigger weapon to deal with those aliens!" demanded Who.

"Unfortunately, you are right, Who," agreed What.

"Look! The reporter said a Navy train never arrived at the intended destination," stated Scooter. "The train was carrying military and commercial nuclear waste to the Idaho holding facilities. The train has been tested and complied by the Association of American Railroads, AAR, regulations governing the transport of radioactive material. The US Department of Energy and the AAR couldn't prevent the disappearance of the transport train.

"Oh my! We are losing our control of these serious radioactive materials. This is a very serious situation," gulped Hannibal. "Earlier, there had been reported UFOs appearing to be spying on nuclear plants and the locations as to where they are transported."

Because, who was helping Amy in the kitchen, came into the living room to see what everyone was excited about.

"Stella, you are resting in my spot! Could you take it to the floor?" demanded Because.

"Stella, then whimpered while moving off the sofa to the floor.

Because, I Don't Know and I'm Not Sure came into the living room just in time to hear a reporter tell a story about a close encounter.

While on a golf course, a foursome saw a creature with four arms pick up two golf clubs and he was trying to hit the ball. The reporter asked if the creature made par for the hole.

A witness said, "No, he was escorted off the fairway by officials and taken to the clubhouse where the creature touched himself and disappeared."

Later, spectators saw a distant dot getting smaller in the sky and then it was gone!

"Wow! That was a good one," laughed I'm Not Sure as the rest of the detectives were also laughing.

Stella abruptly stood up, with his ears pointed and ran out of the living room.

The reporter then concluded, "It is safe to say, there are strange things happening going on around this country. Wait! Here's a story I missed from the bottom of my stack... Well, what do you know? Man has landed on the moon."

Chapter Fifty

THE MEETING WITH FRANK
AND JOE INCIDENT

"Ring-a-ding-ding! Hearing this, everyone was looking for their cell phones.

"It's for me," announced Scooter. "Frank just told me that Joe is back from Iowa City and they want a meeting with me and Hannibal."

"Tell Joe that we can come to a meeting, tonight at 8 p. m. OK, Scooter?" suggested Hannibal. "We will be done with supper by then."

After supper, Hannibal and Scooter left for the meeting in their blue Explorer.

"It's awfully dark tonight," exclaimed Scooter.

"You almost hit that truck. Why don't you turn the headlights on, so you can see where you're going?" asked a disgusted Hannibal. "What are you trying to do? Sneak up on Frank?"

"Oh yeah. That's much better," declared Scooter. "Now that I can see where I'm going, we can meet Frank Mixer and Joe Stargate at the By The River Hotel on time."

"That's Frank Stargate, Frank Stargate and Joe Mixer, Joe Mixer, Scooter," laughed Hannibal. "You're always mixing things up. By the way, did you bring my lamp with you. I don't want anybody else to get their hands on it or I will have a new master. If that happens,

I'm sure my new master will be smart and not a bonehead who gets lost in the dark and forgets names."

"Don't worry. I always bring it along with my bricks," reassured Scooter. "I don't want anybody to be in control of my best buddy."

"You better stay in control of me and my lamp or I'm going to turn you into a brick," laughed Hannibal.

Ten minutes later, Hannibal and Scooter, carrying a brick and a lamp in a bag, knocked on Frank's door.

"Come on in," said Frank. "Joe is busy eating a sandwich, with his lucky hat on."

"Why would Joe eat a sandwich with his lucky hat on it?" asked Scooter. "Why doesn't he just make two sandwiches and wear his lucky hat?"

"Why doesn't he make two sandwiches with his lucky hat on?" laughed Frank. Later on, Joe will be here with your findings from your samples, then you can ask him that question."

"Is he going to talk with his mouth full of his lucky hat and the sandwich?" asked Scooter. I've done that before, but I never ate my lucky hat. You don't need a college education to figure that out. He must be from the FBI. Hannibal and myself want answers. People want answers and now!"

"Scooter, that was a mouthful of questions. You sound like a real mental giant," answered Frank. "I'll go tell Joe what you asked about eating his lucky hat and be right back."

After Frank came back laughing, Hannibal asked," Have you been watching the latest national news about aliens?"

"I've been keeping track of the news," answered Frank. "All galaxies have planets, so one might have the ingredients of life to support it. These planets are being investigated by the Earth's instruments. I believe the aliens are treasure hunting in different universes."

"We're not going to let that happen in our world," insisted Hannibal. "We may have to look deep into the mountains, oceans and outer space to find them."

"We won't have to look hard, because they are finding us," frowned Frank. "We will monitor them from by way of signals, listening from satellite transmitters. Most of the public do not believe in the superior intelligent alien theory. There may be truth out there that the public can not comprehend or do not want to know."

"OK, I'm done eating," interrupted Joe as Frank was talking about the alien theory conversation. "I'm ready to tell you what I found out."

"I see you didn't eat your lucky hat, so let it fly," encouraged Scooter. "What did you find out? What's the pitch, the catch, the delivery, the curve, the angle?"

"I found out that the blue liquid is so special and rare, that its uses are unknown," explained Joe. "Further experiments are needed to determine its uses.

The solid pink material is so hard, it can't be compressed to break. It can be flaked off, however. There is an unknown element in it, not found on Earth. Hydrochloric acid affects it. In summary, we don't know everything about the samples. It's definitely extraterrestrial."

"What are we to make of it?" asked Scooter.

"More experimentation is needed," instructed a satisfied Joe. "I thought you wanted to know, what I know so far."

"Thanks Jughead, I mean Joe, murmured Scooter. "Keep in touch."

On the drive back home, Scooter promised he would find the use for these samples, that are in the basement. The basement will be a very busy place.

The gray alien, Uffey, using his finger to pulverize the boulder

Chapter Fifty-One

THE BUFFALO SAND QUARRY INCIDENT

While trying to sleep, Scooter was tossing around thinking about what to do with the samples. It came to him in a dream he could use the samples to improve the bricks he uses, extraterrestrial bricks. "I will teach them to do as I want."

It was 2:30 a. m. when a phone call was heard in Hannibal's bedroom.

"I know it's late. I was awaken too," greeted an apologizing Uncle Columbo.

"I'm OK. What is it Uncle? Did a family member die?" asked Hannibal.

"No, thank goodness! I was awaken by a call from the Scott County Sheriff's Department that there was a crash in the Buffalo sand quarry, just a half hour ago. I would like you and Scooter to go and investigate it.

A county trooper saw a white ball fall into the quarry. He called for backup thinking it might be an alien spaceship crash. He called me and then I called you."

"OK, me and Scooter will be there within the hour."

"If it turns out to be an alien crash, you will thank me later for the experience," declared Uncle Columbo.

"It's really dark in this hole of the sand quarry," reasoned Scooter. "I don't see any signs of a crash, like debris and fire."

"I see some movement over there, maybe about 200 yards away," calculated Hannibal.

"When is a black dog never called a black dog?" joked a nervous Scooter, with a belt full of bricks.

"When it's a red dog," whispered Hannibal, who was carrying a handgun.

"Not that I know of," suggested Scooter. "it's when the dog is a greyhound."

"Now, that we're coming closer to the movement, shine a beam of light over there," whispered Hannibal.

"Yikes! Scooter, do you see that spaceship and the what you call it?" exclaimed Hannibal.

As time came to a sudden stop, Hannibal and Scooter were face to face with what you call a gray alien.

"Why shouldn't you trust stairs?" joked a nervous Scooter.

"Because they are up to something," replied Hannibal. "and they will always let you down."

"How did you know that?" asked Scooter.

"It seems to fit the situation we are in, as of now!" replied Hannibal.

"Hannibal, I'm going to make a wish for us to understand the alien and for the alien to understand us."

"How did you crash?" asked Hannibal.

"The alien then replied, "I was coming into this hole too fast to take samples of the contents, then I lost control of the spaceship, the explorer."

"For my report, I need to know your name?" asked Scooter.

"My comrades call me Uffey," answered the alien.

"How will I know it is you among the other aliens?" asked Hannibal.

"I have a scar on my face," answered the alien.

"You just can't come here and do what you want. We have property rights and laws on Earth," explained Scooter.

You need to get permission from the owner of this sand quarry. I new that."

"Says who?" replied Uffey who laughed and said, "Well, I didn't know that. I'll take anything I want, any time."

"OK, alien. That's all," declared Hannibal. "I want you to put up your hands and drop any weapons, you have on you. I'm goina' warn you, I'm a dead shot and if I shoot you, you will be a dead, gray alien. Then I'm goina find out if your blood is gray or red."

"That's right, Goofy" added Scooter. "We sure are. We're going to find out if you're a gray hound or a red hound."

"I told you my name is Uffey, not Goofy. I can't drop any weapons from me," replied the gray alien. "I can lower my four hands, but you told me to raise my hands."

"Alright, Mr. Alien. I have a super brick that will force you to keep all your hands up, so we can see them," demanded Scooter, The Brick. "Why don't you guys get out of town and leave us alone?"

My gun is bigger than your gun," interrupted Hannibal. "You have sunrise to leave."

Hannibal then pointed his gun at a boulder and fired a round, chipping away, pieces of it. Uffey then lowered a hand, showing one finger.

"Are you the same alien I saw in the space ship at the ball diamond?" asked Scooter.

"That was me," replied the alien. "I tried to be friendly, but I saw the terror in your eyes. You ran away like a scared little purple alien, who are labeled cowards. My supreme leader told me not to make a show of it at the ball field, so I quickly flew off into outer space.

I extremely enjoyed the look on your face. I would love to study you. I can't take you with me now, because my spacecraft is broken. But I can call some friends up there to help me. I can show you how powerful my finger is!"

"What's with a finger?" laughed Hannibal and Scooter.

Uffey then pointed the finger at the same boulder and a flash of blue light pulverizes the boulder.

"There sure are a lot of you on Earth with different shapes, sizes and color and ugly like you two," emphasized Uffey.

"Those are fighting words. Same to you weirdo," challenged Scooter. "You creatures are out of this world, with your peanut shell shaped head, big eyes, pointed ears, four arms and two feet on each leg."

"What are you going to do about it?" responded Uffey.

I'm goin' give you a gift of bricks and I'm goin' to throw them on your four feet," declared Scooter.

"Ouch! Ouch! That's killing me!" screamed Uffey.

"It serves you right Goofy!" exclaimed Scooter.

"Ouch! Ouch! My name is Uffey, not Goofy, you dumb Earthling," screamed Uffey. "Ouch! Ouch!"

"Then go on home and leave us alone, before I have you turned into a brick, you dumb alien," declared Scooter. "Go on. Now git or you will be facing, though ugly a worst fate than my bricks."

"Why can't we be friends?" pleaded Uffey, as he pointed his finger at Scooter.

"Hannibal, I wish Goofy to be in outer space and out of range to hurt us," wished Scooter.

"That's Uffey, not Goofy," corrected the alien.

"Scooter, your wish is seconded by me and granted now."

"That's Uffey!" screamed the alien. "Not Goofy! Poof! Uffey was nowhere to be found.

With Uffey gone, the detectives were standing in the hole, in the dark, with a spacecraft in front of them. They didn't care where the alien went as long as he was gone.

Within a minute after Uffey disappeared, a Buffalo policeman arrived with the first responders asking why Hannibal and Scooter was at the crash site. Both Hannibal and Scooter used the excuse that they got lost and climbed into the huge pit. They were told that it was a strange place for them to be.

"Shine your flashlight over there," demanded Hannibal.

All the first responders and the Buffalo policeman saw the semi-truck size shape craft. With their eyes and mouth wide open, they did not hear or see the men in black come with huge equipment to take away the spacecraft.

"Let's find our Explorer and go home," suggested Hannibal. "Maybe we can get a few more hours of sleep, before the Davenport Quest sends some reporters for interviews."

Chapter Fifty-Two
The Incident of The Big Question

Later that morning, Hannibal and Scooter woke up in time to smell food, being cooked by Amy, while Ann was cleaning in the living room.

Mm, Mm, the food smells good", exclaimed Scooter. "I'm glad you"re here to help us, sis. A belly full of your cooking will perk me up and give me the strength to fight the aliens."

"It also works for me," added Hannibal.

"Hi Ann. It's good to see you," acknowledged Scooter. "I hope we don't make too much of a mess for you to clean up. Have you had anything to eat today?"

"Yes, I just finished eating," replied Ann. "Amy is a very good chef."

"Scooter, we need to have a meeting with Uncle Hannibal, Rex, Joe and Frank to make a plan to deal with the aliens," proposed Hannibal. "We should also invite the military personnel. Now that I think about it, we should also invite What Do You Think and Michael Eight to our meeting."

Later on at the meeting, the big question was, how to get rid of the aliens, who are hurting people, stealing our water and our nuclear material.

Frank Stargate began by saying, "We know the aliens are on a mission to take what they want and to continue to travel to other galaxies. It's the gray aliens who would destroy humans to get what they want."

"I witnessed the power of the finger weapon," informed Scooter

"Where did you see this, Scooter?" asked one of the Army's Major Generals, who was at the meeting.

"In the Buffalo sand pit where an alien crashed its spaceship," explained Scooter.

"He used his finger to fire a light source that pulverized a boulder, then he disappeared. I think he ran so fast, that we didn't see where he went."

"We have a plan to launch a rocket from the Davenport Airport, when it comes to that," said the Major General. "All those abducted people were defenseless. Some have come back home, only because the aliens wanted to use them."

"Nobody would want to use me," expressed Scooter. "I'm so stupid I can outsmart any alien."

"What Do You Think and Michael Eight, what do you have to say about this group meeting?" asked Sgt. Tarillo.

"I know that the town of Burlington has been seeing more UFOs now, than ever," replied Michael Eight. "I also believe in the supernatural. I need to think what's going on."

"I've also seen UFOs on my radar and some people have been affected by the aliens, in person," added What Do You Think. "My younger brother, why are you thinking about the supernatural when we have real space aliens to deal with."

"I think it is some form of the paranormal theory," reasoned Michael Eight, alias Dr. Zodiac. "The aliens come and go without us noticing them."

"I will help the Major General report the information, from this meeting, to the Pentagon," acknowledged Capt. Columbo.

"I'm going to eat some burgers and then go back to Iowa City, to work on the samples again," reckoned Joe Mixer. "There must be some use for these samples. But I think there is more use to sample the burgers."

"I'm gonna stay here and see what can be done around here," proposed Frank.

"After I send all this information to the Pentagon, I'm leaving for the Davenport Airport," said the Major General of the Army.

"While everybody else is doing their thing, I'm going to do my thing and work on the samples in my basement," added Scooter. "Then together we can do our own thing together and that will be the whole thing."

"You don't say, Eagle Beak. While you're working in the basement, make sure you don't drop any bricks on your feet," laughed Hannibal. "While you're playing with your chemicals, I'm gonna assist Uncle Columbo. We have bigger fish to catch."

Chapter Fifty-Three

THE INCIDENT OF THE NAVY FLEET

While the meeting was going on, the Navy fleet was being followed along the coast and the aliens were disrupting the ships' computers. The Navy ships tried to communicate with the spaceships, but the spaceships wouldn't respond. The Admirals decided to go to the manual system and fired warning rounds next to the spaceships. The spaceships plunged into the ocean and disappeared.

The Admiral reported to the Pentagon about the confrontation. The President of The United States decided to declared an alert of all military forces, including Space Force.

After hearing about the Navy issues from the government officials, Scooter became nervous and excited at the same time. He just had to lighten his mood, by telling a joke.

Scooter then began with a nervous laugh as he began to tell his joke. "The doctor asked his medical assistant, if she took the patient's temperature?"

She responded by saying, "No, I didn't know it was missing!" Scooter then started to laugh harder at his own joke.

"Anyway, does anyone know where Aquaman is?" questioned Scooter. "He will teach these aliens in their spaceships, under the ocean, a thing or two."

"Don't be silly Scooter! Aquaman is a cartoon character in the movies," chucked Hannibal.

"I knew that," declared Scooter.

"Hannibal then suggested, "With all the strange UFOs and aliens affecting our lives, I think we need to step up on our plan."

"What plan?" asked Scooter.

"The one about security, knucklehead. Now it's security for everyone on Earth," declared Hannibal. "We need to be working together. The news isn't good and I miss Pockets. He would know what to do."

"We need to find him quick," declared Scooter. "I don't care where he is. We need to git him back here, even if we have to shut down the Blue Jinn s."

"How do you think we should shut him down?" asked Hannibal.

"You know. Bury him. No one will find the lamp he comes from," exclaimed Scooter. "It will probably free Pockets from his bondage. It's worth a try if it comes to that! The Blue Jinn s thinks he is such a big shot! We'll fix him!"

"I looked up on the internet to find out where genies are from," explained Hannibal. "There are several suggested places in Turkey and Syria. We need to go there to find Pockets. I engraved a special marking on his lamp. It's 'SH' for Scooter and Hannibal."

Chapter Fifty-Four

THE INCIDENT OF THE REPORTS AND THE LETTER

While cleaning the upstairs rooms, Ann entered a room that had memorabilia of a person, named Pockets. She thought it was just another nickname of another relative or a ballplayer.

While sweeping the floor, she noticed an envelope under the bedside nightstand. She picked it up and read who it was addressed to. It read, "West Side Kids, my family." She took it downstairs to give to Hannibal, who decided to read it at an all inclusive agency meeting.

When all the detectives arrived in the living room, Hannibal informed them that Ann found a letter in Pockets' room.

Ann excused herself and went into the kitchen to see if she could help Amy with anything.

Hannibal then read the letter to the detectives. "I want to thank everyone of you for accepting me as a normal person. You were great tolerating my naive behavior. It was the best of times ever! However, I knew it could end at any time, because the Blue Jinn s is hunting me. I appreciate all your kindness and acceptance as a regular member of your detective agency. If I am gone all of a sudden, I will always remember you. When you find and read this letter, I will probably be gone."

"That is a very touching letter!" sniffled You Don't Say.

"I want everyone to know that Hannibal and me are going to find Pockets and break the bondage of the Blue Jinn s on him." responded Scooter. "Pockets can add power against the aliens."

With that information over with, Scooter suggested a report from Who and What about the missing wife and what Smiley and You Don't Say about the murder.

Who reported that Stella helped with the case of the missing wife of a security guard at the Davenport Airport.

"We visited the guard's home to get the scent of the wife's clothes, then we started our search at the airport," explained Who. "She was last seen watching airplanes take off and land at the airport.

What, Stella and me searched the grounds, buildings, fence line bushes and a grove of trees, east of the runway. Stella's nose was on the ground most of the time until he stopped in the middle of lane 3 and started barking at the sky and also looking at us.

With all the strange happenings going on, we think she was abducted by aliens on that spot. We told the guard, we could only pray that she comes back, like other abductees. We recommended immediate transport to the hospital if we find her."

"OK, there is nothing else to do but wait for her safe return to Earth and keep checking on our computers, about anyone found elsewhere," stated I Don't Know.

Now, Smiley and You Don't Say, what have you got to say about this murder or the suicide of the woman?" asked Hannibal.

You Don't Say spoke first and said, "We got permission to look into her medical records and we asked her neighbors about her life style. The medical doctor said she was in a borderline depressive state.

The neighbors said in a social gathering she had loose lips about several debts, incurred when she was younger and had a carefree lifestyle. The neighbors also said that several different men had visited her home over several months. The autopsy report, wasn't pretty."

Then Smiley went on to say, "I'm usually a happy-go-lucky-guy, but I became serious after reading the autopsy report and seeing the picture.

Money seems to be the root of some murders and I believe it is, in this case. We now need new witnesses from the neighbors, who could identify the men that visited her.

You Don't Say and me are at this point in finding the identified men. We can use the computer to find the backgrounds of these men, with the help of the Davenport Police."

"That's great guys," praised both Hannibal and Scooter. "Keep detecting to solve these cases."

Then, I'm Not Sure interrupted the serious talk and asked if the meeting is over, because he had a date with Ann.

"Where are you going, Lover Boy" asked Whatever.

"I'm going to take Ann to a drive-in movie theater in Blue Grass," answered I'm Not Sure. "Throughout America, people are trying to live a normal life. They don't believe in aliens and spaceships. It's a hoax about the UFO sightings and the aliens' presence on Earth."

I'm Not Sure then asked You Don't Say to cover his shift in the computer/security room. In that room, What was given an alert from the radar system of What Do You Think and Michael Eight.

The message from them stated that there were moving bright objects in the area of the Quad Cities. What thanked them and relayed the information to the other detectives.

"Be on alert tonight for any action!" demanded What.

Chapter Fifty-Five
THE INCIDENT OF THE DATE

Later on, I'm Not Sure picked up Ann at her apartment on campus and he drove to the drive-in theater in Blue Grass. The movie title was, "The Invasion of The Aliens". It wasn't a full house watching the movie.

"OK, I'm Not Sure. Now since we're here on our first date, you promised to tell me what your real name is," requested Ann.

"My name is Dean Waterfall," answered Dean. "What is your last name, beautiful lady?"

"My last name is Feathers," volunteered Ann.

"It's nice to meet you Ann Feathers," replied Dean.

"It's nice to meet you, Dean, I'm Not Sure, Waterfall," acknowledged Ann as they both reached out to hold hands.

"I heard that you are going to be an author of short stories and that your first book will be a children's book about aliens. What are the aliens going to look like?"

"My idea of what an alien will look like," answered Ann, "will be they will have smooth gray skin, heart shaped heads, with large eyes and no external ears. Their mouth will be similar to ours. They will have two arms, two legs with webbed feet. Their body will be slim and their hands will have only one thumb and two fingers.

They won't be scary and the aliens will explore the Earth in several places and different situations to teach children to be kind and respectful. The aliens will interact with many kinds of living beings."

"That sounds like an interesting book for children to learn about sharing the Earth with extraterrestrials!" exclaimed I'm Not Sure.

While Ann and I'm Not Sure were watching the movie, they were interrupted by a phone call from You Don't Say.

"Hi, I'm Not Sure and Ann. Are you guys safe? I just received a message from What Do You Think and Michael Eight, that they saw an enlarging white spot on their radar, getting closer to Blue Grass. You may be seeing it now, in the west skies. The white ball of light is zigzagging and may be out of control. Tell the people working at the drive-in to warn their customers."

"Roger that. Thanks for the warning, You Don't Say. I'm going to take care of that right away."

After everybody in their cars were warned, I'm Not Sure explained to Ann the danger of the situation and that they better leave and go to the Ice King Restaurant, in Davenport, for some ice cream. As they were leaving the drive-in, I'm Not Sure looked into the rear view mirror and saw many other people leaving.

As Ann and I'm Not Sure were sitting at the restaurant eating their ice cream, they had a long conversation. After they finished eating their ice cream, I'm Not Sure took Ann back to her apartment, when they saw a flash of light, in the direction of Blue Grass. Neither one, thought anything of it.

After reaching the apartment door, I'm Not Sure said that he had an exciting date with Ann. Ann agreed and the two of them decided to have another date. They hugged each other and said, "Good night".

When I'm Not Sure arrived back at the agency, the gang was watching the news, about an alien spaceship crash, that destroyed the Blue Grass drive-in theater. A couple of people had to be taken to the hospital. The TV news reporter said that no alien was found in the debris. In the background, several men in black, were sizing up the situation.

"I wonder if it was scar face again? He's having a hard time flying around here," laughed Scooter and Hannibal, who joined in with the other detectives.

"I'm going to the basement for a while," declared Scooter.

"Don't blow it up!" jested I'm Not Sure.

Chapter Fifty-Six
The Incident of Looking For Pockets

In the basement chemistry lab, Scooter began mixing several chemicals, with the samples from the spaceship. One mixture made him a strong muscular person and another was an explosion, that destroyed Sgt. Tarillo's car. Another mixture allowed a person to be invisible. But currently, his goal was to make another brick, that could not be destroyed and bouncy enough to come back into his holsters, on the belt he wears most of the time. That is why he is called, Scooter, The Brick.

Tonight, he mixed powdered chemicals, with the blue liquid and pink material, to create what he wanted. He was so overjoyed that he fell over a stool, hitting the floor and stayed there sleeping, until 8 a. m. the next morning. What woke him up was the smell of Amy's cooking. He climbed up the basement stairs and asked Amy if there was any coffee to drink, because he had a short night.

"I just made some coffee," stated Amy, as she was focusing on making omelets.

"Aha, you must have found the chickens!" laughed Scooter as he stumbled on a kitchen chair. "Where is the coffee?"

"I found the coffee on a cupboard shelf," giggled Amy.

"I hope that it's black coffee," reasoned Scooter.

"No, it's coffee beans, mostly brown," proclaimed Amy.

"What are you trying to say, sis?" asked Scooter.

"I'm trying to say that the coffee isn't made yet," admitted Amy. "You will need to grind the beans and make the coffee for all of us."

"What else. Now wasn't that easy!" exclaimed Scooter, with a slight headache.

As Hannibal walked into the kitchen, he saw Amy and Scooter wearing smiles on their faces and said, "Oh what a beautiful morning!"

"That's a matter of opinion!" barked Scooter. "You may think it's a beautiful morning, but I have to make the coffee."

"Leave the paint out of it," joked Hannibal.

The smell in the kitchen was getting so overpowering, that a person could hear their stomach growling.

"The coffee is brewing and the smell of it is already relieving my slight headache," informed Scooter.

After breakfast, Scooter, you and I need to do some planning to find Pockets," requested Hannibal.

"Roger that!" beamed Scooter. "We all miss, the old boy and we just have to find him."

After everybody was done eating, Scooter said to Amy, "Sis, your food is great and it uplifts the energy of our gang every time they eat your cooking."

"You can say that again, Scooter. Every time you do the cooking, we all end up with a slight headache," exclaimed Hannibal, as he grabbed Scooter by the ear and pulled Scooter out of the kitchen. "If you're done eating, master, let's go to the security, camera room, to plan our journey."

As they sat in the security, camera room, Hannibal began to tell Scooter, the start of his plans.

"First of all Scooter, we need to dress like the people from Syria and Turkey," stated Hannibal. "When we get there, remember, we're detectives, so don't do anything stupid and behave like a turkey."

"What else. What's the catch?" asked Scooter. "Are you trying to tell me that we will have to wear turbans and not have to comb our hair?"

"Now really Scooter, you knucklehead," exclaimed Hannibal. "Just bring yer comb with you and comb yer hair, while you still have hair on yer head."

"If you keep rubbing my head with your knuckles, I'm agona send you to your home, away from home," exclaimed Scooter. "You know what I mean. That broken down teapot you live in!"

"If you do something stupid like that to me, we won't be figurin' a plan to find Pockets," challenged Hannibal. "Now let's get down to business, before I turn youse into an alien."

"The lamp that we are looking for, has the 'SH' on it. Can you narrow down the location where we should search, instead of the whole countries of Syria and Turkey?" asked Scooter.

"I think our best choice to find Pockets is Aleppo, Syria," suggested Hannibal. "If we can't find Pockets there, then the next thing we'll have to do, is to go across the border into Turkey."

"I like that plan," exclaimed Scooter. "When we get to Turkey, can we buy some of their eggs to bring back to have with our coffee?"

"Can we buy some turkey eggs to bring back with us?" laughed Hannibal. "Of all the people, I need to have me help look for Pockets, I'm taking a bumbling idiot with me.

When we get to these countries, don't say nuttin'. You let me do the talking. Youse don't see nuttin'. You don't hear nuttin'. And most of all. Don't let anybody over there find out that you don't know nuttin'.

Now let's go tell Ann, Amy and the rest of the detectives that we're gonna be gone for a day, so they can party while we're gone."

After informing the other detectives of their plans and getting the thumbs up, Hannibal and Scooter wished themselves to Aleppo, Syria and disappeared.

"Hey Hannibal, where are we?" asked Scooter.

"It looks like we are in an empty alley," acknowledged Hannibal. "Judging by the sounds and smells, we are here at an open business market. Let's walk out of here and join the crowd."

While Hannibal and Scooter were walking, people were bumping into them and pushing them away from the vendors. Seeing a vendor selling shiny lamps and teapots, they decided to move to that vendor.

"Remember, 'SH' on the lamp will be where Pockets is," reminded Scooter.

"There must be at least a hundred lamps here," reckoned Hannibal.

"Don't ever call me stupid again," reasoned Scooter, with a glow of light in his eyes. "I just thought to have you and me wish for the 'SH' lamp. It's as simple as that."

"Poof!" Now where are we Hannibal?"

"I think we are in a special area, where we would call at home, a junk yard," reasoned Hannibal.

"There is a reason why the genie power placed us here. So let's search for Pockets," instructed Scooter. "Here's a lamp. It's not shiny and I don't see the 'SH' markings, however. Oh shucks!"

"Over here Scooter. I found a lamp that's not shiny either, but I see the markings that look like 'SH'.

"Give it a good rubbing, Hannibal."

"It worked!" shouted Hannibal. "I see a puff of smoke and there he is, Scooter."

"I never thought I would get out of this lamp," exclaimed Pockets. "I'm the slave of the lamp. I'm a magical spirit and you just freed me from my imprisonment of the lamp. To reward you, I will grant you a wish for anything you want and I will get it for you. What do you wish for, gold, diamonds, dancing girls?"

"We wish to have Pockets, a genie and a friend with us," wished both Hannibal and Scooter. "Don't you recognize us, old buddy?"

"Give me a minute and let me rub my eyes," requested Pockets. "It is really dark in the lamp. Now that I can see you, I remember you. Hooray, you have come for me!

The Blue Jinn s has kept me here for breaking a cardinal rule of the genies. That is to never be in human form and act like a human."

"Poof", the Blue Jinn s appeared.

"You humans can't have him," explained the Blue Jinn s. "He hasn't completed his punishment. He can't leave and he can't grant wishes and you should not call him Pockets."

"Where have you been, tyrant?" shouted an angry Scooter. "The world is being attacked by these unfriendly aliens. You, Pockets and all the genies of this world should be defending the Earth, that is home to all of us.

Wake up! You have a lot to lose of your mythical powers."

"I was unaware of the aliens and I wasn't listening to people," replied the Blue Jinn s. I personally will grant you a wish. Make it a thoughtful one. We do not have the power above the Earth's atmosphere, but we can deal with aliens here on or near Earth."

"I don't like you very much for what you have done to Pockets. I trust you will help us to protect all of Earth's people. My wish and Hannibal's wish is to have Pockets come back with us to Davenport, Iowa and he can be who he wants to be," wished Scooter.

"Your wish is my command," acknowledged the Blue Jinn s. "Be safe and prosper!"

"Poof". Hannibal, Scooter and a lamp, labeled 'SH' were found to be in the basement of the agency.

"Quick Hannibal, rub the lamp and let Pockets out, before anyone sees the transformation," requested Scooter.

"Poof". A puff of smoke comes out of the lamp and Pockets is standing in front of Scooter and Hannibal.

"Now that you're back home, you don't need to tell us about being a slave of the lamp," instructed Scooter. "We know who you are. What does it feel like to be at the agency?"

"It feels great to be home again. Do I still get the same upstairs room?" laughed Pockets, along with Hannibal and Scooter. "Now that you're home, we need to introduce you to my twin sister, Amy and our new housekeeper, Ann, as our friend from Des Moines, who is concerned about the strange things happening around the Quad Cities," explained Scooter.

"OK Scooter. Now that we're back at the agency, we can get rid of the turbans," declared Hannibal.

"I'm glad it's time to take it off of my head. It was smothering my scalp," reasoned Scooter. "I could have lost all of my hair and then my mustache, oh my!"

"What time is it?" asked Hannibal. "I believe it must be close to 10 p. m. The gang could be upstairs, watching the news, before hitting the hay."

"Is that the same meaning as to going to dream, the dreams of wishes?" asked Pockets.

"I've never heard it said that way before," exclaimed Scooter. ""But you're right. Let's go upstairs to meet the gang! Hey gang, look who's here!"

Chapter Fifty-Seven

THE INCIDENT OF THE
MEETING OF THE MINDS

The next morning, Hannibal received a call from Uncle Columbo, stating that he was invited to a meeting of the minds with the local, federal, and military advisers.

"Can I bring Scooter and Pockets with me?" asked Hannibal.

"Bring them both. Is that Pockets, who I met before?"questioned Uncle Columbo. "The three of you will be representing the West Side Kids' Detective Agency, who was assigned to the alien theory of activity in the Quad City area. The meeting will be at 2 p. m. today at the National Guard Armory."

Later at lunch, Amy was catering to Pockets and winking her eyes. Ann was curious as to who Pockets was. She wanted to know more about him, but she was hesitant to ask several questions of him. Both girls thought they could get along with Pockets, especially Scooter's sister, Amy, who kept refilling his plate.

The meeting at 2 p. m. at the National Guard Armory started on time. A massive amount of people were attending, given credit to the news media and the eye witness experiences in the area. Several high ranking military officers were there, too.

Hannibal and Scooter were given chairs on the stage in front of the public. Military and local federal officials were seated into a straight line on the stage.

Capt. Columbo and Sgt. Tarillo introduced each one to the public and opened the meeting with comments about the alien theory. Pockets, What Do You Think and Michael Eight sat with the audience.

After hearing what the citizens have experienced, the military officers revealed the defense protection provided at the Davenport Airport. It was noted that there were options to fight the aliens, who were taking our natural resources, mainly water and people to control their minds and behavior for their advantage. It was stated that the aliens would take what they wanted, even if that meant destroying humankind.

Many people stood up and shouted, "We can't have that happen!"

When the crowd settled down, Hannibal and Scooter went to the podium on stage. Scooter told Hannibal to start first.

Hannibal then began talking to the crowd and said, " I have it from unbelievable resources that the aliens can be handled on Earth and in our atmosphere. It will be a force that will convince the aliens not to come here again."

Scooter then interjected by saying, "Whatever fear I have inside me, my ambition to win is always stronger. There will be a plan to take care of them in outer space, so they won't not never think of ever coming back here again."

Everyone in the audience was listening with their mouths open. They didn't know what to believe. The silence was broken when Joe Mixer and Frank Stargate walked to the podium.

Frank began by saying, "After these crashes were investigated, there is some evidence that the spacecraft crashes weren't because of the malfunctioning craft, but of the aliens, themselves. There is something bothering the alien's thinking and coordination."

"Upon further detailed investigation in the spaceships," added Joe Mixer, "remnants were found of insects and peanuts. It might be that aliens are affected by an insect and food allergy carried into their spaceships by the abductees. I don't think they are aware of this yet."

A news reporter then stood up in the crowd and said, "It may be saving the Earth and humankind then."

"You got that right. Our own detectives, Hannibal and Scooter will have a plan also, to get rid of the aliens," praised Uncle Columbo. "It will be very important to have us stay at home, as much as possible in the next several days, for the plans to be carried out. Thanks for coming. Relay the message to everyone you know. We will stay for any questions now."

A person in the far back raised his hand and said, "I can give you my experience to support the assumption that peanuts have an allergy affect to the aliens."

Capt. Columbo of the Davenport Police Department invited the person to tell his story.

"My name is Officer Dustin Edkin, of the East Moline Police Department. Thank you for letting me tell you of my experience.

I was patrolling the streets of East Moline and I was at a stoplight one night, when I noticed a red car rapidly approaching me in the lane beside me. I couldn't see the driver because of the dark tint of the windows. He sped right through the red light. I turned on my flashing lights and followed him to a park beside the Mississippi River. I walked over to the red car after it stopped and asked the driver to step out of the car. Nothing happened as if he didn't hear me.

It was a silent dark night in the park. A bright light over the river appeared suddenly and the car door opened. It was a shock of a lifetime.

The supposed human driver looked like he had a peanut shell shaped head and blue skin. Otherwise, he looked like a normal human shaped body. I've never seen this before. I shook my head several times to refocus on my duties.

I asked the whatever it was, "Do you have a license to drive and do you own this car? Show me your driver's license and registration."

He stared at me with his huge eyes and pointed to the river.

Then I said, "Come on talk. Put your hands on the hood of the car and spread em!"

I knew something seriously was going wrong here, because he didn't move.

The morning police briefing warned us to look out for human

look-a-likes disrespecting the traffic laws of Illinois and stealing whatever they wanted.

I turned my flashlight to the back seat of the red car and found it was full of bottled water and large repair tools. Not knowing what powers these creatures have, I decided to offer salted peanuts in the shells to get it to cooperate.

"It's just as good as salted sunflower seeds. I carry them everywhere I go!" I said to whatever it is.

I know the blue whatever it is didn't know about the peanut allergy, but I knew of its possibility.

The blue guy placed the peanuts in a hole in his face. Within seconds, the blue guy was acting like it was standing on a vibrating floor. His arms were swinging up and down. All this happening without a sound. I then saw it streak to the river and the bright light came closer to shore.

I shouted, "Don't you like my peanuts?"

The blue guy and the light beam became one and it rocketed into the dark night, to outer space. I felt like I was in the Twilight Zone. I asked myself, how was I going to write this incident about my experience with the peanut shell shaped head blue guy.

I think this event helps to support the theory that the aliens are affected by the peanuts."

Chapter Fifty-Eight
THE INCIDENT OF THE PATROL RIDE

Before everyone left the meeting at the National Guard Armory, Officer Dustin Edkin mentioned to Hannibal and Scooter that he would like to talk to them.

"Hey guys, I would like to invite you two to come on a patrol in East Moline with me?" asked Officer Edkin.

"Yah, we could do that," responded Hannibal. "How about tonight? We will meet you at the East Moline Police Station, let's say 8 p. m."

"OK, that sounds good," replied Officer Edkin. "We will join up for a look see, in the streets of East Moline."

At 7:30 p. m., Hannibal once again beat Scooter in the game of rock, paper, scissors, to drive the new Ford Explorer to the East Moline Police Station.

"I know your driving skills, Scooter. You couldn't follow the signs to the police station. There are one way streets that will confuse you," reasoned Hannibal.

"That might be, slave of mine," bellowed out Scooter. "We will take this up later."

Officer Edkin wanted Hannibal in the front seat of the police car, because he knew from the meeting that Scooter would be the type to touch all of the equipment in the front seat.

While cruising the streets of East Moline, Officer Edkin received an emergency call from the police dispatcher. The dispatcher said there were people marching around to a popular park, in East Moline. An alien was guiding the hypnotized people, like a border collie dog.

With sirens blazing, Hannibal, Scooter and Officer Edkin raced to the park. People were walking around like zombies and the alien was their leader. It was easy to find the alien, in the line of people.

The threesome approached the alien and Officer Edkin demanded an answer to his question, "What are you doing with these people?"

Scooter wished Hannibal to have everyone understand each other. Poof, the teapot in Hannibal's bag vibrated and the wish was granted.

"I'm arranging for a group party in my spaceship, you imbeciles. Now, don't bother me," shouted the angry alien.

"How did he say that? I didn't see his mouth move," wondered Officer Edkin.

"I don't know," acknowledged Scooter. "Watch out. He has surprising powers."

"These people have our tracking chips in their necks, explained the alien, stumbling on a rock.

"You're a pain in the neck," offered Officer Edkin. "You can't do this and I won't let you! Did I just hear him right?"

"Don't even try! I have more power," demanded the alien as he raises his finger at Officer Edkin.

"Look out, Dustin!" shouted Scooter.

Hannibal then pushed Officer Edkin out of the way of the alien's killer light beam, which hit and destroyed a picnic shelter.

"Who are you?" asked Scooter of the alien.

"My comrades call me Uffey, a great warrior from Orion"

"Wait a second! You are scar face, Goofy, from the Buffalo sand quarry incident," exclaimed Scooter, who throws two bricks, that causes the alien to swing his arms upward.

Officer Edkin fires three rounds into the alien and one round severs the finger, responsible for the light beam.

"We got him now! He's defenseless like a tiger without teeth and claws," cheered Hannibal.

At that time, a spacecraft showed itself above the park. It was expecting the party goers that scar face arranged in a group for abduction. But the spacecraft was in a different search for the injured alien.

"Watch out for that light beam from the spacecraft. It will abduct you Officer Edkin," yelled Scooter. "We know that the spacecrafts and aliens are unstable from the peanut allergy and the disease-carrying mosquitoes, so their aim is off."

Officer Edkin, block the streets and call for several ambulances and back up policemen, while Scooter and myself deal with Uffey and the zombies," instructed Hannibal.

"Hannibal, I wish that Uffey to leave the universe and that the zombies return to normal humans, with no tracking chip," wished Scooter. "The people will think they were on a friendly group walk in the park."

Poof. Uffey, the Goofy and the spacecraft were sent into outer space and the people returned to their normal selves. Officer Edkin showed the EMTs where the people were. Then he walked over to where the alien was and picked up the dangerous severed finger.

"Wow! What will the guys back at the station think of this?" murmured Officer Edkin.

Hannibal and Scooter weren't paying attention to what Officer Edkin said. They were making sure the spacecraft was disappearing into the dark sky, with shining white stars.

"This time, the aliens didn't get the people," chimed Hannibal. "I need a pat on the back."

"So do I!" stated Scooter, who wanted credit too. "I threw the bricks that saved us."

Officer Edkin joined the two looking at the dark sky.

"What are you two arguing about now?" asked Officer Edkin. "This was a successful mission. My family and the police department will be proud of me."

"Make sure you tell them about shooting the finger off the alien. That finalized its fate," smiled Hannibal.

"Scooter, how far can you throw the bricks?" asked Officer Edkin, feeling like the world was saved tonight.

"I'm Scooter, The Brick. My bricks will go as far as needed, upon my command."

Scooter picked up his bricks and placed them in his holsters and then smiled at Hannibal and said, "Let's go home, my friend, the genie!"

Chapter Fifty-Nine
The Incident of War With The Aliens

The aliens weren't at the meeting, so their activities did not stop, even though some aliens crashed and were lost. The spaceships kept sucking up fresh and salty water, abducting people, stealing nuclear material and changing people's behavior. The aliens actually, were confident enough to walk on the ground, scaring citizens.

Well, the governments of the world had enough. It was decided to try force, even though they knew the aliens had the technology to have an unknown force, like that which caused the boulder to be pulverized.

The President of the United States interrupted television and radio programs to announce the decision to launch missiles at the spaceships.

"We cannot afford to accept failure but if it comes, we will learn what to do next."

The Davenport Airport's staff, maintenance crew, military soldiers and scientists became very business-like preparing for action. The underground launch pad was getting ready for deployment of missiles. What they needed now was a reason. Any threatening spaceship entering into the Quad Cities was a sitting duck. These missiles could fly at supersonic speed to intercept any UFO.

Luckily most UFOs will come close enough and hover over an interesting area, for samples and water. Their prime target is the Mississippi River. Ocean water would take time and special equipment to desalinate.

The night came suddenly. The stars were bright and the moon was looking like a giant volleyball, in the darkness of space.

"We have a nibble on radar," said What Do You Think. "It's moving from North to South. It hasn't been growing larger. What do you think Hannibal?"

"It may be the International Space Station," replied Hannibal.

"Oh, I see another bright ball of light traveling faster than the International Space Station. I don't know where it is going, but it passed the International Space Station and it is getting larger. I bet the International Space Station has notified the military." replied Chris Seven Murphy, nicknamed What Do You Think.

Meanwhile, the Davenport Quest and local news channel reporters were at the Davenport Airport ready to record any action. They all looked up to see the fast spinning lights of a spacecraft slowly moving south to the Mississippi River.

The section of the landing strip opened up quickly, without sound and no lights were activated til the ten second countdown. At zero, the missile roared to the spacecraft in seconds and exploded on the perimeter of the spacecraft. It did not damage the craft! A second missile was fired toward the spacecraft with the same result, but this time a laser beam was directed toward the launch pad. It missed by 200 yards and forced reporters to take cover. All of this was recorded. It did not take long for the spacecraft to hover over the river and take water without serious interference. The Rock Island Arsenal used their howitzers, but no damage was caused to the spacecraft, which took what it wanted and shot a laser beam in a warning effect.

It was a frustrating night for the military. However, no casualties were reported. The military learned that the aliens have force fields around their spaceships, that can't be breached.

The large headline in the newspaper read, "No Deal, What Next!" The smaller print read, "We Need Another Plan."

The Davenport Police Department received a call from the Secretary of War. The Secretary of War said he got permission from the President of the United States to try the unknown plan, presented by Hannibal and Scooter. A meeting should be arranged to disclose the plan.

Chapter Sixty

THE INCIDENT OF THE MOSQUITOES AND PEANUT PLAN

Those invited should be the mayor of Davenport, Capt. Columbo, Sgt. Tarillo, Joe Mixer, Frank Stargate, Hannibal, Scooter and the Secretary of War, who will bring General Olson, an Army veteran, as a body guard.

Uncle Columbo was hoping that Hannibal and Scooter had a definite plan. The world will depend on its success. The West Side Kids' Detective Agency was in a conference with Pockets, the genie from Turkey/Syria area.

"Gang, we will have to drop all of our detection cases for now," explained Hannibal. "We have bigger fish to consider, like extraterrestrials."

"We have our own weapons to defeat the extraterrestrials," declare Scooter. "We have disease-carrying mosquitoes and peanuts."

"There is strong evidence that the aliens are allergic to peanuts and the mosquitoes that are carrying the diseases, not yet known to them," added Joe Mixer, the biochemist. "They have no defense or vaccinations to treat the disease, therefore they will die. By chance, the people who were abducted carried the peanuts and mosquitoes with them to the spaceships."

"Don't forget a very important part of the plan is genie power," included Hannibal. "How could you forget that Scooter?"

"You didn't give me time to," replied Scooter. "I would put you in the teapot, but we need you out of it."

"I hate being in that teapot!" answered Hannibal.

"You ain't telling me anything new," responded Pockets.

"You can say that again, Pockets. Now, let's get back to the plan," instructed Hannibal. "Scooter and my own self will carry a gallon of live mosquitoes and a large bag of peanuts with us. Scooter will wish us to be in the mothership, located above the 60 mile outer space limit from Earth. These are the weapons along with the Scooter's super bricks.

Pockets and the other genies around the world can handle the rest of the extraterrestrials on Earth and below the 60 mile limit. The genies can become invisible and be where the aliens can't see them. The genies can prevent what the aliens are up to and then send them into another galaxy, far, far away. The aliens can't win!"

"Hannibal and myself will use the leverage of mosquitoes and peanuts to convince the aliens to leave our galaxy," explained Scooter. "Now that they have been exposed to these weapons, I will have a bug whacker and Hannibal will grant the wish to have the peanuts gone and the air will be cleaned inside their spacecraft. They can't refuse to get out of town or out of our universe. It's a win-win proposition. Are there any questions?"

"I don't know, what are we suppose to do?" asked I Don't Know.

"Well, lets see," contemplated Scooter. "The rest of you can spread out in different directions and be the bait for the invisible genies."

"Wha, wha, What?" shuddered What. "You want us to sacrifice ourselves?"

"No, you don't understand the plan," chuckled Scooter. "You will be protected by the genies."

"Hold your horses and listen up," answered Hannibal. "What Mr. Smiley Face is trying to tell you is that all the genies around the world will need to hear from any person that they wish to have the aliens gone, as in poof, good-bye and don't ever pester us again.

You can work with What Do You Think and Michael Eight to

project this message on all communication systems. The sound of the wish should be heard around the world!

When me and Scooter git to the mothership, we will offer the ultimatum, to die or go away!

If we don't git back to earth, do tell my parents, George and Jean Columbo, that I love them," requested Hannibal.

"If I don't git back and I don't know why I wouldn't, because the extraterrestrials ain't going to like me, tell my parents, Henry and Henrietta Hickenbottom, that I love them too," announced Scooter.

"Why don't you tell them yourselves?" asked Because.

Both Hannibal and Scooter looked at each other and replied, "Then I would have to answer their questions."

The plan was then explained by Hannibal, Scooter and Pockets, who wasn't invisible yet. Everyone agreed to try it. But what the hey? What other choices were there?

While at the scheduled meeting with the mayor, Frank Stargate, Capt. Columbo, Sgt. Tarillo, the Secretary of War, and General Olson, Joe Mixer was absent for the first fifteen minutes.

Joe said he smelled some food down the hall, so he had to re-energize!

While the aliens were walking on the ground every which way, because their feet pointed in all directions, the people were trying to fight back. The aliens had control of those people, still with tracking chips behind their necks. The aliens were getting all kinds of secret information about water resources and nuclear plant locations.

Because one genie couldn't handle all of the aliens and didn't have the power, it was a surprise to know and see how many teapots actually had genies in them.

Hannibal and What Do You Think noticed what was going on, so they agreed to set loose the invisible genies. The "Wish" was universally spread throughout the world.

Pockets was in charge of the United States genies. Along with the bait, the invisible genies were turning the tide of the extraterrestrial domination of Earth. Many people watched the flying saucers, jet out of sight. It was like meteors in reverse!

Chapter Sixty-One
THE INCIDENT OF THE
ANSWERS TO THE ALIENS

"Before we decide to go to the mothership, I would like to take a minute to talk with Professor Boblit," demanded Scooter.

Ring a ding ding. "Hello, this is Professor Boblit. "How may I help you?"

"Hi, this is your buddy, Scooter."

"Oh, that's wonderful! Do you have the answer to the alien invasion?" asked Professor Boblit. "I keep wondering if I will have a radio station. You know, the aliens are sky adventurers and they upset the frequencies of radio transmission."

"Me and some friends are going to put an end to the alien theory, today! I have some questions you might have some answers to."

"Don't shoot me, but go ahead and ask," said a nervous Professor Boblit.

"Do the aliens have a soul?" asked Scooter.

"I don't know," answered Professor Boblit.

"Do they have a pulse?" asked Scooter.

"I have no idea," answered Professor Boblit. "The next time you meet an alien, you can feel his pulse."

"How does a person distinguish between a human cloned alien, hybrid, from a normal human?" asked Scooter.

"This one I know," exclaimed an excited Professor Boblit. "The hybrids have no belly buttons, no navels. The world will have to watch out for them. No telling what powers they may have! What does it feel like to be abducted?"

"First there is a crackling sound of electrical charge, making my skin crawl," answered Scooter. "Then, well let's say, I know how a bug feels trapped by a net."

"Did we have contact with the aliens, before now?" asked Scooter.

"The Majestic 12 found out, so they say, that there was an actual alien contact in 1948. Their purpose was to study the UFOs. The documents of 1952 describing the study of 1948 aliens, were a top secret cover up.

In 1988, it became declassified as a secret. Why a people of twelve studying UFOs, I don't know. Throughout history, the number of twelve was frequently used."

"OK, thanks for your knowledge. I have to go now. Nothing will be top secret anymore!"

"See you later on the phone, buddy!"

"Click."

Chapter Sixty-Two
THE INCIDENT OF THE RUCKUS

Capt. Columbo got word that there was a ruckus going on along the Mississippi River. There was a spaceship hovering near the Davenport Water Works. Some aliens were on the bank of the river pointing a finger at a group of angry citizens.

Sgt. Tarillo, Frank Stargate and the invisible Pockets went to investigate. Joe Mixer decided to have a snack time after smelling the food in the By The River Hotel. Joe said he would join them, after he ate.

The aliens pointing fingers said, "If you fight us and try to prevent us from taking what we want, we will create disasters, like destroying the Hoover Dam and Area 51."

"Go ahead, try! You'll make my day!" shouted Capt. Columbo.

"I got your back," said the invisible genie, called Pockets. "I will beam them up to a different galaxy, to where they can't hurt Earth and its people. All the other genies around the world will do the same."

After getting to the ruckus, Joe Mixer said, "I'm gonna enjoy watching this."

Back at the detective agency, Stella was nervous, growling and barking.

I'm Not Sure stayed at the agency to protect the girls, Ann and Amy. The only way to stop Stella from barking was to cuddle him and feed him his favorite food.

After the confrontation at the river, the detectives, with Joe and Frank, went home for lunch.

"With Joe's good sense of smell and hunger to eat food, I think he is an interesting guy," commented Amy, Scooter's sister. "I might want him to come back here often, from Iowa City."

"Joe, do you have any reply?" asked Who.

"What? I wasn't listening while I was eating," chuckled Joe.

Hannibal and Scooter then came out of their bedrooms dressed for warfare. Scooter had his super bricks, fine tuned and trained, in his holster belt. Hannibal was dressed in a camouflaged uniform, carrying his bug whacker, a large bag of peanuts and the teapot. Hannibal told Scooter he had to carry the bottle of mosquitoes.

"Scooter, you will have one hand free to handle the bricks," demanded Hannibal.

"OK, I guess we are ready to go on a journey of a lifetime," responded Scooter. "I just hope we will enjoy it."

"Remember to keep an eye on the pitch," suggested Who.

"The catch," said What.

"The curve, recommended Because.

"The angle," responded Smiley.

"And when you come back home, we'll do the penguin waddle!" shouted Whatever.

"Where did What Do You Think say the biggest dot in outer space was?" stated Hannibal. "Because that's where we are going."

"I wish we was in the mothership of the aliens orbiting Earth, Hannibal," wished Scooter. "Give us a ride, Hannibal. Give us a ride."

Chapter Sixty-Three

THE INCIDENT ON THE ALIEN MOTHERSHIP

"Wow, this is a big ship. Where are we Hannibal? asked Scooter, ready do drop some tricky bricks.

"I think the door says human lab research," answered Hannibal.

"Hey Hannibal! Let's get out of here!" panicked Scooter. "The first one back gets to play with Stella!"

Hannibal and Scooter then walked down an empty hallway, with Scooter timidly walking close behind Hannibal, til they were seen in an open chamber room. Three gray skinned aliens grabbed them on several parts of their body and carried them to their leader of the alien fleet.

Hannibal reminded Scooter that he arranged for the aliens to understand them and they understood us.

Scooter whispered, "Is he like the five star general of aliens?"

"I think so," answered Hannibal.

Then the alien general started to yell at Hannibal and Scooter and said, "Why have you come here and how did you do that?"

"Why are you hollering at us?' asked Scooter. You only work here. We're the guests."

"I asked you what are you doing here," demanded the leader.

"Curiosity killed the rat," answered Hannibal.

Hannibal then whispered to Scooter, "Don't tell them too much", as he touched the teapot to make sure it was close at hand.

"My friend, Hannibal has the power to be here and the power to throw you into another galaxy!"

"I don't believe it. You humans are a weak race without advanced technology to defeat us."

"We're not weak. You don't know who you are messing with!" demanded Scooter.

"You better know what you're talking about," reasoned the leader.

"You'll feel silly when you find out. Don't you see your spaceships are crashing and being tossed into outer space, disabled?" explained Hannibal.

"I see my aliens are affected by something not found in other planets," reasoned the leader.

"We have with us, those things that are causing it. Mosquitoes with viruses that you can't control and an allergy to peanuts, which both have come to you, because you have abducted humans with them," threatened Hannibal. "We can turn these things loose in all of your spaceships and you will float out into the universe with no live aliens in them."

"They have already begun!" shouted Scooter. "It's a die or go away ultimatum."

"If you promise to leave us alone, we can help you survive. You must leave our universe!" boomed Hannibal. "The bug whacker here will kill the mosquitoes and I can take all the peanuts back to earth.

Don't you see, you already have weak warriors around you. They couldn't hit us with a laser beam if they tried!"

"We're sticking right here," acknowledged the leader.

"Why, have you got stock in the Earth?" answered Scooter.

"Attack them! cried the aliens' leader.

Before they could lower their fingers, Scooter quick drawed all the bricks from his holster and hurt them so bad, that they laid on the floor moaning. The bricks automatically recoiled back to his holster, ready for action again.

The alien leader saw this as a lack of control and eyed the humans with more respect.

"I see now you are over powering my weakened warriors. You humans may not yet have our technology, but you have the fortitude and bravery to overcome your weakness. You are determined to save your planet. We will leave your galaxy. Will you please leave many more mosquito whackers and take all the peanuts from the spacecrafts with you?" begged the alien leader.

"That's not so easy, buster! We will give you many more mosquito whackers, if you send home the people, you kidnapped, before leaving our galaxy," demanded Scooter.

"I will give all human-snatching spaceships the word, to return them back to Earth," acknowledged the alien leader.

"One more thing," added Scooter. "I took samples from a spaceship that helped me create a formula for these bricks. I want them on Earth for the building of highways and other roads. Place them in a sand quarry, near Buffalo, Iowa.

"You got it Earthling. Now may I leave the galaxy? I'm feeling a little weak myself."

"Well, we did it Hannibal. We saved the world," declared Scooter. "Now I wish to be back on Earth. Let's ride!" Poof!

"Now, where are we Hannibal?" asked Scooter.

"It looks like we are in the Buffalo sand quarry!" exclaimed Hannibal.

"Hannibal, did you remember to bring your cell phone?" asked Scooter. Please call my sister to come and pick us up by the highway in Buffalo. It must be about 10 p. m. here."

After Hannibal called Amy, Amy then told the gang, that Hannibal had called to say they needed a ride back home. Hannibal was too tired to transport them home.

The gang decided to take both Explorers, to greet Hannibal and Scooter at the quarry. It was a well played out plan. The gang penguin-waddled to the two space travelers and hugged them both.

The detectives heard from What Do You Think that all alien spacecrafts left our world and many missing people were found and taken to the hospitals.

"Not a bad days work," said Scooter, just before he passed out.

"Tomorrow is another day," exclaimed Hannibal. "Take me home!"

To The Reader

This is an alternate ending to the story.

"Take all the peanuts and leave the mosquito whackers," begged the alien leader, when Uffey and a couple other aliens moved behind Hannibal and Scooter. The aliens hit them from behind and knocked them out.

Scooter and Hannibal were then taken to the tables in the Human Research Laboratory. The alien leader decided to switch Hannibal and Scooter's brain with two aliens, who would go back to Earth as Hannibal and Scooter.

The pink and blue aliens wrapped an electrical band around Hannibal and Scooter's heads, which were electrically connected to the two alien heads. Scooter's brain was interchanged with the blue alien. Scooter now has the alien brain and the alien has Scooter's brain.

Scooter was then accidentally sent back to Earth with the alien brain, by Hannibal. He was still wearing the holster full of bricks and his favorite baseball cap, with the brim up.

The leader thought a blue alien brain in Scooter's body could find out many secrets the humans have in the fight against them.

Scooter, with the blue alien brain, was sent to the chemistry lab in the basement of the agency. He walked up the stairs to the 1st floor. The detectives and Amy saw him looking up, down and side to side rapidly. He acted as if he was trying to use his two hands to grab many kitchen items. Everyone was shocked to see Scooter acting this way.

"What happened to you up in the spaceship?" asked Amy.

"I don't know, but it was a wild experience," said Scooter with the alien brain. "Where is your source of water? I'm thirsty!"

"You don't talk like Scooter and you know where the water comes from, the faucets," responded I'm Not Sure.

"I ask the questions and you give me the answers," demanded Scooter, with the alien brain. "How are the aliens being defeated?"

"You know just as well as us," answered Pockets. "You helped us with the plan to save all of humankind. By the way, where is Hannibal?"

"He said he would come later after he took care of the affairs in the mothership," answered Scooter with the alien brain.

Stella looked at Scooter straight in the eyes and started barking wildly.

"Grab him guys!" shouted I'm Not Sure. "Tie him up!"

"Don't hurt him!" yelled Amy. "His body is still my brother!"

"We won't," exclaimed Pockets. "He's coming with us to the mothership to get Scooter's brain back in his body and to rescue Hannibal. Each one of the detectives will have an invisible genie with them."

By genie power, Pockets, the detectives, with the invisible genies and Scooter, with the alien brain, arrived in the human research laboratory of the mothership. Hannibal was found tied up on the table, with the electrifying band around his head.

"It is not your right to do what you have done to Hannibal and Scooter!" shouted Pockets to the alien leader. "We will reverse your brain interchange and take our friends back to Earth to continue their normal lives."

"Let's git them! Charge!" shouted Smiley.

All the detectives avoided the gray aliens fingers and rendered them helpless, in a frozen coma, thanks to the help of the genies. While the fight was going on in the human research laboratory, Who raced to Hannibal and removed the band around his head, therefore preventing the brain transfer.

Pockets moved quickly throughout the mothership, causing all aliens to be stopped in frozen time, except one. The alien, with Scooter's brain, was found in the ship's control center. The alien, with Scooter's brain, was trying to find the button to push that sounded the alarm, but it was too late.

Hannibal recovered quickly and he broke the glass window of the control center. He tackled the alien, with Scooter's brain, but he couldn't quite drag him to the research lab. The alien's four arms were too much, so Hannibal yelled for more help. What and Because came over to help Hannibal escort the alien to the lab.

"Look dummy, you're going to give up your brain to Scooter with the alien brain.

The alien, with Scooter's brain, said, " What about the left body?"

"You're talking just like my best friend, Scooter," exclaimed Hannibal.

"Now that, that's confirmed of who has what, Hannibal, I give the honors to you," instructed Pockets.

"I wish Scooter's brain to be placed in Scooter's body and the alien's brain be placed in the alien's body," directed Hannibal.

"Your wish is my command, stated Pockets. Poof!

"Welcome to your body, Scooter!" shouted the detectives.

"Alright, alien, with your own alien brain, you are the only one to deal with now," added Hannibal. "You know what we can do so in order to stay alive, you must transport the alien fleet to another galaxy," demanded Hannibal.

After adjusting to his body again, Scooter demanded one more thing.

"You will return all the abducted people back to Earth," instructed Scooter.

"OK, OK! That sounds fair!" gulped the alien, now the leader.

"OK Scooter, do your part," suggested Pockets.

"I wish we all get safely back to Earth," declared Scooter. "Hannibal, now it's your turn." Poof!

After they returned to Earth, Scooter, Hannibal and the detectives pleaded with the Blue Jinn s to allow Pockets to be a human and be able to stay in Davenport.

"Well, since we worked so well together, saving the Earth from the aliens, it is the same for genies limited to this world also. Pockets' relationship to people on Earth as a human can be granted." answered the Blue Jinn s.

"Yea, hooray!" cheered the detectives.

Pockets was smiling from ear to ear, while Amy was winking at him.

"I bet you all want a feast to eat after saving the world. Let's go out to eat!" cheerfully suggested Amy.

The military and the local authorities were pleased to have relief of the aliens. Capt. Columbo and Sgt. Tarillo were very busy answering questions from the press. The military secretly gave the West Side Kids' Detective Agency a sizable amount of money for eliminating the aliens, in the fight to save the Quad Cities and the world.

As months went by, the hearts of several detectives couldn't live without their sunshines. A group marriage was arranged at the Vander Veer Park, where flowers were plentiful, the grass was green and the pond rippling from the spray of the fountain. The sounds of nature became the symphony of life.

Now that you have read the story with two separate endings, I want to tell you the rest of this part of the story," smiled Stella, the Doberman Pins her.

"Now, I am going to tell you who married who," barked Stella. "Scooter married Kelly. Hannibal married Betty. I'm Now Sure married Ann and Pockets married Amy.

All the parents attended the wedding, along with Uncle Columbo and his wife Janet, Sgt. Rex Tarillo, Chris (What Do You Think) Seven Murphy, Michael Eight Murphy, Tim Murphy, Joe Mixer, Frank Stargate, the Blue Jinn s and me, Stella. And wouldn't you know it. I was with an adopted female Doberman, named Goofy."

After the ceremony, the gang was dancing and singing, "The space aliens have come and gone away, gone away....!"

About the Author

David Dorris had retired after working 35 years at Ralston Purina. He got a 2- year degree from Scott Community College in 1992 for General Studies. He was a newsletter editor for Dads' Club, his church, and the Junior Chamber of Commerce over the years.

He coached Dads' Club softball for 30 years. He always taught the kids that played for him that life is like a sport, which encouraged him to write several books.

He has a sense of humor portrayed in his West Side Kids book series. He is a kind and generous person. Happiness can be found in making the best of everything you have. Laughing can ease the downs in life and help you find sunshine in life. Treat people with respect and help those in need. These facts guide his life.

The West Side Kids Series Books by David Dorris:

- The West Side Kids Meet The Small Fry
- Stunning Stephen Edwards and The West Side Kids in The Invisible Man
- The Adventures of Stunning Stephen Edwards as The Stunning Kid in The Time Traveling Marshals
- Stunning Stephen Edwards as Detective Steven Edwards in Wrestling With Death
- The West Side Kids in A Pocket Full of Wishes

About the Co-Author

Co-author of this book is Michael Boblit.

He is a retired dentist, who had been writing in patient records for 38 years. Each patient has a story in his or her own record.

With two college degrees, he has read many educational and recreational books. He has a great powerful magnetism toward a variety of books. He can't leave a store without looking at books and purchasing some. He likes being in a library. He also admits to watching adventure, mystery and military programs on TV.

It brings great satisfaction in the accomplishment to see his work be successful. He is looking forward to having this book be enjoyed by all the readers. He thanks David Dorris for having the opportunity to be involved in helping to write this book.

About the Illustrator

Norah Bell is an artist from Burlington. She uses digital media to create her artwork, and she gathers a lot of inspiration from comic books and manga. You can follow her at @houseintheriver on Instagram.

About the Book

West Side Kids in Space Aliens Are Coming, Space Aliens Are Coming, written by David Dorris and co-authored by Michael Boblit is a fun book to read. It has mystery, comedy and space aliens invading Earth. It has genies that turn invisible to help fight the aliens. Romance is obvious between several characters. The West Side Kids have funny nicknames that play into the content of the story. Scooter, The Brick has his own arsenal of weapons against the villains. The police and the military investigate the concerns of the public. A male dog, named Stella, gives a speech at one of the two endings of the book. The book tells how the aliens get sick and why they have come to Earth. This is a great story with so much more. It's a fun book to read.

Printed in the United States
by Baker & Taylor Publisher Services